NOW

THAT

IT'S

OVER

NOW THAT IT'S OVER

a novel

O THIAM CHIN

EPIGRAM BOOKS
SINGAPORE · LONDON

Epigram Books UK
First published in 2016 by Epigram Books Singapore
This Edition published in Great Britain in May 2017 by Epigram Books UK

ISBN
978-1-91-209869-9

Printed and bound in
Great Britain by Clays Ltd, St Ives plc

Epigram Books UK
55 Baker Street
London, W1U 7EU

10 9 8 7 6 5 4 3 2 1

www.epigrambooks.uk

For my parents

"All water has a perfect memory and is forever trying to get back to where it was."

—TONI MORRISON

"The heart is but the beach beside the sea that is the world."

—CHINESE PROVERB

PART ONE

1

Ai Ling

The body lies on the quiet beach, its long hair wild and brittle, streaking across the face and back. It has floated for a day on the waves, before finally being deposited on this stretch of fine, pristine sand, the shoreline of a tiny island that lies nine kilometres southwest of the coastal town of Phuket, Thailand, one of over four hundred such islands sprinkled all over the Andaman Sea. Until the body arrived, the only presence on the island has been a family of crabs that found refuge there—digging holes in the sand, multiplying in great numbers—as well as the occasional seagull that would pause and rest on its way to or from Phuket.

In its wake, the body—a woman in her mid-thirties—has brought along a school of dead fish, mostly red snappers and garoupas that the fishermen in the vicinity hunt for their livelihood; the decomposing piscine bodies litter the beach, their silvery corpses sparkling under the sun, already starting to reek.

A seagull flies down and lands on the lower branch of a coconut tree. It eyes the sea with a weary, suspicious stare, and then scrutinises the woman's body, as if waiting for her to stir. But she remains motionless.

∞

It had been Ai Ling's idea to go to Phuket for a vacation.

"It would be a nice change to our usual year-end holidays," she told her husband Wei Xiang over breakfast. "The price of air tickets is cheap, thanks to the promotions going on for the December holidays. It'd be easy to get tickets to Phuket."

"It's already November, isn't it too late to plan? What about work?" said Wei Xiang, looking up from the newspaper. "And you were in Thailand just last month."

"I'll get someone to cover for me," she said.

For the past four years, Ai Ling had worked as a preschool teacher in a childcare centre, taking care of children aged one to five. It was the longest she'd been in a job after graduating from the National University of Singapore with a Social Sciences degree. The job market was in a bad shape the year she graduated, and for years all she could find were temporary contract jobs that only lasted from two to six months. Fortuitously, she was able to find something more permanent, as a secretary at a mid-sized air-con repair company—a job recommended to her by Cody, a close friend from university—which she held onto for a year before quitting out of boredom. She hated the idea of taking calls, making coffee and scheduling her boss' calendar as a long-term career, even though the pay was decent enough and her boss treated her well. When she told Wei Xiang she wanted to quit, he tried to reason with her: the job was stable, regular hours, no overtime, good salary. But with her mind made up, there was nothing he could say to change it.

The teaching job at the childcare centre came along just a few months later, reinforcing her belief that she had made the right decision.

Once Wei Xiang agreed to the Phuket trip, Ai Ling went about checking the prices of tickets online and borrowing Lonely Planet guidebooks from the public library. Cody had visited Phuket two years before with his boyfriend Chee Seng, and over coffee one afternoon, Ai Ling asked him to join them on the trip.

"It will be fun, just like old times. God, how long has it been since we last travelled together? Since our university days?"

"Yes, years ago," Cody said. "To Bangkok, for our secret getaway, where I broke your heart, and then you married Wei Xiang after. Do you still remember that trip?"

"Asshole, still dare to say. Lied to me and dragged me into the mud with my little crush."

"You were too blind to see it, so obvious to everyone else. I made it very clear to you, but you didn't pick up the hints."

"How could I know? It's not as if you had a sign over your head screaming 'gay'," Ai Ling said, mock-punching Cody in the arm. "So how, you want to join us?"

"I don't know. Does Wei Xiang mind if we tag along?"

"He's perfectly fine with you guys, you know that. He won't mind at all."

"Let me ask Chee Seng then, see whether he's interested. He hates when I make any decision without asking him first."

A few days later, Cody called and told Ai Ling to go ahead and book the tickets for him and Chee Seng. His voice over the phone was upbeat but somewhat restrained, as if he were carefully mulling over his words. When she asked if anything was wrong, he said, "There's a lot of shit going on in our lives right now. So I think we really need a break to get away, you know? To sort things out."

When Ai Ling pressed for more details, Cody became cautious and vague in his replies. She gave up trying after a while and put the whole matter aside; she'd take it up later when the time was right.

Fortunately, there were still available seats on flights to Phuket during the Christmas period, after she checked with several budget airlines. It would be a good idea to spend the holidays away from Singapore, she convinced herself, to leave behind their busy lives, even for a short while. Good to take things easy, and maybe then she could drum up the courage to break the news to Wei Xiang. She did not think she could keep it from him any longer.

So Ai Ling bought the tickets. They would fly to Phuket via a nine o'clock flight on the morning of Christmas Day and come back four days later.

2

CODY

Your eyes snap open as the television suddenly flares to life. First there are only faint voices, a static buzz of broken, disconnected vowels. Then images appear on the screen, wavy and distorted. Disoriented by the intrusion of light in the dark hotel room, your thoughts scatter in every direction. You peer at the television screen from your position on the floor: the patches of darkness floating on the fuzzy sea of white have slowly assembled themselves into vague shapes and forms. You stare at this ghost of a ghost until your eyes hurt.

The images resolve into a hazy shot of a middle-aged Caucasian man in a tailored suit, sitting behind a desk. The man is nodding his head, his mouth moving, the sound of his words breaking up in stuttering bits. The image jumps and scrolls upwards. You can't make sense of it. In the corner of the screen, a video is playing within a rectilinear frame: shaky images captured with a mobile phone of the waves sweeping in to shore, toppling huts, smashing into trees and buildings, swallowing everything in sight. The image shifts, now showing the wall of water approaching, with people in the foreground, unaware: food hawkers milling around, a bunch of skinny children drawing in the dirt with their sticks. The video is cut off mid-scene, and the man behind the desk appears again. You pick up the remote control next to you on the floor and switch the television off. The hotel room returns to tight silence, broken only by the rasp of your breaths.

How long have you been lying here?

As long as you keep breathing, time is immaterial. There is nothing else to consider; every memory or thought is held at bay. The only thing you can feel is a debilitating heaviness, seeping into every part of you—it is a deeply familiar sensation, from a time long ago. A distant memory surfaces: the death of someone—but whom? Your mind is blank.

The curtains are drawn and the lights remain off even with the return of the hotel's power. All you want to do is to sleep, to slip away and become nothing; there, nothing can touch you. Outside the hotel room, in the flooded streets, the world has turned to water; the infinite sea that thrums with life has taken everything away. You've been spared, while Chee Seng—

You blink rapidly. The curtains lighten—weak morning light seeping through the worn, dirty fabric—and then darken again. You feel no thirst or hunger—only the tightening knots of guilt and numbness in your stomach. You turn on your side, pull your knees to your chest. Maybe if you can stay like this, you'll disappear, slipping into something similar to death, a realm of non-existence. But only if you keep very, very still.

A knock on the door, followed by a pause, and then another few quick raps. Vague shadows in the narrow gap between the bottom edge of the door and the floor. A voice deep and urgent—someone calling out—the words indistinct. Another two knocks. The shadows hesitate, then move away, footsteps fading down the corridor.

You stay very still, close your eyes and wait to fall into the deep well of your dark, swirling thoughts.

3

A sharp smell assaults my senses as I stir awake. The hard, wood-planked bed beneath me creaks as I try to move; every stiff muscle in my body shrieks with pain. A frayed stale-smelling blanket is draped over me, looking as though sewn together from different rags. The air in the room is warm, almost suffocating. I manage to lean up onto one elbow; I appear to be in the living area of a small, sparsely furnished hut. Slender beams of sunlight stream through the only window in the room, illuminating the dust motes that dance languidly in the stuffy air.

Directly opposite the bed, a dented soot-stained pot is boiling on a stove, with soft plumes of steam rising from its jumping lid. A sharp hunger comes alive inside me, though my body is too weak to move. No one seems to be around; everything is still. Outside, a songbird is trilling. I open my mouth but no sound comes out; my tongue is thick and my throat feels scraped raw.

I turn my head and see a ceramic bowl holding some kind of dark liquid, on a wooden stool beside the bed. I inch towards it. I try lifting my hands, but they are so sapped of strength that they barely move. I lean over the edge of the bowl and sip—and almost immediately my gag reflex kicks in, and I vomit up the little that was left in my stomach, leaving behind a rancid aftertaste. I spit onto the floor, strings of yellowish saliva sticking to my chin. I start to cough, which causes me to double up in a knife-sharp convulsion of pain. Once it subsides, I lean back and sink deeper into the folds of the rag blanket, and close my eyes, exhausted.

I hear something, the scuffle of someone stepping into the room, and crack my eyelids open to see a figure in silhouette. It approaches the bed and presses a hand to my forehead. Then the hand moves to the back of my head, raising it up. My lips meet the rim of the ceramic bowl. The bitterness of the brew once again causes me to gag, but before I can retch, the foul fluid is poured down my throat, forcing me to swallow it all. Then my head is laid back down, and I fall instantly into a sleep as deep as death.

∞

Dipping in and out of wakefulness, I lose track of the reality around me; the only thing that makes any sense is the recent memory that keeps looping through my mind.

I was lying on the beach after a long tussle with the sea. I could feel the gritty texture of wet sand on my face; my lips were crusted with salt, and a residual metallic taste lingered in my mouth. My stomach churned, and I began to tremble violently, as though I were still trapped in the sea's undercurrents, whipped and tossed about, drowning.

I forced myself to calm down, then opened my eyes again and surveyed the beach. The harsh sunlight had bleached everything of colour. I had no clue where I was; the long expanse of beach seemed to stretch without end in both directions. Apart from the rhythmic sound of the lapping waves, it was utterly silent.

With great effort, I flipped onto my back. The sky was smothered with billows of heavy rain clouds. I could have lain there forever were it not for the sharp little flints of raindrops now hitting my face. I jerked backward on the sand, away from the breaking waves, suddenly overcome by the primal fear that the water would take me again. I had to leave the beach immediately; despite the pain, I struggled to my feet.

Past the beach was a thick grove of palm and coconut trees, a forest that led to a hilly, craggy ridge via a narrow dirt path. A world of shadows beckoned from within. I took a step, and then another, and stumbled my way into the dark forest.

4

WEI XIANG

The man hears a deep rumbling coming from the distance, a collision of noises that grows into a forlorn, bewildering cry. And he understands what it is, after a while: the crashing of waves.

The sea is coming for him.

The man is standing in a hotel room, looking out of the glass-paned door to the balcony. A woman lies on the bed, deep in slumber. Her pearlescent naked body shines against the white bedsheet; her fingers twitch, the wedding ring catching the pale light from the window, flashing once, twice. The man bends down to the bed, hesitating over whether to wake the woman. He breathes in the warm, musky smell emanating from her body.

The sound of waves grows louder, more insistent. He turns back to the window, to the world outside the room. The sky is grey, made impenetrable by a thick bank of ashy clouds. He opens the balcony door and steps outside. The sight below him is unlike anything he has ever seen before: a tempestuous sea stretching to the horizon. He shivers uncontrollably.

A hand touches his shoulder and shakes the man out of the spell. The woman. The man stares at her, unable to comprehend her immediate presence. The woman turns her gaze to the roiling water, her expression slipping swiftly into disbelief. And for a long time they stand there, side-by-side, mute and unmoving.

The woman lowers her head into her palms, her body heaving as if in deep agony; the man puts a hand on her back, and strokes gently. He can feel the trembles rippling through her, unstoppable, as if the sea itself were churning inside her—urgent, fervent, alive.

Her body, the sea.

The man hears another sound, a cry. He looks out, straining to catch its source, his eyes scanning the surface of the water, and sees it: a small boy enfolded in the waves. The woman looks at the man with stricken eyes, willing him to act. But the man does not move. She takes a step backward, away from his touch, then leaps over the railing of the balcony before the man can even react, and is swallowed whole by the sea below.

In the long moments that follow, the man can only register the silence in his head—a dark, hollow pit that takes in all and gives nothing. The water around him continues to swell. Just as he is convinced that he has lost the woman to the sea, she suddenly breaks the surface of the choppy water, holding the unconscious boy in an arm-lock, their entangled bodies bobbing, appearing and disappearing with every wave. But then, just as abruptly as they first appeared, they are gone again: the waves have pulled backward, as if the sea has sucked in a deep breath, and dragged them both away.

The man lets out an anguished cry. The world he knows is finally gone, and there is nothing he can do to stop it.

∞

Upon waking, Wei Xiang realises Ai Ling's side of the bed is empty. He sits upright and rubs the sides of his throbbing head. Remnants of the dream are still playing in his mind, some parts so clear that when he closes his eyes he can see them again: Ai Ling and the boy in the waves, disappearing under the water, drawn away from him. He is seized by a sharp moment of panic; he breathes deeply and shakes his head, forcing the strange dream to break its hold on him.

Wei Xiang turns to the digital alarm clock on the bedside table: 8.37am. Ai Ling's pillow is slightly indented; he reaches over to smoothen it out. He throws off the blanket, gets out of bed, and shuffles into the toilet. The area around the washbasin is wet, and Ai Ling's toothbrush lies beside the tap; he replaces it in the glass container that they are using to hold their toothbrushes. The room smells of minty toothpaste and lavender-scented talcum powder. Wei Xiang stares in the mirror at the sagging eye bags and days-old stubble of his reflection; his eyes are lustreless, and his skin pale and sallow, the texture of bread dough. How did he get so old, so quickly? Only thirty-eight, yet he feels at least ten to fifteen years older, already a middle-aged man. He sighs, then turns on the tap and splashes his face with cold water, rubbing the skin roughly. He grabs a face towel from the rack and realises Ai Ling has used it that morning. He breathes in her familiar smell, then dries his face.

After stepping out of the toilet, he wonders where Ai Ling could have gone so early. She has always been a morning person, waking at least an hour before him, even on weekends. Sometimes, while half-asleep in bed, Wei Xiang could hear her moving through the flat, doing laundry or getting ready for a five-kilometre run around the neighbourhood park. Maybe she has gone out for a run; her Adidas shoes and running attire are no longer in her luggage. Whenever they travel, she always tries to explore the new surroundings with a short run when the day is still young. "Come on! The air is good!" she would say, trying to drag Wei Xiang out of the hotel bed, but over the many years, he has probably only joined Ai Ling a couple of times.

Wei Xiang checks the time again. Perhaps he should wait for her to come back so that they can have breakfast together at the hotel café. He remembers the porter telling them, when they checked in yesterday, that the continental buffet breakfast was available until ten o'clock. He changes out of his sleeping attire—singlet and boxer shorts—into a white T-shirt and Bermudas, then lies back on the bed. He stares up at the ceiling and recalls their lovemaking the night before: his mouth on Ai Ling's engorged nipples, the fleshy swells of her breasts, her stifled groans as he moved within her. His skin tingles from the remembered pleasure, and an erection stirs in his shorts. He reaches in and gives his cock a few tugs, then stops himself. This can wait; it is still early.

Even with the windows closed and curtains drawn, Wei Xiang can still hear the sounds of the town coming through, soft and muffled. He thinks of the places they will go to later; Ai Ling has already planned a long day packed with activities and sightseeing. They only managed to check out Phuket's shopping district yesterday after arriving from the airport, with a trip to its wet market and bazaar, and ended their day with dinner at a beachfront restaurant showcasing a panoramic view of the sea. Wei Xiang reaches for the printout of the itinerary on the bedside table; under one column, Ai Ling has listed some restaurants and cafés, and directions to get to them. She has also printed out a map of Phuket Island and marked down these eateries, highlighting each with a different colour for different days. So typical of Ai Ling, to plan everything down to the smallest detail.

The night before, after dinner, they took a walk along the beach, and stopped at a clearing of rocks on the shore. He noticed the worried look on her face, but when he tried to cajole her into telling him what she was thinking, she became taciturn, even evasive. Her moods can sometimes turn dark, as he has learnt over seven years of marriage, and leave her distant and distracted for days on end, even weeks. Each time she slips into this state, she pushes away from him, retreating into a secret place inside her to which he does not have access; it always pains him to think that his wife does not trust him enough to share whatever is going on in her life. He does not want his marriage to slip into that of his parents', one that was virulent, destructive.

Even when he was just a young boy, Wei Xiang could clearly sense his parents' profound unhappiness, flinching at the hurtful words they constantly hurled at each other. His parents' lives had drifted apart, taking separate paths, until they were practically strangers living under the same roof. For a long time, Wei Xiang could not understand the causes behind his parents' frequent fights, and where all of it would eventually lead. All he can remember is the fear that ate away at him, that the world was no longer stable and at any time would collapse. He carried this fear as a warning to himself, an old wound which he kept scratching.

Wei Xiang took it upon himself to do whatever he could to keep his family together. Without any prompting, he cleaned his room, neatly put away his shoes in the cupboard, washed his eating utensils, did his homework, folded his clothes, showered and ate and slept at the same time every day, and nailed down his daily routine into exactness and precision. He listened to his parents, obeyed their instructions, came home on time, did not ask to watch television, kept to the rules (and made some of his own), helped out his mother with the housework and went out on errands to buy newspapers or cigarettes for his father or a bottle of soy sauce for his mother. He passed his tests and examinations with flying colours, and received praise from all his teachers for his results in the year-end assessments. He performed as the lead in the school play in Primary Six, which his parents attended together; they even clapped for him. He kept everything in check and in order, and firmly believed that if he did everything perfectly, down to the tee, nothing would ever go wrong, not in his life or in his parents'.

And yet, the fights persisted, worsening in severity and frequency; Wei Xiang would hold himself responsible, believing that his actions, or inactions, were to blame, that he had not done the right thing at the right time—an unseen and unknown catalyst that had sparked off yet another chain of regrettable events. And he would redouble his efforts, adhering even more staunchly to his quest for perfection; he would not give in to negative thoughts, thoughts he would never share with his parents in any case. His faith in his own actions always depended on this belief, and he never swayed from it, even in adulthood.

Later, of course, he came to know the reason for the collapse of his parents' marriage, a reason that caught him completely by surprise: the death of a brother he never knew. One night when he was in his early twenties, his father told him everything in a state of drunkenness: when Wei Xiang was seven, and still an only child, his mother went away for two months to stay at her sister's to recuperate from a miscarriage. Alternating periods of sadness and neediness and silence ensued after his mother came back home, strange baffling episodes in which she would pull Wei Xiang into a hug as easily as she would push him aside or ask him to stay in his room and do as he was told. This had also been the beginning of the long stretches of fights that took place between his parents, their angry voices penetrating the walls of his room.

Wei Xiang was stunned by the news, and by the fact that he had been kept in the dark for such a long time, and at the same time he was intrigued by this secret part of their family history. He wondered how his parents had worked in tandem, through the long years, to keep any hint of the death from him. He felt betrayed by the secrecy that had led to nothing but pain for all of them.

Yet, even the birth of Wei Xiang's younger brother, two years after the death of the secret brother, did little to obviate what was ultimately the end of the marriage. His parents had hoped that the new son would take on whatever the dead son could not, but this was an unfair expectation, a false hope. The shadow of death loomed over the family, even if Wei Xiang and his younger brother were never consciously aware of it.

"But still, we tried, we really did," his father slurred as he peered into Wei Xiang's face, seeking some sort of penance, perhaps even forgiveness. Wei Xiang turned away, not knowing what to say.

In the end, Wei Xiang's mother was the one who decided on the divorce, which was finalised when Wei Xiang was seventeen, in his first year in junior college. His parents sat him and his younger brother down to break the news to them. He asked all the questions that could be asked about the causes and outcomes, but his parents provided only what he needed to know, and nothing more. Wei Xiang was furious at this obfuscation, but was even angrier with himself for not being able to forestall the divorce, for his faltering faith in his own beliefs and actions.

After signing the papers, his mother migrated to Hong Kong, where one of her sisters was living, and within two years she was romantically involved with a man who owned a chain of watch shops. Always the dutiful son, Wei Xiang kept in contact with his mother, and took two trips every year that his mother paid for, visits in which Wei Xiang took pains to be as obliging and accommodating as he could, to present his best self to his mother. But when she invited him to attend her wedding, a simple church affair followed by a reception, Wei Xiang politely declined, citing his year-end examinations.

After a brief period of uncertainty and adjustment, Wei

Xiang and his brother continued on with their lives in Singapore. Wei Xiang fought hard to get back the life he had before, to achieve the sense of balance and control that had been hugely unsettled by his parents' break-up, and to this end he devoted himself, sticking to his routine and habits with a doggedness that left little to chance.

His father, on the other hand, became a pale shade of the man he was before the divorce, cautious in his ways, defensive and prone to anxiety attacks. So different from the man that Wei Xiang grew up with: wiry, greasy-haired, bent over the nightly Chinese newspaper, his plastic-framed thick-lens spectacles perched on the bridge of his nose; dozing on the sofa after a meal, snoring like a drill; leaving for work, his shoulder blades sharp and visible under his short-sleeved shirt. His father had worked as a clerk in a heavy machinery firm that loaned out tractors, digging rigs and lifting cranes on long-term lease to construction and building companies, until he was retrenched when the company had to downsize. He never found a permanent job after that, making do with odd jobs here and there to support the family. Apart from his drinking—he now limits himself to two bottles of Tiger Beer daily—Wei Xiang's father has little comfort or enjoyment in life, defeated, buckled by the forces of life.

These impressions of his own father have affected his thoughts on becoming one himself. He told Ai Ling more than once of his decision to delay their parenthood after they were married, and he knew Ai Ling silently took heed of it, though he could see it hurt her and conflicted with her growing desire to be a mother. He has softened his stance in the last two years, after seeing how affected Ai Ling was when one of the kids from the childcare centre went missing; it was clear how much she denied herself the pain of this loss, the disappearance of a boy she had grown very fond of.

Wrapped in the silence of the hotel room, Wei Xiang feels something constrict in his chest, an imperceptible ache that spreads across his body. He turns to face Ai Ling's side of the bed again and runs his hand over the pillow. He plucks a strand of her hair and tosses it aside, then notes that half an hour has passed while he was daydreaming. What is taking her so long? A random image from the dream comes to him then—the sorrowful expression on Ai Ling's face, her eyes drilling into him, before she plunged into the water after the boy, and disappeared.

Wei Xiang leaps up from the bed, suddenly uneasy. A wave of fear and nausea passes through him. Muted sunlight filters through the curtains. He opens the glass-paned door, steps out onto the balcony, and sees the new world outside the hotel room.

5

CHEE SENG

When I open my eyes, the world around me is shadows, and it takes a long time before they start to rearrange themselves into shapes and dimensions, shades and colours. The sounds, and then the smells, begin to make themselves known, little by little, as my mind struggles to make sense of these new, strange sensations. Slight movements out of the corner of my eye: a figure bent over a soot-blackened stove, swathed in layers of rags, stirring a pot, somewhat familiar. Steam rising from the pot shrouds the face.

I shove away the dusty blanket, and pain shoots through my arms. I attempt to push my body upright and fail; I fall back on the bed, drained. The figure at the stove does not turn around or show any sign of noticing me; it keeps stirring the pot. The smell of garlic and eucalyptus hangs in the air, prickling my senses. My stomach rumbles with hunger, and then I remember the ceramic bowl, the bitter concoction.

Nearby are a small wooden table and two benches; on the table is a bundle of tiny yellow flowers with red berries—herbs?—and a water jug. At the ankle-high threshold of the doorway, two brownish-grey hens are clucking and pecking, sneaking glances into the hut. Morning light reaches in to expose the grainy texture of the cement floor. Near the far wall, three wooden chests are stacked one on top of another according to size. The dark figure trudges towards a latticed larder, and from one of the compartments takes out a glass jar. Removing its cover, it sprinkles the contents into the pot with two light shakes and continues to stir it with the ladle. Then turning around, it finally acknowledges my presence with a steady gaze.

I have a hard time deciphering the face looking at me. With a scarf covering the hair and deeply creased lines around the eyes and lips, the face looks ancient, otherworldly, like a stone carving that has weathered seasons of rain and sun. The eyes, however, set deep within the folds of wrinkled skin, beam with a sagacious, ageless intensity, the eyes of a cat in the dark. As the figure steps towards me, I notice that one of the eyes is actually a glass eye, slightly larger, unmoving in the socket; the other is assessing me closely.

It is an old woman.

Putting the ladle down on the wooden table, she pours some water into a cup and brings it to me. I drink it very slowly, but want more. The old woman brings the jug over and fills the cup again. I drain it. After I finish, she points to the boiling pot on the stove. She places the jug on a stool beside the bed, then goes over and ladles the contents of the pot into an earthenware bowl, the steam rising visibly. It is a thick broth, almost gruel-like, rich with herbal spiciness; I scald the tip of my tongue in my haste, and it leaves an acrid aftertaste in my mouth and a sizzle on my chapped lips. Holding the bowl, the old woman encourages me to eat more. It takes a long time to finish it all; by the time I'm forcing the last granular dregs into my mouth, the soup has turned cold. I lie back down; a warm, effervescent sensation infuses my insides, spreading out to the rest of my body. Once again, I feel drowsy, the irresistible pull of sleep dragging me under. The soft, nearly incorporeal touches of the old woman as she arranges the blanket around me and smoothens out my hair come to me as if from a distant place.

The next time I wake, the old woman is nowhere in sight. How long have I slept? A few hours, a day? There is no clock to tell the time. How long since I was carried off by the waves? I try to recall something else—anything—but my memories are all fuzzy and loose, untethered to any semblance of reality. I slowly sit up on the bed, some of my strength returned, and listen to the surroundings. Apart from the clucking of the chickens outside, there is hardly any other sound. At the foot of the bed are my shirt and jeans, dried out and stiff like pieces of a discarded husk. The old woman has dressed me in layers of dun-coloured robes, held together with frog buttons. Though it is warm, I can't bring myself to shed the layers.

The cement floor is cool to the touch. I try to stand and the blood rushes from my head; I waver unsteadily, my knees almost buckling, as though the earth is shaking under my feet. Once the moment has passed, I hobble towards the doorway in small, tottering steps. The soles of my feet are raw and tender. Narrowing my eyes against the light, I look out, resting my shoulder against the wooden doorframe.

Outside the hut is a small, compact courtyard, bordered
on one side with ramshackle wire cages with missing or
unhinged doors, and on another side by a tidy garden plot, its
perimeter marked out with trails of stones and pebbles, and
a brick well in one corner. Budding knots of yellow flowers
bloom in the garden, along with hanging fruits of berries,
green limes and chillies. The raked soil looks freshly turned
over; a brood of chickens prances and pecks on the ground
beside it, seemingly aware of the boundary of the garden,
taking care not to step into it. A stone-cobbled path, perhaps
smoothened by years of footsteps, leads out of the courtyard
and into a thick grove of trees about fifteen metres away.
Beyond that, the hills rise and dip in smooth undulations,
stretching to the distant coast.

The old woman is sweeping the fallen leaves with a
short rattan broom into the thick undergrowth of shrubs
bordering the compound of the hut, stooping from time to
time to pluck weeds from the ground. Despite her apparent
advanced age, her strength is evident in the manner in
which she is able to easily yank out the weeds, the roots still
clutching clumps of damp soil. Across the sloping hills, the
sun is descending, drenching the sky in yellow, purple and
orange. The old woman continues to work, undisturbed,
oblivious to my presence. I sit near the threshold in the shade
of the overhanging eaves of the hut—standing has become
unbearable—and watch her move across the courtyard,
finishing her sweeping, then tending to the garden and
herding the chickens back into the cages. She surveys the
whole courtyard and walks to the brick well; she removes
the wooden cover, picks up a small bucket attached with a

rope to the side of the well, and throws it in. A hollow sound echoes from the mouth of the well, a watery slap. With a few tugs, the bucket reappears, water overflowing the brim. She splashes the dry, hard ground of the courtyard with the water, then repeats the motion. The water spreads across the cracked surface in dark, rapidly moving tentacles, until the whole ground glistens like a shining coat of oil. From somewhere deep in the forest, a melancholic howl pierces the air.

The old woman unties the rope from its metal handle, hefts the bucket of water and walks towards the hut, nodding at me as she crosses the threshold; her shrunken, furrowed feet are caked with grains of wet soil. I follow her inside.

She empties the water into two large earthenware jars and a cooking pot on the stove. With a quick strike of a matchstick, she lights a handful of dried chaff and shoves it into the hole of the stove, provoking the flames with a straw fan. Flickering orange embers glow from within. She starts to cook, taking out rice, eggs, cloves of garlic and stalks of leafy vegetables from the larder, and seasons the food with sauces taken from bottles coated with a sticky layer of grease. The smell of cooking conjures up fragmented memories of my childhood, of time spent in the kitchen watching my mother prepare dinners, a miasma of smells that lingered in the air long after the meals were done and the dishes put away.

The old woman performs the task briskly, knowing exactly when to add a pinch of salt or a dash of sauce, and how long to keep the lid on the pot to allow the soup to simmer. She does not ask for my help, though she throws pithy glances at me every so often. Sitting at the wooden table, I rest my cheek on my arm and drift in and out of sleep.

My dream is a broken reel of images and sounds: random faces, the terrible sound of waves crashing in my ears, a deluge of noises that shatter the silence. Amongst the images, I catch a glimpse of Cody's face, staring into mine, expressionless, vanishing and then appearing again. His mouth moves, but nothing comes forth. I reach for him, but he is pulling away, receding farther and farther. I start to shout—in the dream?—and suddenly feel a firm pressure on my shoulder, shaking me, and I leap back into wakefulness with a gasp. The old woman is standing over me, watching me intently. She gives me a cup of water, puts her hand on my forehead, and motions to me to lie down on the bed. I fumble my way to the bed and collapse into it. Though I'm bone tired, I try to keep myself awake this time, afraid to slip back into my dream.

When the food is cooked, she heaps the rice and stir-fried vegetables onto a metal plate and brings it to me. Though I'm hungry, I can barely eat more than a mouthful of rice. She serves up a bowl of egg soup and nudges me to drink. I take a few sips and push the bowl away, suppressing the urge to throw up. I lie back on the bed and stare at the ceiling. The old woman returns to the wooden dining table and eats quietly; other than the chirping of crickets out in the gathering dusk and the nervous clicking of darting geckos, the hut is silent.

The old woman has still not spoken a single word to me, yet I do not find it in any way strange. It has briefly crossed my mind that perhaps she is mute, or if not, that she has chosen not to speak for reasons of her own. Perhaps since she lives alone—I have not seen any other person in the hut or its surroundings—she does not need to speak at all, and maybe has already given up the ability. I myself am still too fatigued to speak, and even if I could, what could I say? Even the simple act of opening my mouth and forming words with my tongue seems like an impossible feat, one that requires a reserve of strength that I do not have.

After our meal, the old woman puts the leftovers in the larder, and washes the plates and bowls. When she is done, she dunks a rag in a small pail of water, then takes out a glass bottle filled with a dark liquid from a wooden chest beside the wall. She places a small stool before me and rests my feet on it. She starts to clean the dirt from the cuts and wounds on my soles and calves, causing me to grit my teeth against the pain. After pouring a small amount of the dark liquid onto another rag, she dabs gently. Some of the injuries are inflamed, while others are starting to ooze yellow pus. I bite my lip and taste blood. The pain tips over into numbness. For some of the larger wounds, the old woman applies a salve—from another jar—with her fingers. By the time she is done with my legs, and then my arms, chest and back, I have been reduced to a mass of worn, frayed nerves, beyond exhaustion, and I pass out.

Waking up later—is it the same night?—I immediately sense the absence of the old woman from the room. In the near darkness, I listen for any sounds of movement amidst the nocturnal noises. A flute-shaped kerosene lamp is placed on the wooden table, emitting soft, feeble aureoles of light that throw the shadows of the objects in the room onto the walls in sharp relief. The wooden door of the hut is partially open, letting in the cool night air. I stumble to the entrance, using the lamp to guide me.

Outside, I can barely make out anything in the darkness, which has sealed the surroundings in a thick, impenetrable cloak. The sky is a lighter shade of purple-blue, and the scattering of stars seems to pulse with an irregular rhythm, like weak heartbeats. A wedge of light emerges from a gap in the tiny shed beside the hut. In daylight, the shed looked nondescript and run-down, constructed out of uneven planks of wood and a corrugated-zinc roof; but now in the dark, it seems ominous, foreboding.

I hobble towards the shed, careful not to trip over any unseen objects or make a sound. The door is unlocked. I pull it open, adjusting my vision to the wan light provided by the lamp on the floor. The old woman is squatting just inside, her silhouette shaky on the wall of the shed, her body bent over something. I sidle up to her, and peep over her hunched shoulders.

Lying on the ground before us is a young boy, unmoving, his body enshrouded in a coarse blanket, revealing only his bloated face. And cutting across his closed left eye: a deep, red scar.

6

AI LING

The pallid sun peeks out from behind a bank of grey clouds as a trio of seabirds glides across the sky. The waves lap onto the beach, leaving behind broken pieces of bleached wood, dead dull-scaled fishes and tangled coils of seaweed, occasionally touching the woman's feet, leaving behind fizzing trails of bubbles.

The solitary seagull, glancing at the body, and then at a distant point in the sea, flies down from the branch of the coconut tree and lands a stone's throw away from the woman. It ambles towards her, hesitant, as if wary of startling her.

The woman is wearing a white T-shirt, smeared with dirt and grease and in shreds around the neckline and sleeves, and a pair of lavender-coloured shorts that hug her hips snugly. Specks of grimy sand pepper the woman's arms and legs; her exposed skin has turned darker. The seagull appraises the woman for some time before it ventures closer. It pokes its beak at her shoulder a few times and pulls back, waiting for the woman to move. Then it jabs her neck, harder this time, as if wanting to stir the woman out of her stasis. A tiny hermit crab skitters out of the shadow of the woman's neck, its claws extended and snapping, and scrambles towards a nearby hole in the sand. It moves quickly, hardly leaving any mark. The seagull watches its movements for a moment, and then, in a swift motion, picks up the crab, crunches it down and swallows in a gulp.

Emboldened by the quick meal, the seagull lowers its beak to the woman's face, its dark outline reflected in the dull surface of her right eye. It pokes at the eye, assessing its jelly-like texture. The half-shut eyelid reveals a brown-tinted iris. The seagull regards it for a second, and then in a sudden move, it strikes in sharp, precise thrusts until the eye pops out, restrained only by the optic nerve. Thick dark blood dribbles out of the socket and down the woman's cheek. The seagull bends and holds the eyeball with the tip of its beak, giving it one last tug, freeing it. The eye catches the sunlight and seems to be taking in the seamless, thriving sea.

In the next moment, the seagull jerks back its head and consumes the lifeless object.

∞

Her eyes were what Wei Xiang had loved most about Ai Ling, what most attracted him when they first met during a school reunion. They were attending the twentieth anniversary of their secondary school in Ang Mo Kio; Wei Xiang was three years older than Ai Ling, and although they had been in the same uniformed group in school, the National Police Cadet Corps, they had not known each other then—Ai Ling, being in lower secondary, attended the morning session while Wei Xiang came to school in the afternoon. The uniformed group was the largest activity club in the school, with hundreds of members, and had different activities for different secondary levels.

At the reunion, Ai Ling bumped into Wei Xiang as she was leaving the buffet table, almost spilling her plate of fried egg noodles and chicken curry on him.

"I'm so sorry. I'm so careless sometimes," Ai Ling said. Wei Xiang stood a head taller than her, and his hair was neatly trimmed. She smiled up at him.

"No, no, it's me," he said. "I kind of surprised you there. It's my fault, really."

"It's okay, no harm done," Ai Ling said, suddenly feeling self-conscious. Her green-and-black geometric-print dress felt too tight on her hips. She should have worn a different ensemble, perhaps the blouse and skirt she had bought last month; she knew she would have looked better in it. She tried to smooth out the creases in the dress with her free hand.

They introduced themselves and traded abbreviated stories of their school days: graduation years, mutual friends and acquaintances, teachers they remembered, extra-curricular activities. That was when they discovered they had both been in NPCC, and puzzled over why they had not met before.

"I wasn't really the most popular guy in school, maybe that's why," Wei Xiang said.

"Maybe," Ai Ling said. "Although it's not as if I was the most attentive person in school either. I was very blur and clueless then."

They laughed, and Wei Xiang took a step forward.

"You have very nice eyes," he said, holding his smile. "Your irises are light brown, very unusual."

"Yup, I know. My parents' eyes are black, so I don't know where I got mine." Ai Ling looked down at her black pumps, embarrassed by the attention that Wei Xiang was giving her.

A salvo of noises erupted from the stage, where the emcee was adjusting the microphone on its stand, testing the volume. After clearing his throat, the emcee asked the guests to take their seats, so that they could commence the line-up of performances.

"Where are you seated?" Wei Xiang asked. Ai Ling gestured to a table with a nod of her head, where her old classmates were sitting and chatting animatedly among themselves.

"Can I join you?"

"Sure, of course," Ai Ling said, and they walked to the table.

∞

Ai Ling wanted to take the courtship with Wei Xiang as slowly as she could; her previous relationship had been a shaky, tumultuous part of her life that she wished to erase. Ian, her ex-boyfriend, was also someone she had known back in secondary school, and they dated during their last year in school through their junior college days; for a while, they seemed destined for marriage. At least, it was what Ian had planned, after he settled down with a full-time job in a bank, after serving his two and a half years of National Service in the army. Ai Ling, on the other hand, was not so certain about their future. Part of her doubt had risen while Ian was still in NS and after she had just started her course of study at the National University of Singapore; there, she made new friends and was exposed to different kinds of lives that were more interesting and nuanced than what she had known before. With Ian, Ai Ling felt constrained by the ever-narrowing possibility of her choices, as if she were slowly working her way into tight corners and dead-ends. She was fearful of how her life could be neatly parcelled into fixed pigeonholes that would define it: career, marriage, children. Yes, these were things that would matter to her in the long run, but she was only twenty-one then and had not yet seen the world, and she did not want to settle just yet.

Perhaps, in an unconscious reaction to her gradual drifting away, Ian began to hold on tighter to their relationship, to demand more time, effort and commitment. He wanted to spend every available second together when he booked out of camp on weekends, just them without their friends, as well as to have shared hobbies and activities, like badminton and swimming. For a while, to compensate for her waning interest—she did not dare admit to herself how she felt—Ai Ling often put in more effort to be more involved, to pay more attention to what Ian wanted. She gave in to him time and again, until her own wants and desires nearly disappeared.

"I feel like I'm losing you," Ian told her once, over a dinner to celebrate one of their many anniversaries, one which Ai Ling could not remember. Ian bought her some flowers and a small plush bear. She had come to the dinner empty-handed.

"No, I'm just busy with schoolwork, that's all," Ai Ling said, pretending not to understand what Ian was implying.

"Is everything okay with us?"

"Yes, of course. Why would you ask that?" Ian shook his head and took hold of Ai Ling's hand, giving it a squeeze. Ai Ling smiled, knowing that she had, once again, pushed back the inevitable; yet it gave her no relief whatsoever.

∞

When Ai Ling met Wei Xiang, she was in her mid-twenties, and most of her friends had already got married, settled down, had a kid or two. A steady tremor of restlessness reverberated in her life; Ai Ling had expended much of her energy in her twenties trying to make sense of what she wanted, moving from one job to another, never staying longer than six months in each job. Her parents had frowned on her decision every time she quit, but left her alone. Sometimes, she would feel that she was wasting her life, and that anything that followed was just mere existence. Yet, despite this, Ai Ling rarely envied her friends' decisions to make do with what they had—husbands, children, good jobs.

With Wei Xiang, Ai Ling was motivated to grow out of her usual self, to move in an entirely different direction. She was a better version of herself with Wei Xiang, more competent and decisive. Wei Xiang was always sure of what he liked or wanted to do; he was the kind of man who, once he decided to take a certain path in life, would stick to it, and would never stray from it. He laughed at the thought of lost opportunities or opportunity costs: "I make my own opportunities." At a different stage in her life, Ai Ling might have rolled her eyes at the bland, narrow truth of this trope. She had, in fact, done that with Ian, but with Wei Xiang, she could see the conviction of his actions, the force behind his words. She was drawn to it, attracted to something that she knew was lacking in her own personality.

"So, what was your ex like?" Wei Xiang asked her on one of their early dates. Ai Ling wanted to dodge this topic, but did not know how to avoid it.

"He's okay. We had different priorities. I think he's married now."

"Oh, do you still keep in contact with him?"

"No. I heard about him getting married from another friend."

Ian had got married barely six months after Ai Ling had broken up with him, to a girl he knew from work. Apparently, it had been a whirlwind courtship, something that Ian had orchestrated. He had even called Ai Ling to tell her about his wedding plans, his voice higher than usual: "I'm happy, and I want you to know that."

"Yes, I can tell that you are," she'd said.

"Will you come to the wedding?"

"I don't think so."

"Why?"

Ai Ling had remained silent.

"I don't know what's the matter with you. You never seemed to be happy with me, and now you can't be happy for me. Why? What's wrong with you?"

"No, really, I'm happy for you."

"You were never happy, and you will never be happy with anything. You don't know what you want, and it's really frustrating."

"That's not true. I just don't think that what I wanted was something you could give me."

"You are lying to yourself. And you're lying to me."

Ian had swiftly ended the call, and in the wake of it, Ai Ling felt battered by his accusation. Ai Ling had always known what she wanted, or at least what she did not want:

her relationship with Ian. She had tried almost everything to keep them together: putting Ian's needs before hers, being more loving, letting him make all their decisions, giving in to his requests for sex. But the more she committed to this role of being a good girlfriend, the more she felt out of touch with her own self, as if she were living a fabricated life divorced from her inner state.

"Do you still miss him?" Wei Xiang asked her.

"What's there to miss?"

And Ai Ling believed the truth of her own words.

∞

When Ian had brought up the topic of marriage, in their sixth year of courtship—he was working his first job, as a junior credit analyst with a local bank, while pursuing a part-time degree in business studies at a private tertiary institution—Ai Ling knew she had to make her decision sooner than planned.

So, over dinner one night, when she had drunk enough wine to calm her jittery nerves, she told Ian her decision. For a brief moment, Ian laughed, assuming it was a joke. And just as Ai Ling was about to take back her words—maybe she had gone too far—Ian saw something in her eyes that made him quiet down, to fully absorb what he was hearing. He stared at Ai Ling.

"Why?"

"I don't think I'm ready," she said.

"Then we can talk about this another time. No hurry in rushing into marriage."

"No, Ian, I don't want to get married. I don't think…"

"Why? What do you want then?"

"I want us to think about what we both want, really. What you want. What I want."

"What do you mean?"

"I don't know. I think we should just take some time to think about all this."

"Bullshit," he spat. "Just tell me what's on your mind."

"I want to be alone for a while."

"Alone? Why?"

"I'm tired, Ian. I'm tired of being your girlfriend. I'm tired of where we are going. I'm tired about what's to come."

"You're just fucking selfish. You only think of yourself. You never think about us."

Whenever Ai Ling recalled Ian's words, she remembered how they had struck a part of her that knew, despite her resistance, that he was right, that she was only thinking of herself, of how she had wanted to get out of something that no longer meant anything to her. She was only being fearful of what she did not know or want. And for a long time after their break-up, Ai Ling did not dare to date anyone. Even when she began to date again, she was often afraid of taking the next step in commitment, afraid that even at her age, she could still make mistakes that might have worse consequences than those she had encountered with Ian.

"So you are telling me that after Ian, you dated many guys casually?" Wei Xiang had joked over coffee later. He made a face at Ai Ling, feigning incredulity.

"No! Come on, the way you put it sounds so wrong. I'm not that kind of woman. I just went on some dates, that's all, nothing serious."

"Then what kind of woman are you?"

Ai Ling pinched Wei Xiang on his arm. He winced playfully.

"So, this is not serious too?"

"Well, no, not serious at all, just a casual date," Ai Ling said, before breaking into a laugh.

Wei Xiang, too, had gone through a break-up that took a while to get over. His last girlfriend had cheated on him with a colleague, her supervisor at work, a married man with three children. And she had broken up with Wei Xiang, because she had wanted another life with the married man, which was something that Wei Xiang could never wrap his mind around. He could not imagine why anyone would want to live like this, and after the break-up, like Ai Ling, he had refused to keep up any contact with his ex.

Once, when Ai Ling was over at Wei Xiang's place—he had decided to cook a meal for them—she peeked into one of his photo albums, curious about how his ex looked. She had expected to confirm some of her suspicions—to have Xiang's ex marked out in some obvious ways—but the person she saw in the photographs was no different from any woman on the street: pretty, yes, but not special in any way that was physically apparent.

Yet, Ai Ling still felt a sort of fascination about what the woman had done, to give up what she had with Wei Xiang to be a mistress to a married man.

∞

The break with Ian was not as clean as Ai Ling had wanted. Though she had ignored all his calls and emails, he still turned up unannounced on her doorstep several times; once, he had made such a ruckus that her parents had no choice but to let him in, and she had to shut herself in her room while he pleaded with her parents to talk some sense into her, to make her change her mind. He cried on every occasion. Ai Ling's parents had asked her to resolve the issue with Ian, to get back together, because Ian was a good man, and it was hard to find someone like him. Ai Ling ignored her parents' advice, and even in the heat of her inner conflict, she chose to stick to her resolve, to not budge from her decision.

The months that followed the break-up were a long period of adjustments, changes and coming to terms with her new status, as if whoever she was when she was with Ian had to be remade in the light of the current circumstance. She had chosen to avoid any contact with Ian's friends; some had chosen to take his side, and Ai Ling was told in no uncertain terms, from their messages and emails, about how they felt about the whole situation. Others were more sympathetic, and it was the latter group who Ai Ling did not want to see. She did not feel the need to justify herself to them. Apart from this, Ai Ling took to her new life with as much enthusiasm as she could muster, with an unspoken, underlying hope that whatever she was doing would somehow, one way or another, lead her to a clearer perspective of her life, a deeper understanding of her own actions and decisions. It was a long way to go, Ai Ling had to admit, and she had to watch herself, lest she get distracted by a thousand and one things.

"And you don't have any regrets after the whole incident, after the break-up?" Wei Xiang posed this question to her, more than once.

Ai Ling had often wondered about Wei Xiang's longstanding interest in her failed relationship with Ian. They had been dating for five months then, and Ai Ling liked the pace the relationship was taking—consistent, steady, unhurried. They had taken their time to know each other, and after the first flush of romance had come and gone, what remained was a growing bond of affection. What they agreed upon was to be frank with each other, no matter what.

"What's the point of regret? Regret is for something you did not do when you should be doing it. And I did what I did. The rest is history to me. It doesn't matter. A lot of things don't matter after a while."

"But surely you must have felt something like regret, during the months after the break-up."

"I can't remember now. Maybe I did. It doesn't matter anyway."

Sometimes, Ai Ling wondered whether Wei Xiang saw something in her that she could not see. Was she the kind of woman a man would feel an instinctive need to protect, to take care of, or did she appeal to a type of man who liked her assertiveness, her independence? Ai Ling knew how she looked—her lanky frame, small breasts, shapely nose a few degrees from aquiline—but how the different, unequal parts of her body added up to something that could tell the whole story of her character was never apparent, something that remained a mystery to her. Sometimes, when she looked deeply into herself, she would feel a brief alarm at the chasm that existed between her external and inner selves.

"But why do you like me?" she asked Wei Xiang in bed, while spending her first night over at his place.

"Well, you are really beautiful and sweet and gentle and caring and…"

"No, I mean, what do you really like about me?"

"You are very special…"

"Are you sure you know anything about me at all?"

"I don't, but I want to, a bit at a time."

"You know I can be stubborn and petty at times, right? And I've my moods, too."

"Yes, I know. But…"

"But what?"

"But I still like you."

"You're hopeless."

∞

When she said yes to Wei Xiang's proposal, Ai Ling knew she was making the right decision. She had expected it for some time—they had been going out for three years at that point—and she was already preparing herself mentally for it. She had just hit twenty-eight then, and knew she was happy with Wei Xiang, a happiness she knew she had a role in its nurturing.

And at that moment—when she said yes—she had meant exactly what she had said. And, for once, in a long time, she had not doubted herself, or the choice she had made.

7

Late at night, you stumble out of a recurring dream, like a suffocating man breaking through an invisible barrier, your breaths laboured, your body covered with a film of sweat. Shards of the dream have lodged themselves in your fevered mind. Turning to face the blank wall, you can see in the faint illumination hairline cracks creeping up like railway tracks, disappearing into the ceiling. You stare at the wall for a long time to calm yourself down.

You drift into overlapping states of wakefulness and sleep—you can no longer tell which impressions are real or dreams. You can still feel your body working, like a well-tended machine: the breaths in your chest *(in-hold-out, repeat)*, the tiny pulse in your wrist *(tick-tick-tick)*, the curl-in-curl-out movements of your fingers *(twitching, twitching)*. Life as a machine, going and going and going, persistent, dumb, unbearable.

You look up at the expanse of the white wall, all the way to the ceiling. Space, so much space—how could one ever fill it up? You stare until your eyes—dry like sandpaper—start to hurt, tiny specks floating across your vision. You study the unmoving shadow on the wall, a dark mountainous ridge.

You stretch out your hands, and the muscles in them ache anew. Triggered by the sudden movement, your body stirs to life—a forest catching fire. Flashes of heat flare at your joints, moving outwards. With the quickening of blood through your body, you can feel your cock hardening. You reach into your shorts and stroke yourself, mind still dazed. Slowly the act itself takes over, demanding every ounce of your attention, sinking you into the vagaries of desire. You find yourself masturbating to images of Chee Seng, salvaged from the depths of your memories.

∞

"Really, you have to meet him," Ai Ling had gushed over the phone. "He's a catch. You'll like him."

She had called Cody during his lunch break, bursting with the news that she had met an old friend from junior college, a teacher, and over coffee with him, found out that he was gay and single.

"I don't know," Cody said, playing down her enthusiasm. In the past, Ai Ling had tried unsuccessfully to fix up blind dates for him, whenever she met gay men from her previous jobs or from other friends and acquaintances. She had believed, without checking the person's background— as long as he was gay—that he would be suitable for Cody. To get her off his back, after her first few attempts, he had gone on a date with a guy she had highly recommended, only to find him a complete bore, with no other interests besides his job as a stockbroker in a securities firm.

"I'll be your chaperone, to take the pressure off. You really need to meet him," she said.

"Come on, you're making me seem desperate."

"Well, you're always complaining to me about being single, and how there are no longer any good men around. Or am I wrong?"

"Fine. Why don't you arrange something and I'll come along."

"You won't regret this, I promise. He's very cute, definitely your type: tall, dark and handsome."

"Isn't that every gay man's type?" Cody shot back. Ai Ling let out a cackle and ended the call with an update-you-later.

The date was set for a Sunday afternoon, coffee at Starbucks outside the Orchard Cineplex. Cody was running late, and as he approached the table at the café, he had a few seconds to observe his date before Ai Ling saw him and got up to introduce them.

Chee Seng was tall and solidly built, with a tanned, almost sunburnt complexion. Over coffee that afternoon, he kept up a brisk, low-key conversation, able to hold his own without Ai Ling's help, directing most of his questions at Cody, basic questions about his life, work and leisure. Every time Chee Seng smiled, lines would frame the contours of his mouth, his teeth bright against his dark skin.

Cody discovered that Chee Seng had been a teacher for about a year, and before that he had worked as an air steward for three years. "Too long," he stressed.

"Why did you quit?" Cody asked.

"I wanted to do something else," he replied, "something more meaningful."

"And so you chose teaching?"

Chee Seng raised his hands in a gesture of I-don't-know-what-I'm-doing, grimaced and laughed.

After two hours in the café, they left. Chee Seng insisted on driving all of them back. He dropped Ai Ling off at her place in Bishan before driving Cody back to Ang Mo Kio. Along the way, he asked Cody whether he was keen for another round of drinks since it was still early, only slightly after six.

Cody agreed, and Chee Seng turned into the McDonald's drive-thru, near the block of flats where Cody lived, and bought two iced coffees. After parking the car, they walked to a nearby park, alternating between light conversation and companionable silence. Chee Seng touched his shoulder to Cody's as they walked, sometimes brushing against his hand, grazing it lightly. Chee Seng's laugh was full, unabashedly robust, and Cody found himself laughing along with him, caught in the undertow.

When the daylight started to fade, they turned back and walked out of the park. Cody glanced at his watch, undecided on whether to end the date, when Chee Seng asked if he would be interested to have dinner with him sometime.

"Of course," Cody said.

"How about tomorrow?"

Cody agreed without hesitation. Chee Seng smiled, and for the first time that day, he looked shy, almost awkward. At the lift lobby of Cody's block, they hesitated, unsure how to proceed.

"So this is where you stay," Chee Seng said.

"Yes, my whole life."

"Well, I hope to visit one day, if it's okay with you."

"Sure, one day."

Then Cody moved to kiss him, a light peck on the lips, before pulling away. Chee Seng looked surprised, his eyes wide. Then he flashed a grin and started walking backward, waving at Cody as he headed back to the car. When he was gone, Cody took the lift up, and felt the nascent stirring of desire kicking at his heart.

∞

Chee Seng was getting ready to leave, slipping on his white Jockey underwear. He rarely stayed over at Cody's place on weekdays because of his work.

"I need to go. It's getting late," he said.

"Why don't you stay for the night and save yourself all the travelling?" Cody said, patting the empty space on the bed. The crumpled bedsheet still retained Chee Seng's body heat, warm to the touch.

"Not today, okay? I got a long day at work tomorrow, some teacher-parent meeting to attend. This weekend, definitely," Chee Seng said, tucking the tail of his striped shirt into his dark pants, checking himself in the body-length mirror behind the bedroom door. He gave his hair a few tousles. Cody sneaked up behind him and put his arms round Chee Seng's waist. They studied themselves in the mirror. Cody kissed the nape of his neck, breathing in the muskiness of his skin.

"You look sexy in your work attire," Cody said, stroking Chee Seng through his pants.

"Come on, you're horny again?" Chee Seng said, but did not stop Cody when he unzipped the pants, and fished out Chee Seng's semi-hard cock from the tight underwear. Dropping to his knees, Cody took him into his mouth. Chee Seng held Cody's head with his hands, raking his hair. Cody looked at their reflections in the mirror as if he were someone else—a stranger—watching a secret, private act. He watched how his mouth moved, how his hands slid up and down Chee Seng's legs and waist and ass, the flickering of tongue over the swollen head of the cock. Chee Seng closed his eyes and stood on the balls of his feet, immersed in the pleasure.

Cody pulled back for a moment. "Look," he said, nodding towards the mirror.

Chee Seng opened his eyes and watched as Cody took the cock into his mouth again. Cody hastened his movements, and Chee Seng's cock contracted involuntarily, a quick spasm.

"I'm coming," Chee Seng said, tilting Cody's chin so that their eyes met. An agonised expression streaked across Chee Seng's face as he came hard. Cody loosened his grip as the convulsions slowed and stopped. Then he swallowed.

Chee Seng grabbed Cody by the shoulders, pulled him up and kissed him full on the lips. Then he pushed Cody onto the bed and pulled down his underwear brusquely. By the time they were both finished, Chee Seng was so tired that he ended up staying the night.

∞

"Where are you bringing me?"

"You'll know when we get there. It's not far from where you stay," Chee Seng said, turning into the car park beside Yio Chu Kang Stadium. At eleven-thirty, it was deserted, the streetlights barely illuminating the empty parking lots between the few cars and vans. Several had window curtains drawn, which made Cody wonder whether this was a haunt for couples to make out. How did Chee Seng know about this place? Had he brought other guys here before?

Before Cody's mind could raise more doubts, Chee Seng pulled into a lot, at the farthest end of the car park. Switching off the headlights, the car went dark except for the panel of red-orange lights on the dashboard. Chee Seng reached over to pull the lever under Cody's seat and slide it backward; it went three-quarters of the way down. The next moment, his hands were on Cody, unbuttoning his shirt, fingers cold on his skin.

"I thought we were having a chat."

"Yes, we can chat, or we can do something else," Chee Seng said, his breath landing on Cody's cheek. Cody leant in to kiss him.

"Okay, let's chat then," Cody said, nibbling Chee Seng's right earlobe, moving down his neck, taking in the scent of his cologne. Extending his body, Chee Seng accidentally pushed the air-con button to high, and cold air gushed out of the vents. He fumbled to turn it down.

"It's so cramped. I can't even stretch," Cody said.

"Let's go to the back," Chee Seng said. Cody crept across the lowered seat, trying not to bump into anything. Chee Seng was close behind, his hands never leaving Cody's body, guiding him gently to the back seat. Turning around to face him, Cody felt a sting of self-consciousness as Chee Seng hurriedly began to take off his clothes. Cody looked out the darkly-tinted side windows, scanning the surroundings for movement, keenly aware of the risk that they were taking. His heart pounded, and he froze.

"What's wrong?" Chee Seng asked, lifting his head.

"Do you do this often? We might get caught."

"Don't worry, there's no one around. It's safe."

Not wanting to sound too insecure, Cody did not ask again. *I don't have to know everything about him,* Cody reminded himself. *It's only been two months since we started dating, and there's plenty of time to get to know him, so why the insecurity?* Brushing aside his uncertainty, Cody focused on getting back into the moment, to what they were doing.

In the cramped space of the back seat, they moved tentatively; they were still new to each other's bodies so they took their time, with Chee Seng leading the way. Quickened breaths interrupted the silence of the quiet car, and their skins broke out in perspiration, tingling with rawness. Holding down Cody's body with his, Chee Seng coaxed him into a fierce, quavering orgasm.

"Does this turn you on?" Chee Seng asked, after they had dressed and were back in the front seats, ready to leave. The headlights were on, casting a pool of buttery light on the tarmac in front of the car. Cody's body, softened by the heady release, was still sticky, still yearning.

"Yes, but..." Not knowing how to finish the sentence, Cody laughed and leant across to give Chee Seng a long kiss.

8

Ai Ling

Swallowing the eyeball, the seagull turns its attention back to the woman's body, assessing it with unfaltering concentration. It pecks away a stray strand of hair from her sand-speckled forehead. The woman's face is swollen and discoloured, bruises darkening into islands of deep green and indigo on her sunken cheeks, and around the eyes. In the mute sky, a fellow seagull, newly arrived, sounds out a mournful cry, dipping and rising in the wind. The seagull on the beach looks up and regards the other bird. Then it flaps its wings forcefully and skips up into the sky, disappearing in the direction of Phuket, in pursuit of the other seagull.

The blood seeping from the empty pit of the eye socket has hardened into dark crusty trails on the woman's face, and stained the patch of sand around the head into a crimson peninsula. Already the body is transforming, breaking down quickly in the heat and humidity. The muscles have finally relaxed, causing the body to sag, giving it a languid, restful demeanour. Rising from the body: a complicated mixture of smells, strong and overripe.

An agitated gust of wind blowing in from the sea lifts the woman's torn shirt, revealing the bulge. The gastric acid is gradually eating out the stomach, dissolving its contents into a slushy broth. Bloated with noxious gases produced by the digestion, the stomach has grown distended, like a balloon, pressing itself against the sand. The woman's hands, claw-like and protective, rest on it.

Suspended in the quiet sea inside the woman's body, the tiny form remains inert, enclosed in a shrinking world.

∞

During the second year of their marriage, Ai Ling had a miscarriage that she kept secret from Wei Xiang, barely a week after she had tested herself with a home pregnancy kit. She had wanted to tell him on several occasions, but the moment was never right. Then one morning, she woke to terrible cramps and bleeding, and had to call in sick after Wei Xiang left for work. Over breakfast, he had commented on how pale she looked, which she shook off with a smile. She stayed in the toilet and did not come out until she heard the front door close.

Ai Ling tried to staunch the bleeding with sanitary pads, but they were completely soaked through in no time. She threw on a loose-fitting shirt and left for the neighbourhood polyclinic, numb with pain and fear. She held her dark thoughts at a distance and focused only on her breathing. Two hours passed before her number was called. The polyclinic doctor, a short, balding man with a stern expression, was surprised that Ai Ling had endured so long—she should have called an ambulance instead—and gave her a strange, sympathetic look. The doctor asked about her husband, but Ai Ling gave a vague, noncommittal reply and looked down at her hands. She was transferred to the nearest hospital for the operation.

Ai Ling checked out of the hospital the very same evening after she was stitched up. While standing in the taxi queue, she called Wei Xiang on her mobile phone, telling him that she was running late and would not be cooking that night, that he should buy something back for dinner. In the taxi, she told the driver to switch off the air-con and roll down the rear windows. She pressed herself against the door, the warm rush of air hitting her face, and put her hands on her tender abdomen, feeling nothing except for a fist of pain inside her. *Everything happened so fast*, she thought, *but now that it's over, I don't want to think about it.*

She felt her skin go cold and clammy; something tightened inside her, leaving her out of breath. She had to ask the driver to stop by the side of the road so that she could get out to vomit whatever was still inside her stomach.

Ai Ling carried on as usual after the incident. She went to work at the childcare centre every day, knocked off at six, prepared dinner and ate with Wei Xiang. Sometimes she would watch TV programmes with him, and sometimes she would read the books she had borrowed from the library. At night, she stayed to her side of the bed, quiet and still. The rush of happiness she had felt when she first held the pregnancy test indicator was now a distant memory, something that might have happened to another person in a fleeting scene in a movie. *What a silly person*, she would have said if she had seen such a character. She would have clucked her tongue and rolled her eyes, reaching for the TV remote to change the channel.

Sometimes, when her mind drifted as she was picking up the toys after the kids at the childcare centre, or stir-frying a dish at the stove, Ai Ling would wonder why she had kept the pregnancy and the miscarriage from Wei Xiang. Just after they got married, Wei Xiang told her in passing that they ought to hold off on having a baby in the first few years of their marriage, so that they could enjoy their couplehood, just the two of them; since then they had not talked about it. Now her silence was sealed, and she would have to carry the burden of her secret stolidly.

For a long time after the miscarriage, Ai Ling avoided having sex with Wei Xiang. She could not bear the thought of it; her body felt depleted, sapped of any desire, and she did not want to do anything that might cause it to hurt in such a terrible way again. So she remained rigid and tense when Wei Xiang tried to initiate sex, brushing off his advances. She would stay up late on weekends, watching reruns of Taiwanese drama serials on TV till the wee hours, only going to bed after Wei Xiang had fallen asleep. One time, in a fury of lust, he overpowered her, clamping down her flailing fists and legs, reaching into her shirt to grope her breasts, and she had to fight him off with every bit of strength to get away from him.

In his confusion and frustration, Wei Xiang spat: "What is *wrong* with you? You *have* to tell me."

Ai Ling threw a pillow at him, left their bedroom and slept in the spare bedroom for a week.

∞

Three months after the miscarriage, while she was clearing out the wardrobe drawers in the bedroom, she felt something behind a stack of old clothes. Pulling it out, she saw that it was a pair of infant shoes, still held together with a plastic band, the price tag of $5.90 on the sole. Ai Ling stared at the shoes as if they were a relic from ages ago, one that had suddenly landed in her hands, although she could not remember when or where or who had bought them, or why they were kept at the back of the drawer. She did not hear Wei Xiang until he was standing behind her, looking over her shoulder.

"What is that?" Wei Xiang said.

Ai Ling spun around and held out the pair of shoes, like a thief surrendering her loot, unsure of the punishment awaiting her.

"Wait, I remember. I bought them a few months ago when I was at the mall. Aren't they adorable?" Wei Xiang said. Ai Ling stared at him, still holding out the shoes. She could feel the immense weight in her hands.

"Do you still want them?" Ai Ling said, putting the shoes into his hand and stepping back. Wei Xiang adjusted the laces and chuckled to himself, as if amused by his impulsive decision to buy the tiny shoes. Ai Ling bit her lip. She wanted to laugh, all of a sudden, at this scene playing out in front of her, at the absurdity, the irony. She let out a choking noise.

"Let's keep them. It's a waste to throw them out," Wei Xiang said, tearing away the price tag. "Just in case we plan to have kids when the time is right."

Ai Ling said nothing. Then she turned away and returned to the task of clearing out the drawers.

Wei Xiang kept the shoes, hanging them by the laces near

the dresser table, where Ai Ling could not avoid them. She decided one day, when Wei Xiang was at work, to throw them out. She put the shoes in a plastic bag and left for the neighbourhood park.

It was late afternoon, and the park was quiet except for several runners and a few mothers pushing strollers or chatting on the benches near the children's playground. Ai Ling walked past them and avoided looking into the strollers. She headed for the large pond located near the south exit of the park. The water was jade-green, overrun with water lilies, arrowheads and duckweeds, giving off a raw, earthy smell. There was no one around as Ai Ling made her way down to the edge of the pond. The water touched the tips of her toes, darkening the fabric of her sandals. She could step in and sink right to the bottom, and nobody would notice or save her.

Ai Ling stirred the water with her fingers and watched the ripples rouse the clump of duckweeds. Taking out the pair of infant shoes, Ai Ling placed them on the surface of the pond, making footsteps on the water. She relaxed her hold—the shoes seemed to float for a moment—and then quickly pulled them out and put them beside her on the soggy ground. Slipping out of her sandals, Ai Ling sank her feet into the water, feeling the coldness permeating her skin. Stirring the water, she could imagine the disturbance her feet were causing, scaring away the tadpoles and fish. She waited for something to bite her, to pull her down into the depths.

But all she could feel was the slow, heavy movements of her kicks. She picked up the infant shoes again and dropped them into the pond. The bright colours of the appliqués on the shoes—of an elephant and a bear—were quickly darkened by the water. The shoes floated for a breath of a second in the water before sinking. She stared at the spot, watching the bubbles form and then pop.

Ai Ling heard a cough and saw an old man with a cane looking at her from the pebble-strewn path a few metres away. She withdrew her feet from the pond, the sensation of chilliness lifting off her wet skin. Without looking back, or paying heed to the old man, Ai Ling walked away. It was only when she was almost out of the park that she realised she had been walking barefoot, having left her sandals beside the pond. She considered heading back to retrieve them, but gave up the thought. She could always buy a new pair. There was no rush.

As Ai Ling had hoped, Wei Xiang did not notice the missing pair of infant shoes, and she did not care to remind him about them. He was forgetful, she told herself, and it was not necessarily a bad thing.

9

CHEE SENG

It was Christmas night, and I was alone. The moment I stepped from Exotica's main hall into the tight space of the toilet, the sound of loud dance music became muffled. My battered eardrums hummed, as if a field of insects were chorusing inside. No matter where I turned in the dance club, the volume of the music was uniformly deafening; it would take a few days for the humming to fade. I checked my watch; it was almost two, maybe time to make my way back to the hotel. The amount of alcohol I had consumed numbed my thoughts, but still I wasn't ready to face Cody just yet. I washed my hands at the shallow aluminium trough that functioned as a wash basin, and splashed my face with water. I dried off, then made my way through the thumping music and writhing bodies to the front door of the club.

Cody and I had planned to check out Exotica together, but he suddenly changed his mind. We were back in the hotel after dinner with Ai Ling and Wei Xiang—they had headed off for a walk—lazing around and watching the local news on TV. He wanted to stay in and rest, claiming exhaustion from a whole day of activities.

"Come on, it's Christmas," I said. "There'll be lots of people there, it'll be fun. You said you wanted to go just now."

"I'm pretty tired though. Why don't you go and enjoy?" he said.

"It won't be the same without you," I said. "So typical of you, agreeing to something and then backing out in the end, so fickle-minded."

"I'm just really tired now. Anyway, you know clubbing is never my thing. I only ever went because you wanted me to go."

"Fuck, now you tell me this."

"Chee Seng," Cody said, but I had turned away, storming into the toilet.

I sat on the edge of the bathtub, waiting for the anger to run its course. My mind was a train wreck from the events of the past few days, after discovering the chat messages on Cody's computer. The guise under which I kept my emotions in check had been rudely ripped away, and all the old hurts had resurfaced. More than anything, I was angry with myself for losing my cool yet again. I closed my eyes and took a few deep breaths, but it was hopeless.

When I opened the door, Cody was standing right outside. He stared at me, and said, "Okay, I'll come with you."

"No, don't. I don't want you to go. I don't want to force you to do something you don't want to do. I'd rather have a good time at the club, without you sulking and hating every second of it."

"But I want to go," he said weakly. And because I knew he was doing this only to pacify me, it infuriated me even more.

"I don't want you to go, you understand? Just fucking do

what you want to do." I grabbed my wallet and watch from the bedside table, slipped past him and left the hotel room.

Outside the club, someone took my hand and pressed his mouth to my left ear. "Hey, what are you thinking?"

I turned around and looked at the young man, the same one I'd been dancing with for nearly an hour; with the thunderous music sweeping over us, I could not get his name—was it Danny, or Benny? He had approached me at the bar, where I was downing my third bourbon and Coke, and pulled me onto the dance floor. Danny or Benny, twenty-six, Malaysian, was holidaying in Phuket ("second time here") with some friends ("all straight, and boring"). With his toned frame and pale, smooth complexion, he looked much younger than his supposed age.

"I thought I lost you after I came back from the bar," he said, gripping my hand. "Are you leaving already? It's still early." His face was flushed. I kissed him on the cheek; my head was spinning from the alcohol I had consumed. Even standing on my feet was becoming a challenge; the world shuddered under my feet, seemingly about to give way.

"Yes, this old man needs to have his rest soon. He's not getting any younger," I said.

"Aw, you're not that old. I like you. Come with me," he said, pulling my hand, dragging me onto the sidewalk. A few locals, chatting and smoking under the club's bright signboard, looked in our direction; one of them laughed and threw his cigarette to the ground, crushing it under a heel.

"Steady, steady," Danny or Benny said, pulling me closer to him. I detected faint cologne, mixed with the scent of cigarette smoke. Exotica's house music gradually softened as we moved away from the club. Under dimly-lit lampposts, the busy streets, lined on both sides with bars, clubs and drinking holes, were still choked with people at this time of night—a bevy of drunk Caucasians arguing outside an Irish pub, two locals haggling with a youngish-looking prostitute at a corner, street hawkers hollering and delivering food orders to customers sitting around rickety, makeshift tables. In the muggy air, the smell of pungent spices, diesel oil and dusty tarmac mixed in my nostrils. Someone called out. I glanced back to see where the sound was coming from: a crash, and a burst of laughter. The bright neon lights scorched my retinas, and the music continued to ring in my ears. The night was alive in a thousand ways, fragmented into light and music and movement.

"Down this way," Danny or Benny said. We slipped into a dark alleyway, between a beachside hotel and a three-storey shophouse. He pressed me to the wall, his hands moving down my back to my ass, his tongue frantic in my mouth. He pulled back—a gaping pit of desire opened up inside me— and grabbed my hand, then led me through the darkness. I followed, drunk on lust.

As we progressed, I could feel the dense, salty air of the sea on my face, the night breeze tunnelling through the alleyway, through our hair and sweat-drenched clothes, touching our warm skins with light, ephemeral brushes. And then, as though we had finally broken through the diaphanous veil of the night, we were out in the open, on a patch of sand, facing the sea. The waves, glittering with moonlight, broke on the shore, sending up sprays of froth. I stopped, out of breath, and stared mutely at the dark sea.

Danny or Benny was looking at me, a smile on his face. He stretched out his hand, sweeping across the view.

"Beautiful, right?" he said.

He took two steps forward and glided down the small dune, swinging his arms to balance himself. I followed him and fell on my back into the sand. He reached out to pull me up, and guided me towards the deck chairs hidden in the shadow of a wide umbrella on the beach.

There, he held his body against mine on the deck chair and straddled me, his hands kneading my chest and arms. He lifted my head and pressed his lips to mine; I tasted beer, cigarettes and mint. I bit his upper lip. Our tongues met. I moved my hands across his muscled back and into the back of his tight jeans. He arched to allow my hands to slip easily under his underwear, breaking our kiss, releasing a soft breath into my ear. I felt the firm curve of his buttocks and trailed down the smooth groove between them with my fingers. He pressed his erection to my stomach, grinding it against me, then unbuckled my belt and unzipped my jeans. Already I could feel the dampness on my underwear, the strain of my erection against it. Tracing the contour of my cock against the underwear, he whispered into my ear: "I want you to fuck me."

He removed his shirt, and I licked his chest, tasting the salt on his skin, nibbling at his hardening nipples. The sea breeze swept over us, drying the sweat on our skin, raising goosebumps that heightened the sensitivity of each touch, each kiss. Against the lapping of the waves, we could only hear our own breathing, and the soft groans that escaped our mouths.

He reached into my underwear to free my erection,

touching his forefinger to the tip of my cock. "You are dripping wet," he said, and brought his finger to his tongue, licking it. Then, throwing me back on the deck chair, he bent down to kiss my chest, moving down my torso till he came to my crotch. I arched towards him. Teasing the head of my cock with his tongue, he looked up at me suppliantly, as if waiting for me to give the go-ahead. I grunted my approval; he took my cock all the way into his mouth, slowly. I closed my eyes and sank into oblivion.

After a while, he stopped and looked up at me. "Let's go back to your hotel room," he said, his look expectant.

"Sorry, I can't."

"Why? Don't you like me?" he said, his hand gripping me tighter.

"My boyfriend is staying with me."

"Oh." His voice registered a hint of irritation. He released his hold on my cock and pulled away, putting his shirt back on. After straightening up, he planted a light kiss on my cheek.

"You should have told me earlier," he said. And then he left.

I shook my head, suddenly overcome by a surge of crippling lethargy. I sank back onto the deck chair and stretched out the heavy sack of my body. The wind had turned chilly, stinging my face and arms, but I made no move to leave. The light of the crescent moon played on the rippling surface of the sea. I folded my arms across my chest, curled up my legs and closed my eyes. As I listened to the waves, I could only think of Cody, alone in the hotel room, waiting for me to come back to him.

Yet, even if I could muster all my strength and brace myself for what was to come, I knew it was impossible to return to the way things were before, to the lives we had.

10

Your mind is raw and foggy, skinned of any real memories, floating without thoughts. You close your eyes and, almost instantly, they flash wide open, unable to rest. Your shorts are damp, and the fabric sticks to your legs. Have you pissed without knowing it?

Your body is now a separate being, acting on its own will, keeping your mind hostage. You force your mind to sharpen, to will your arms to move. Your fingers twitch and your hands tremble; you ball them into weak fists. It's enough to send a tightening ripple along the length of your arms. Slowly you lift your hands to your face, and stare at the creases on the palms, the deep lines that crisscross the surface of the skin.

It's bewildering to think how the years can pass so quietly, so mercilessly; you looked up one day and noticed the deep, unseen shift in the things of your life—the places, the people, how they had changed, imperceptibly and fundamentally, over time. You know, in the core of your heart, that you too have changed, and in ways that are completely unknown to you; and in this newly-unravelled knowledge, you are left grappling, surprised not by the facts—because these changes have taken place right before your eyes, even though you could not truly see them yet—but by the realisation that time changes everything in its sweep, always moving in one direction, ahead of you, leaving you behind, stranded.

Your life is in your own hands—but how foolish it is to think that one could have any real, permanent control over one's life, over every aspect of it, when life is as random and faithless and fragile as it comes. For a moment, your existence is a thick fog that hangs in the air, obscuring the landscape; in the next, it lifts and vanishes into nothing.

∞

What Cody remembers from his nine years with Chee Seng: late-morning breakfasts, ten-kilometre runs around Bishan Park, Chee Seng's failed attempts at baking raisin scones, visits to the rental shop to get DVDs for their Saturday movie marathons, three-hour games of badminton with friends on Sundays, and the urgent lovemaking of their early years. They did almost everything together, because they wanted to be with each other all the time—and never stopped to consider where they were going, and soon became forgetful, careless, complacent.

First year: they watched movies, ran, cooked meals, made love everywhere, travelled, pooled circles of friends together for gatherings, read the same books.

Second year: they opened a joint savings account and split the bills equally. They travelled to places they had always wanted to visit: Krabi, Hanoi, Shanghai.

Third year: they took up volunteering and different activities, to "broaden their lives": aikido for Chee Seng, rock-climbing for Cody. They became more visible to their respective families and attended family gatherings together—weddings, funerals, baby showers. More places: Taipei, Tokyo, Sydney.

Fourth year: Chee Seng was promoted to subject head in school, and Cody quit for a new job as an editor in a trade magazine that specialised in aviation news. For travel, they decided to visit Paris, Madrid and Barcelona, and used up two eight-gigabyte memory cards for photos. They had a huge fight that year, and did not talk for a week, but things got back to normal in the end; the cause: money.

Fifth year: they went to numerous property launches to see whether they could find a place to buy, but could not reach a mutual agreement; with Chee Seng it was always money and whether they could afford it in the long run, while with Cody, it was all about convenience and accessibility and privacy. They adopted a dog from the animal shelter, a black Labrador they named Ninja, and took turns to pay for its upkeep: veterinarian visits, food, grooming. From the start, the dog liked Chee Seng more than Cody. They limited their travel to only Bangkok that year, and only for three days, because of the dog.

Sixth year: a quiet year of domesticity. They both changed mobile phones and upgraded their data plans. They babysat Cody's three nephews and niece. They went for walks in Bishan Park with Ninja; he had grown bigger and friendlier, and less demanding, and was greatly loved by the children of Cody's sisters. They signed up for a marathon at the end of the year; Cody finished an hour faster than Chee Seng. They explored eastern Malaysia, Sabah and Sarawak, its quiet beaches and lazy, rustic towns.

Seventh year: they finally found a flat that they both liked, within their budget; after a longer than expected renovation, caused by unnecessary delays and several arguments with the contractor over material defects and poor workmanship, they moved in. The flat wiped out almost all their savings, but they finally had their own place, and they hoped things would get better; they had been fighting more and more, and over increasingly trivial things. Travels: again Barcelona, and five months later, Taiwan. There, they had a threesome with a twenty-eight-year-old Taiwanese man who worked as a software engineer in an online-gaming company. Cody chatted up the guy at Funky, a dance club, and he took a liking to both of them. Chee Seng was apprehensive at first, but Cody convinced him that it was just a one-off thing, nothing more, and he gave in eventually. They brought the guy back to their hotel, and took turns to fuck him. The guy left after they were done, but expressed interest in meeting up again, no strings attached. They did not pursue this, in any case. Chee Seng and Cody talked about what happened after they came back, and because they were both averse to the idea of an open relationship, they left things as they were. Ninja had missed them while they were away, and so they bought him a chew toy shaped like a bone.

Eighth year: Cody was promoted to senior editor, and started sending out résumés for other better-paying jobs. Less than two months later, he received an offer to work in a company that handled custom publishing for government-linked agencies. Job scope was not much different, but he did get a twenty per cent pay raise. Chee Seng was promoted again, to head of department, and complained incessantly about the increase in workload. They still fought, naturally, and when it got worse, Cody would sleep on the sofa in the living room, or go back to his father's flat for a few days. Reasons: money and housework and Ninja. They took longer to reach a truce, and when they could not find common ground for a ceasefire, they turned the other way and pretended otherwise. The days passed, and they would still have meals together, and from time to time they would still make love, quickly and efficiently. Sometimes, to avoid the trouble or inconvenience, Cody would masturbate in the shower. Always, there were things to do, to make do, to follow up: the leaking air-con, the weekly groceries, Ninja's vaccinations. And then Ninja died that year of heatstroke, which was primarily Cody's fault. He brought the dog out for a run around the neighbourhood, forgetting that Ninja had grown both old and overweight. After less than a kilometre, the dog collapsed to the ground, whining in agony, his mouth lined with froth. He shat all the way to the animal hospital, and the vet kept him under tight watch for twenty-four hours, but Ninja did not respond to any treatment, so they had to put him down. Chee Seng and Cody were inconsolable, grieving for Ninja as though they had lost a son. They cremated him and brought his ashes back in a porcelain urn, keeping it at the back of the wardrobe. They threw away all of his stuff, but Cody secretly kept his leash. Chee Seng did not blame him for what happened, but Cody had already assumed the guilt. That year, they took separate trips overseas: Chee Seng to Phnom Penh, and Cody to Bangkok.

Ninth year: they went to work every day and ate out most evenings. They still talked, but about things that were of little consequence. They ran, and occasionally caught a movie at the cineplex. They went to bed at the same time, and paid the bills through the joint savings account on time. They planned to get another flat, but this time for rental income. They kept themselves busy the whole year, and tried to stay sane and healthy. They were close to the ten-year mark, an achievement, something to be proud of. Then Cody's ex-boyfriend Terry called one day to invite him out for dinner; he was going to be posted to Shanghai for a six-month job assignment and wanted to celebrate it with Cody, for old times' sake. Things fell into place swiftly afterwards: a few drinks after dinner, a long, nostalgic talk about their shared past, an innocent enough kiss, then the familiar touches of an ex-lover. Everything that was bound to happen happened, and that was that, the oldest act of betrayal in the history of love.

So when Ai Ling suggested the trip to Phuket at the end of December, Cody was more than willing to take it up. He needed some more time to carefully think through what he wanted out of his relationship with Chee Seng, and was hoping things would take a turn for the better.

∞

Somewhere in the dark room, the ringtone of a mobile phone sounds: the opening chords of the Coldplay song

"Clocks". Chee Seng's phone. The song plays for a minute or so, before it stops, and then resumes again a moment later. This happens another three times. You creep over to the pile of clothes strewn on the floor beside the cupboard, pick through the clothes—the song's getting louder—and find the phone in the pocket of Chee Seng's Bermuda shorts. The song cuts off just as you're fumbling to see who the caller is. Seven missed calls from Chee Seng's mother.

You grip the phone and sink back to the floor. After accidentally touching a button, the main screen comes on with a photograph: you and Chee Seng, taken at the beach on your first day in Phuket, the sunset draining away behind you, the sky a dark blue. Chee Seng's arm is around your shoulder, holding you close so that you could both fit into the frame. You had tried a few times, adjusting postures and smiles, before Chee Seng was finally satisfied.

You click on his message inbox and scroll through the messages. Most of them are from you, several from his mother, and others from mutual friends. All the messages are either very recent or very old; Chee Seng has a habit of clearing his inbox regularly. He once told you that it's because of the lack of memory on his mobile phone, but you know it's just another expression of how he has always lived his life, his singular way of managing things; the fewer things one has, the lesser hold and influence these things have on you, he told you once.

Towards the bottom of the inbox, you see that he has saved all the messages that have come from you. You click on a message, one dated back to when you two first started dating:

Do you wanna come over to my place later? We can order in and watch a movie. Any movie, your choice. I'm fine with anything. Let me know. Miss you.

And further down, as if backtracking in time, another message:

I had a great time this evening. Hope you have enjoyed it too. Can't wait for the next time we meet. When can I see you again? Haha. Good night, dear.

You continue to scroll through the messages. In the earliest ones you glimpse forgotten past events, words of love, the first flushes of emotions. You can't remember most of the messages that you sent to him, yet they clearly mean something to Chee Seng, important enough to keep.

And the more you read, the weaker the grip of your understanding of this person who has sent these messages; it's nearly impossible to comprehend this strange construct of a person that is the younger you, so far removed from who you are now. You hit the Sent box and read the messages that Chee Seng has sent in response. When you're done, you close your weary eyes, your mind strangely empty of thoughts, suspended in a limbo.

And you stay there, in this state, for a long time, willing yourself to feel nothing, to be nothing.

11

By the time he has run down five flights of stairs to the second floor of the hotel—the lift has stopped working—Wei Xiang is completely out of breath, his heart slamming in his chest. There is already a commotion at the makeshift front desk that has been relocated from the lobby to the second floor foyer: a stocky, dark-skinned woman in a sundress is gesturing wildly and yelling at the hotel manager, while the latter is trying and failing to mollify her. Wei Xiang can hear the woman from where he's standing, an intense volley of angry words, and though he does not understand a single word—Spanish? Portuguese?—he can guess at the gist of what she wants, or what anyone in the current situation wants. He, too, is about to do the same thing, if not for the motley group of hotel guests queuing at the desk, staring openly at the one-sided altercation, waiting their turns. Behind the manager, two female receptionists are cradling phones to their ears, talking rapidly and glancing furtively at the guests.

Wei Xiang walks down the final flight of stairs and stops two steps above the standing water that has flooded the hotel reception and lobby. The velvety sofas have toppled, their wooden legs sticking above the water like limbs of dead, stiffened animals; the large glass-paned table in the waiting area has shattered into webbed pieces, and the side tables have floated to the other end of the lobby, jumbled in a tight configuration. Torn magazines, books, newspapers, Lonely Planet guidebooks and travel pamphlets, warped and water-bloated, drift on the surface of the mud-grey water, banging listlessly against one another. A few landscape paintings have fallen off their hooks and bob in the water, the paint dissolving into smudgy blots and splotches of colour, their wooden frames broken. Two Caucasian children, oblivious to the danger around them, are playing in the stagnant water that comes up to mid-thigh, throwing handfuls of dirty water at each other. The wall lighting fixtures and decorative standing lamps have either been short-circuited or switched off; the lobby is shrouded in a palpable gloom.

Five men, hotel staff, are rummaging through the mess, salvaging what they can: shoes and sandals, small pots of fake geraniums and daisies, brochure holders, clothes hangers, rugs, umbrellas. Two of them are carrying black trash bags, into which they throw everything that is broken, tattered, or in an irreparable state. The men go about their task in an orderly manner, as if this were a regular part of their daily work routine. A few female staff, dressed in their black-and-white hotel uniforms, appear with large plastic buckets and metal pails, forming a line that snakes from the lobby into a room at the back of the hotel. They begin to fill these containers with the dirty water, and pass them up the line. Looking at them, Wei Xiang can't help but wonder how long it will take them to clear away all the water. To Wei Xiang, their feeble attempt to relieve the situation seems futile, pointless even, akin to emptying the sea with spoons and ladles. From outside the hotel, overlapping yells and cries can be heard.

Wei Xiang hesitates where he stands, holding the handrail, his feet just above the surface of the lightly rippling water. He watches the commotion around him with detachment, as if what is happening before him is removed entirely from reality, a scene from a dream perhaps, and that if he closes his eyes and opens them again, all this will disappear and everything will return to normal. But the urgency of the harried voices around him is too loud to ignore, piercing through the fog that has veiled his mind. There's no time to wait. Wei Xiang cautiously slips into the cold water, which comes up to his calves, darkening the hem of his Bermuda shorts. A porter, wearing a short-sleeved shirt and rolled-up pants, turns to look at Wei Xiang as he wades towards the flooded reception area. Holding the black trash bag, the man throws in a soggy travel magazine that has come apart in his hands, and regards Wei Xiang with a solicitous look.

"Good morning, sir. How can I help you?" the porter says, straightening his body, giving Wei Xiang a wan smile.

"What happened?" Wei Xiang can't help asking this question, though he has already seen the aftermath of the waves, the destruction that has wrecked the town, from the balcony of his hotel room.

"We hit by big waves, sir. Very big waves. Happened in morning, very early."

"Did you see the waves?"

"No, sir. Happened too fast, very sudden, they said. I sleeping." He points to somewhere behind Wei Xiang, beyond the restaurant, towards the back of the hotel; the staff dormitory. Wei Xiang caught a glimpse of it the day before, a nondescript, three-storey concrete building situated beside a small mango and rambutan garden and a stone-paved footpath, with flapping uniforms, shorts, towels, and undergarments pegged on clotheslines hanging across the balcony. Most of the hotel staff, who come from villages from the northern part of the country, or from the other islands near Phuket, stay there.

Wei Xiang sees a family coming down the stairs, the father putting up his hand to stop his wife and children from stepping into the water, his three young children gasping with delight at the sight of the water-logged lobby. The man speaks to his wife in Thai, who immediately shepherds the excited children up the stairs, while he rolls up his pants and makes his way across the lobby, his arms moving in wide, exaggerated arcs around his chest, as if he were trotting through the water with great effort.

"Have you seen a Chinese woman with long hair, about this height, this morning?" Wei Xiang says, lifting his hand to a height just below his chin. "I think she might be wearing running attire." The porter stares at him, his forehead furrowed. "Have you seen a woman like that?" he asks again.

The porter lowers his eyes, shakes his head. "No sir, I no see this woman," he says.

Wei Xiang feels a passing moment of relief until it strikes him that Ai Ling might have left the hotel before the man came on duty, and his mind begins to crowd with other thoughts. Yes, Ai Ling is still out there, somewhere; perhaps she has found some sort of refuge before the waves came in, and is waiting for someone to find her. Maybe she's waiting for him to get her now. Wei Xiang turns to leave.

"Sir, can't go out, very dangerous," the porter says, a look of concern flashing across his face. "Later waves come back. Stay in hotel, better, safe. Don't go out."

"I need to find my wife. She went out this morning, and I think she is missing. Do you understand? I need to find her," Wei Xiang says, his voice cracking. He looks away, out of the dirt-smeared hotel windows, at the street and the soot-hued sky.

"Sir, messy outside. Water everywhere, hard to walk. No safe."

"It's okay. I can manage," Wei Xiang says, tearing himself away from the porter, and trudges towards the open doors of the hotel. He can hear mutters of "Sir, sir" behind him, but ignores it. Moving through the sluggish water is much harder than he thought. He steps on something soft and squishy, and quickly brushes it aside with his feet. The muddy water is thicker and more viscous at the entrance of the hotel; the glass doors have shattered, leaving behind a skeletal metal frame with a barbed perimeter of glass shards. Crossing the threshold, Wei Xiang looks out into the street. The commotion behind him in the hotel fades into the background as the bustling din of the street assaults him.

The cries of children rise above the clamour of the other noises; they have taken to wandering the street, looking lost and confused, their faces mottled with dried-up mud, tears and mucus. A few kids are crying at the top of their voices, perched on piles of rubble, their clothes wet. In the street, the water comes up to Wei Xiang's hips. Small groups of locals navigate the water with caution; some are staggering in the direction of the beach—Wei Xiang has a hard time telling which direction the sea is—while others head inland towards higher ground.

Wei Xiang sees a young woman moving frantically through the water, peering into narrow alleys, shouting something with every step: "Yari!" A name perhaps. A lean, bare-chested man is pushing a rickety bicycle missing a seat through the water, a large basket of chickens tied with ropes around its frame. The metal-grille gates of the row of shops opposite the hotel are shut tight, their faded signboards askew. Two cats patrol the zinc rooftops of the shops, surveying the sight before them with lazy contempt.

Two old women wearing wide-brimmed, woven straw hats brush past Wei Xiang, talking loudly; one of them gives Wei Xiang a long rueful stare. Standing in the middle of the street, Wei Xiang assesses the two possible routes he can take: towards the sea, or away from it. He can also head down any of the alleyways that branch off into other parts of the town and find his way around. A hard object bumps against his calf and jolts him; he looks down and sees a small dead dog gliding away, the fringes of its matted fur trailing in the water. A group of locals carrying a torn-off aluminium panel knocks into Wei Xiang, almost throwing him off his feet; a hand, white knuckles taut, peeks out of the plastic sheet covering the makeshift stretcher, and he quickly moves aside. The path clears as the crowd makes way for the men to pass. Wei Xiang watches the procession till it disappears around a bend, near the main road. Then he glances down the waterlogged street leading to the beach and sees hordes of people making their way into the interior of the town, away from the wreckage.

Someone grabs his arm and Wei Xiang jumps, staring into the anguished face of the frantic young woman he saw earlier, the one searching for someone. He does not pull away from her touch, certain that he's also wearing the same raw, pleading, desperate look. The woman's voice is hoarse, but she utters the word again, like a chant: "Yari! Yari! Yari!" Wei Xiang shakes his head, and the woman loosens her grip, stumbling away to another passer-by, calling out the name.

Where the landscape has flattened out in the direction of the sea, Wei Xiang can see the ruins of toppled huts, reduced to perilous fragments of walls, carcasses of their former selves. The coconut trees have been stripped clean of foliage, their bare trunks jutting into the sky like accusing fingers.

A dizzying chill runs through him as he registers these images, his clouded mind lacking the ability to process them or put any definite meaning to what he is seeing. Everything is scrambled up, a reel of disconnected images. Yet, amidst all this, an overriding thought shrieks for his attention: *Where is Ai Ling?*

Stirring from his indecision, Wei Xiang takes a step, and allows himself to be pushed along with the flow of the crowd heading towards the sea.

PART TWO

12

Two days after the tsunami, the weather is sultry, the sky a clear expanse with hardly any clouds. In mid-morning, as the sun parks itself above the horizon, the dewy lightness of dawn gives way to the intensifying warmth of a humid day. The seashell-littered sand glisters with a shine, reflecting winks of light, as the coconut trees sway in the breeze that sweeps across the small island.

The body of the woman on the beach has darkened into shades of blue-purple blotches, decorated in livid patterns; the tributaries of veins and arteries are mapped out clearly in red, green and black under the skin. Visceral fluids leak from the body, pooling around the woman's ears and mouth, staining the front and back of her shorts. Under the heat of the sun, the body continues to execute its functions like clockwork, breaking down and tearing apart from within. Life, still persisting, still working, through death.

The sea breeze carries the smell of death across the island and ruffles the long, frizzled hair of the woman. The loose strands leap and dance in the breeze, as if charged with energy. The world around the woman's body teems with little acts of movement, small signs of life.

∞

The first thing Ai Ling noticed about the new boy was his hair—soft coils that hung like cursive loops on his forehead. She patted his head twice when he was brought into the class by the principal. The boy looked up at her, his eyes full of questions. For the rest of his first day at the childcare centre, Ai Ling watched him attentively. The boy was slow to come out of himself, and while the other children largely ignored him, the boy's eyes never left them, watchful and observant as if making mental notes of what they were doing or saying. During mealtimes, he sat quietly by himself eating his porridge, never once staining his shirt or dirtying the table. During the afternoon games of tag and skipping, the boy fell but swiftly got up, brushed his knee once, and ran to the back of the queue, waiting for his turn again. When Ai Ling asked him whether he was okay, he nodded his head, barely lifting his eyes to look at her. The boy perspired freely, and his wet hair was plastered to his forehead like a row of inverted Cs. That day, Ai Ling stayed back late and waited with the boy for his parents. His mother came, a stout, wide-hipped woman with dull, darting eyes, and Ai Ling talked to her for a few minutes and told her about the boy's first day. The mother nodded her head, saying little, before she picked up the boy's haversack and hurried him out the door.

That night, while they were having dinner, Ai Ling told Wei Xiang about the new boy.

"He is really small for his age, the shortest in my class."

"Boys are usually like that, shorter and smaller than the girls, until they hit puberty."

"And he is too scrawny. His arms are so thin, that I'm afraid of pulling them off."

"Maybe he has a higher metabolism than the others. I was a skinny monkey when I was young. A tiny body with a huge head. Try imagining how I looked."

"But he's really adorable and quite obedient. The rest of the children have not taken a liking to him yet, but I guess they will, sooner or later."

"Children are like that, they take a long while to adapt to changes, to new people. I'm sure the boy will be fine, and will get along with the rest when he's comfortable with them."

"I hope so."

In the days and weeks that followed, Ai Ling could not help but pay the boy more attention, keeping him within her sight, noting his movements and behaviours. Her interest was purely professional, she told herself; she was a teacher, and she had to look out for the children under her care. But deep inside, she was aware of something that went beyond her duties, something more instinctual, as if the boy had triggered a latent maternal impulse in her, a seed that had been sown and was now growing of its own will.

"Do you think I'll make a good mother?" she had asked Wei Xiang once.

"Of course, no doubt, you'll make a fantastic mother."

"How do you know?"

"I've seen you with kids. You are wonderful with them."

"But that doesn't mean I'll be a good mother, even though I'm good with other people's children."

"Well, this shows that you possess some sort of a maternal instinct."

"Having a maternal instinct doesn't translate to being a good mother. I know a few teachers at the childcare centre, the younger ones, who are also good with children, but are happy being single, or happy being childless with their husbands."

"Maybe you are at the age where you now want to consider having a child?" Wei Xiang looked at Ai Ling, searchingly.

"I don't know. Are we ready?"

"We can be, if you are."

Ai Ling knew Wei Xiang was being kind and accommodating; he had wanted to enjoy the first few years of their married life, just the two of them, before plunging into parenthood. He wanted to take it easy until they had everything in place: finances, the proper frame of mind, the ideal time. Ai Ling went along with his decision, only because she was still working out her own thoughts about being a mother. They were in their fifth year of marriage, and she was only thirty-two; the years stretched before them with other possibilities, other choices. Maybe she should give herself another year to think; maybe she would have a firmer decision by then. She had heard of women giving birth in their late thirties, even early forties, and the idea took the edge off her anxiety.

When Ai Ling had to stay late at the centre to catch up on her paperwork, she would look out for the boy's mother so she could talk to her. From their brief, truncated conversations, Ai Ling found out that the boy was the eldest of four siblings, and that the mother was working as a part-time retail assistant at a chain supermarket. Nothing was said about the father. While Ai Ling was all praise for the boy's good behaviour, the mother only cited incidents at home when he had misbehaved, how he could never sit still for a single moment, always climbing all over the furniture, how she was afraid one day he would fall and break his neck. The mother's reproachful tone, whenever she spoke of these incidents, was nonetheless filled with bemused affection. It was clear to Ai Ling that the boy held a special place in the mother's heart.

Once, when the mother came to pick up the boy later than usual, she would not look Ai Ling in the eyes, and busied herself with helping the boy put on his shoes. The boy's mood changed in the presence of his mother, becoming more subdued. When the mother finally looked at her as she was leading the boy out, Ai Ling saw the dark bruises near her right eye. Ai Ling asked casually about the bruises, but the mother brushed it aside with a vague reason. She dared not meet Ai Ling's gaze; the boy remained hidden behind a blank expression, his large, unblinking eyes moving between his mother and Ai Ling. The next day, when Ai Ling tried to find out about the family situation from the boy, he remained tight-lipped, turning his full attention to whatever he was doing—drawing with coloured pencils, building wobbly towers out of building blocks, or playing catching with his newfound friends. For a while, Ai Ling felt helpless at being merely an observer, and also angry at the woman for her passivity. But she knew her ambivalent, fluctuating sense of helplessness and anger was fuelled only by speculation— what did she actually know about the boy's family? Nothing, except for what little she had seen. She was being a busybody, and it would do her no good to meddle in other people's affairs. She knew she had to stay out of it.

Then one day, the mother did not turn up to pick up the boy, and after an hour of fretful waiting, Ai Ling decided to send the boy home herself. From his records, she found out where he lived, a housing block only three streets away. The boy, who had been sitting on the bench beside the shoe cupboard and glancing out the window, went submissively with Ai Ling. When she offered to carry his haversack, the boy shyly declined.

It took less than ten minutes to locate the block of flats. The boy seemed hesitant when they were in the lift, his hand clutching the long strap of his Winnie the Pooh water bottle. At the flat, the door was wide open; Ai Ling peeked in and saw a man lying on a sofa, watching a game show on TV, with two younger boys and a girl crowding in front of the screen. The mother was nowhere in sight. When Ai Ling said hello, the man jerked upright on the sofa, visibly annoyed. He stared at Ai Ling for a moment before noticing the boy standing beside her. Ai Ling explained the situation as the man opened the metal gate and invited her in. He was in his late thirties, a paunch evident behind his loose white singlet, with features that crowded in the middle of his long, pinched face. The man seemed friendly and cordial, though Ai Ling could sense a wall of guardedness behind his words and in the even tone of his voice. She asked about the boy's mother, and the short reply she received was that she had to work overtime and had not been able to pick the boy up from the childcare centre. The other children sitting on the floor turned their attention to Ai Ling, curious about the interaction between her and their father. The boy, meanwhile, had disappeared into the kitchen. When Ai Ling left, she could detect a hint of censure from the sharp closing of the door.

When the mother turned up the next day, she thanked Ai Ling for her help and gave her a box of cream puffs. She wore a dark long-sleeved shirt and black slacks, a departure from her usual attire of T-shirt and shorts. When she declined the gift, the woman insisted, pushing the box into her hands. Ai Ling offered the boy a cream puff, which he took after receiving a look of approval from his mother. He ate in small bites, holding the puff in both hands, the cream leaking from the edges.

That was the last time Ai Ling saw the boy's mother. After that, the father came to fetch him.

∞

On some nights after work, and on weekends when Wei Xiang was in the office, Ai Ling would head down to the boy's housing block and linger outside the flat, out of sight. She would stand against the wall, an eye out for any passing neighbours, and listen to whatever was happening inside. Mostly she heard the television and the voices of the children as they played, and several times the severe, scolding voice of the father; never once did she hear the mother's voice. Ever since the mother's disappearance, Ai Ling had tried to investigate the woman's whereabouts, but received only empty stares and imposing silence from the boy or the father whenever she attempted to broach the topic. She had even appealed to the other teachers for more information, but they were as clueless as she was.

The children were often left alone at home on weekends; the father would be away, perhaps for work—Ai Ling did not know what he actually did, though he worked long odd hours and would sometimes fall asleep when he came home without changing out of his clothes. A few times, during periods of long silence in the flat, Ai Ling would walk past, peeking into the gap offered by the ajar front door, trying to see what the children were up to. She took great care not to be seen; only once, when she stepped out of hiding, she came face to face with the boy's younger sister, who was picking up a ball near the metal gate. Ai Ling had to walk away quickly. If she had been discovered, Ai Ling never heard anything of it, at least not from the boy.

It was only when Wei Xiang started to get suspicious about her late-night wanderings and perpetual state of distraction that Ai Ling told him everything.

"Why are you doing this? What were you thinking?"

"I'm just curious about the mother, why she disappeared all of a sudden. The children are left alone most of the time."

"But what you are doing is not right. You have no right to pry into their lives."

"I'm not spying on them, if that's what you're saying. I just want to find out what happened to their mother."

"But you're going too far. You have to stop."

"I know, I know."

Even after Ai Ling stopped the visits, she still thought constantly about the boy and his mother. In her classes, the boy was still the same, behaving obediently, never drawing any attention to himself, yet alert to his surroundings, careful to stay out of trouble; he would relinquish any toy or game that the other kids wanted without a word. When the other children ignored him and excluded him from their games, he would retreat to a corner and read or play by himself. Ai Ling would often reward his good behaviour with sweets or packets of biscuits. Unwittingly, she had stepped into a role left vacant by the boy's missing mother, a role she secretly relished. Of course, she knew being a mother was more than what she was doing, yet she enjoyed every moment of it, and drew a fair amount of satisfaction from performing every task that the role entailed.

∞

When the boy did not turn up one morning at the childcare centre, Ai Ling did not think much of it, assuming he had fallen sick. She followed up with a phone call, but no one answered. When she finally reached the boy's father, and found out that the boy had been out of the house since morning, she began to fret. The father, on the other hand, worked himself up into a rage at the thought of his son playing truant.

"That boy! He told me he would go to school on his own. And now this! He will get a good beating from me when he comes home."

"Please calm down, sir. I'm sure he will return soon. Please call me once he does. I'll leave you my number."

When the father called her later in the evening and told her that his son had not come home yet, Ai Ling advised him to file a police report. *The boy is only five*, she reasoned, *where could he possibly go?* It was likely somewhere familiar, a place he knew well. Unable to sit still or keep herself calm after hearing the news, Ai Ling told Wei Xiang that she wanted to check around the boy's neighbourhood. Though Wei Xiang offered to come along to help, Ai Ling assured him that she would be fine on her own, that she would be back soon. She could tell that Wei Xiang wanted to say more about her involvement in the matter, but he had held back his words, perhaps waiting for another opportunity to voice his concerns. Ai Ling was grateful for the delay of the confrontation she knew was inevitable, but which she did not have the means to deal with at the moment.

In the taxi, Ai Ling remembered an incident from her childhood, an episode which had been dislodged from the tangle of her memories. When she was nine, Ai Ling had run away from home, though her parents never knew about it. She waited for the right moment to make her escape, when the front door of the flat was left unlocked by her mother while watering the plants along the corridor. She had never been outside the flat without her parents, so the idea of venturing beyond her immediate world was a strange, bewildering experience. She took the staircase instead of the lift, and after reaching the void deck, she walked across the car park in a direction that would lead her to a nearby garden. Once there, she decided to go farther, to another part of the estate she had only seen from the school bus; she recalled seeing a playground with swings and a concrete slide. To her nine-year-old mind, it had seemed like a paradise, a place where she could have all her fun.

Even as Ai Ling tried to remember the reason for running away from home, she could not, for the life of her, recall exactly what had made her do it. She had never had any big issues with her parents when she was young, and she was not an unhappy child; what she had wanted was readily provided by her parents, and she was an undemanding child, simple in her needs. While she was curious, like any child would be at that age, Ai Ling could not see her curiosity as the main reason for her to stray out of the known perimeter of her world. Then what? And why? Ai Ling could not fathom her reasons now, across the span of over twenty years.

At the playground, she had sat on the swing, pushing herself outwards and upwards. There were other kids, but they were playing amongst themselves and left her alone. Sensing their wariness, she did not approach them, staying away from their noisy game of hide-and-seek. She did not know how long she stayed there, but soon she got tired and thirsty. Ai Ling had not brought any money, and the immediate reality of her situation began to dawn on her. She started to panic. She looked up and, as if for the first time, saw beyond the playground to the blocks of flats that stretched beyond her vision, the streets heavy with mid-morning traffic, the rows of tall imposing trees. Everything suddenly seemed ominous, full of potential danger. As the world grew out of proportion in her mind, looming like an ever-growing leviathan in her imagination, Ai Ling was also aware, however vaguely, that she was shrinking inwardly, reducing herself to something that was easy to manage, quick to take flight, like a bug burrowing itself into the earth, or a dragonfly taking flight. How small she felt then, how inconsequential, how easily she could lose who she was. Within minutes of this realisation, Ai Ling decided to retrace her footsteps, and in the end did manage to find her way home. When she knocked on the front door of the flat, her mother was surprised at her appearance. Her parents had assumed that she was in her room all this time, reading, and did not want to disturb her; her absence from the flat had been completely unnoticed. She quickly returned to her place in the only world she knew.

As the taxi stopped in the boy's neighbourhood, Ai Ling's thoughts returned to the task at hand. For the whole night, she searched the area, but with no success. She called out the boy's name, whispered it into deserted alleyways, shouted it across dark empty fields; with each utterance, Ai Ling could sense the waning hold of his name, and she was gripped, again and again, by the premonition that something terrible had happened. The poor boy, her boy. She knew she mustn't lose hope, yet hope was like an elusive bird, vanishing out of sight.

When the first light of the day started to seep up from the horizon, Ai Ling called the boy's father; upon hearing his hoarse, sleepy voice, she could tell he had not fared any better.

"I've called her, but she denies knowing anything about this. That damn woman must have kidnapped him. What kind of a fucked-up mother is she? How can she even do this?" Yet his words lacked the heat of firm belief, carrying in them the dark hint of doubt. And Ai Ling suddenly pitied him.

"Maybe she didn't do it."

"You don't know her, or what she is capable of. How could

she just abandon her children and run off with another man? What kind of a mother does that, you tell me?"

Ai Ling could feel the weight of weariness finally descending on her, deadening her bones, and all she wanted to do was lie down where she was and never get up. She hung up the call and started her journey home, heartsick and wrecked.

∞

The police never found the boy, and Ai Ling never saw the father again, except for the final time he came by the childcare centre to pay the outstanding school fees and collect the boy's belongings. Ai Ling had packed everything—the boy's slippers, blanket, his drawings—into a large shopping bag and placed it aside. She excused herself when she saw the father talking to the principal. He glanced in her direction, but did not make any sign of acknowledging her. He seemed diminished, his shoulders hunched, his eyes dull. Ai Ling tried to smile at him, but he turned away.

For weeks after the boy's disappearance, Ai Ling forbade herself to think of him, reining in her thoughts tightly. She had glanced at the short newspaper report before putting it away, and the news soon trailed off; with that, the boy was gone a second time. Ai Ling went through her days at work as if in a daze, moving at a much slower pace, one simple task at a time. She taught new songs, words and games to the children, and wrote down their progress in the little blue books for their parents. She helped them put on their shoes and wiped them down after they dirtied themselves during mealtimes. She comforted those who were hurt and patted the shoulders of those who needed encouragement. She waited with them if their parents were late, and told them stories and fairy tales to pass the time. She did everything right, and the children adored her.

It was only in her dreams that Ai Ling was able to find the boy and bring him home with her and Wei Xiang; the boy would take to this new life with such joy that even Ai Ling was surprised by it. She would cook elaborate meals and give him any toy he wanted. She would watch over him, pat his head, and comb his curly hair. Even in her dreams, Ai Ling could feel the texture of his hair; the lightness and colour, the thickness and the darkness slipped through her fingers, like cool ribbons of water. How beautiful his laughter, chiming in Ai Ling's ears. She would hold the boy, and the feeling that stirred in her was as natural as breathing, and as vital too. Yet the dreams always ended with the boy leaving her; she would turn her head for a second, and he would be gone, disappearing into the world, leaving not a single trace. Every dream had felt like a small death.

Ai Ling soon got used to these dreams and gradually they began to occur less frequently. Over time, her memory of the boy became fainter, receding further and further into her mind, until it became nothing more than a broken fragment of her past, one that no longer caused her unwanted pain.

13

CHEE SENG

I look out of the hut into the courtyard, narrowing my eyes against the morning glare. Drawn by the light, I step out of the hut, into the heat of the day. The old woman glances over at me, and returns to her sweeping and weeding. I stretch out my arms, and turn my gaze to the shed beside the hut. The dead boy must still be in there.

The night before was a page torn out of time, and even as I try to recall aspects of it, everything feels unreal, impalpable: the old woman bending over the dead boy, her expression severe and watchful, motionless for a long time. Stunned with incomprehension, I stood frozen on the spot, failing to understand what was going on. Who was the boy—her kin perhaps, a grandson, or a stranger? Where had she found him—in the forest, or near the sea? What did she intend to do with the body?

The old woman unfolded the blanket from the boy's body as if she were peeling a relic from its protective wrapping. The hard, marble-like skin, speckled with patches of dirt, shone with a luminescence in the light cast by the kerosene lamp. Eyes shut and mouth open, one could mistake the boy being in a deep slumber; his tousled hair, long eyelashes, and a tiny nub of a nose that held a disarming fragility. The deep, long scar.

Taking up a rag, the old woman wetted it in the bucket beside her and began to clean the body, starting with the face. Then she moved down the chest and stomach to the legs and feet, unhurried in her ministrations, as if she were executing a difficult task in precise, calculated steps. The old woman tried to pry open the fingers of the boy's clenched fists, but they were closed as tight as a vise. Then, she tried to prop the boy's body upright, struggling with his ungainly frame. Motioning in my direction, she gestured for me to hold up the body while she cleaned his back. I hesitated briefly before squatting down. The unyielding coldness of the hardened flesh was shocking; it was bewildering to imagine how the body of such a small boy could possess such a severe degree of rigidity.

I mustered the strength to not flinch and let go of the boy's shoulders. The old woman finished cleaning his back. With a broken-toothed comb, she smoothed out the wild tangles of his hair, removing bits of sand and gravel. She hummed a song under her breath, timing each stroke of the comb to the rhythm. Then she poured a coconut-smelling liquid from a bottle onto her hands and applied it to the boy's hair from scalp to tip. Even after the hair shone from the strange oil, the old woman kept running her fingers through it, humming as if soothing a child to sleep. Patting down the stubborn screw-ends, she created a part on the left side, a tiny path through the mass of black hair.

Then taking up another bottle of oil, this one smelling of eucalyptus and sandalwood, she emptied the contents onto the body, rubbing it evenly over his skin, transforming him into a slick being, as if he had just been reborn into the world. With a nod, she signalled me to lower the body back down. In the dim light, I could not take my eyes off the boy's face. The old woman cupped a palm over his eyes and uttered something that sounded like a chant or perhaps a prayer, authoritative yet hypnotic at the same time.

The timbre of the old woman's voice coursed through the very marrow of my bones, resonating with a deep, ancient truth. In the silence between her words, I felt that I understood everything. Life begins, life flowers, and life ends: an endless cycle. I imagined her voice filling the shed as a physical thing, and then drifting away into the night, into the dark forest, to the edge of the sea and then over the waves, to distant, forgotten lands.

When she finally stopped, the shed fell into a deep silence. I was seized by a strange, crippling ache in my chest. The old woman started wrapping the boy in swathes of white cloth, binding his body tightly, leaving only the face exposed. Then, standing back, she looked at him for some time, before covering him with the blanket. She picked up the lamp, stepped out of the shed and nodded at me as she passed. I took a last backward glance at the dead boy, then followed her out.

What did the old woman plan to do with the boy? Did she intend to bury or cremate him? Or perhaps leave his body out in the forest? It was impossible to imagine leaving him in the shed for long, in this humid weather. In a day or two, even the strong smell of the oils would not be able to camouflage the rotting smell of death. Something would have to be done.

Stretching my arms to ease the tension in them, I push these thoughts to the back of my mind. The morning sun is warm and intimate on my skin. I shuffle over to the garden plot, which consists of neat rows of flowering plants, adorned with green calamansi limes and bullet-shaped red chillies. I bend down and help the old woman with her tasks: sprinkling a fine layer of fertilizer on the topsoil, removing the weeds, watering the plants. Despite my weakened body, once my hands touch the damp earth, they slip smoothly into motion, and in no time, I'm working up a sweat. When I feel light-headed, I sit back and rest to gather my strength; the old woman scoops water from the bucket beside her in a cup and makes me drink it.

At midday, we have a meal of gruel, stir-fried long beans and salted cabbage. Then we are back in the garden again, picking up where we left off. Working silently, we manage to complete all the tasks by mid-afternoon. The old woman fetches a pail of water from the well, and we wash our hands and feet as best as we can—the dirt is encrusted under my nails, and has made its way into some of my wounds. The old woman gestures at me to take a break, and I retreat to the shade under the eaves of the hut. Even after the hours of labour, the old woman does not display any sign of fatigue as she starts cleaning out the coops, feeding the chickens and sweeping up their faeces. The chickens, alert to the scattering of dry feed on the ground, come rushing to the old woman's feet. She reaches down and, in one fluid motion, grabs the chicken nearest to her. The other chickens go about their business, nonchalant, unbothered by the slight disturbance.

After walking back to the hut, the old woman takes out a large carving knife and a wooden chopping board and puts them on the ground, while holding firmly onto the struggling chicken with her other hand. Positioning the slender neck of the chicken between her hands, she gives it a quick wring, and the chicken stops moving, its body suddenly slack. She slits the throat and drains the blood into a small urn, filling it to the brim, before putting the lifeless body of the chicken away. Then she covers the urn with a lid and walks over to the shed, nodding at me to follow. In the dusty semi-darkness of the shed, she removes the blanket from the boy and motions for me to carry the body. In the cradle of my arms, the boy's body is solid and unremitting, heavy with death. I hold him close, feeling his weight against me. The sweet, cloying smell of the oils wafts up from the body.

Leading us out of the shed, the old woman picks up the urn of chicken blood and a hoe from a display of gardening tools, and walks behind the main hut. The thick, untamed foliage all around presses in tight around us; a narrow dirt path provides a route between the hut and the forest behind it.

A short distance away, about a hundred metres from the hut, we come to a rise in the land, a mound of red earth that rises up to a plateau, resembling the arched, muscled back of a huge sleeping bear. Climbing a dozen hardened-mud steps, we come to flat ground, where several piles of stones are stacked together, spaced unevenly apart. With a gesture from the old woman, I lower the body to the ground, and glance at the boy's face, half-expecting him to open his eyes. Using the hoe, the old woman marks out a hole in the ground, then passes it to me. I begin to dig slowly. The old woman stands back to assess the hole after I have been digging for some time, and kneels down beside the dead boy. She takes his hand and pats it, then nods at me. I place the body gently into the grave.

Against the damp, reddish soil, the dead boy looks preternaturally radiant, serene in repose. The old woman throws in the first handful of earth, which lands on the boy's chest, spattering outward in a firework of blood-coloured dirt. As we cover him with the soil, and he slowly disappears into the ground, something makes me stop for a moment and choke up; tremors go through me like an electric charge, stinging my eyes. When the boy is completely buried, the old woman pours the urn of blood on the small mound of soil, from one end to the other, staining it in dark streaks. The blood is swiftly absorbed into the earth.

The old woman looks out over the lush sweep of trees that stretches into the distance, to the ridge of hills that serrates the skyline like the teeth of a chainsaw. Then she begins to sing the prayer-chant I heard the night before. The soft cadence of her voice carries through the still, silent air, a sorrowful, primordial sound that seems to rise from the dark heart of the earth.

I close my eyes and listen; the song fills me completely, just as the soil swallowed the boy whole. It feels as if the song will never end, as if it will continue until the end of the world, but it does end, eventually. Even so, I can still hear the old woman's voice in my head as I sit on the ground beside the boy's grave, weeping inconsolably.

14

CODY

Growing up, Cody was often left alone, even though he had two elder sisters. They were eight and ten years older, already in adolescence, when he started school. Distracted with other things—boys, make-up, clothes, exams, extra-curricular activities in school—they did not pay much attention to him. But Cody had not minded, as he was preoccupied with his green toy soldiers, paper planes, and Old Master Q comics. To him, his sisters were like the creatures he sometimes read about in his storybooks, aliens from another planet who looked human but had blue blood flowing under their skin.

Because their fishmonger parents were often busy at the wet market, they left him in the care of his two sisters, who had to make him breakfast every day before school and make sure he got to school on time. Their parents were out of the house by three in the morning and usually did not return until late morning after they had closed their stall. Given their profession, the fridge was well stocked with all types of fish and seafood: sea bass, red snapper, garoupas, tiger prawns, stingrays. They often had a steamed or fried fish for lunch and dinner, and while Cody never grew sick of eating it, his two sisters were always complaining about eating the same thing. Their father would ignore them, but their mother would silence them with a stern, disapproving stare.

Because of the age gap, Cody was left by himself most of the time while at home, since his sisters were either still in school or out with their friends. His father had given him a key, which he wore around his neck in Primary Three, and his parents did not track his whereabouts, unlike his classmates who had to report their every movement to their parents at all times. When he came home from school at one-thirty in the afternoon, his parents would both be taking their naps, and his mother would tell him to eat whatever was left on the stove or dining table—a meal of sweet potato porridge or rice with stir-fried vegetables, braised egg or fish. When he was done with lunch, he would wash the plate and utensils, and lie on the sofa and read comics until his parents woke up, and then he would start on homework.

In school, Cody had friends, though there was nobody whom he was particularly close to. During recess, he would play with a group of boys from his class, usually football on the school pitch—he always played the defender role, since being a striker or midfielder was too strenuous, involving a lot of running and aggressive body contact, which he was not comfortable with—or a game of catching around the canteen and assembly area. Because of his small build, he was often chosen last, or second to last, when the bigger boys picked players. Standing in the dwindling group, he would look at his feet, pretending not to care, even while he could feel himself shrinking inside, diminishing into something insubstantial. Sometimes, he would look at the boys who were chosen after him, or at the boys who stood at the fringe of the school pitch, who, for one reason or another, did not want to play football or preferred to play zero-point or five stones with the girls. Sometimes, the boys who played football would point out this group of boys and laugh openly at them and call them names, and Cody would join in. Though he longed to be part of this clique of boys who was sporty and popular and interesting, his position in the hierarchy was often at the bottom; it was all too easy to be left out, and this fear—felt rather than spoken—was what kept him in line, constantly seeking the approval of those higher up.

In Primary Four, Cody was promoted to a new class after he received better-than-expected exam results. He was assigned to a desk beside Wee Boon, a quiet boy who sat ramrod-straight throughout the lessons, and brought his own food, prepared by his grandmother, for the recess breaks. Milk-pale and skinny, Wee Boon was one of those boys who did not like to play football or any kind of sports or games during recess; he was often alone, reading at the library corner under the stairwell, or walking about aimlessly in the school garden. He seemed happy to be left alone by himself, to do whatever he wanted. Whenever Cody bumped into him, by chance or intention, Wee Boon would break from his reverie and turn his full attention to him, always eager to do whatever Cody asked him to. Sometimes, when Cody grew bored of playing football, he would get Wee Boon to catch grasshoppers or dragonflies near the pond with him, and they would fill plastic bags full of these insects, clicking and beating against the surface like tiny bombs. They would keep these bags in the slots under their desks, and take them out from time to time to shake them up; sometimes they would forget about them, and when they did remember, the insects would all be dead. And they would catch a new batch.

Once, Cody asked Wee Boon to join in the football game, and he reluctantly agreed. The leader of the team chose Wee Boon last, eyeing him with a suspicious stare, and commanded him to take the defender position. Unathletic and uncoordinated in his movements, Wee Boon was slow to chase after the ball and too timid to block anyone who charged at him. Unlike him, Cody had learnt to hide his fear, to steel himself against any shot that was thrown in his direction, masking his clumsy footwork with a slide. He was never good at the game, but that was hardly a reason for not playing it. Wee Boon only played that one time and never again, and Cody did not ask him to join in any more.

An only child, Wee Boon was doted on by his parents and grandparents, and had everything he wanted: sticker cards for *Dinosaurs of the Past*, a box of rubber erasers that featured the flags of the world, new pencil cases and school bags every year. While Cody had to save up to buy a new pack of sticker cards every other week, skipping his recess break once or twice a week, Wee Boon would get a pack whenever he went out with his grandparents. His *Dinosaurs of the Past* book was three-quarters full within two months after they started, while Cody's was still patchy, with many empty boxes. Wee Boon would give him any sticker cards he needed, though he was too shy to ask. In time, their booklets looked almost similar, lacking only those phantom sticker cards that never appeared in any packet they bought.

After school each day, Wee Boon's grandmother would be waiting for him outside the school gates. With her white hair held tightly in a bun, and wearing a rosewood samfoo with frog buttons, his grandmother was a gentle, smiling woman, who would reach first thing for Wee Boon's school bag and water bottle when he came out of the gates. She would smile at Cody and, in a spiel of rapid Cantonese, ask whether they had been good. Wee Boon would look embarrassed and tell her that he was hungry and ask for a snack—an ice-cream or some White Rabbit candies from the provision shop. Since the boys lived in the same neighbourhood—their flats were only two blocks apart—they would walk home together, and Wee Boon's grandmother would buy Cody whatever Wee Boon was having. When they reached Wee Boon's block, he would sometimes invite Cody up to the flat, where he had his own room and several large boxes of toys and shelves of comic books. At his place, he would show Cody his latest toy figurines and allow him to play with them, and they would stage epic intergalactic fights that often ended with everyone but one last hero massacred. When they got bored with these fights, they would lie on the floor and read the latest Old Master Q comics. When it was time for Cody to leave, he would borrow a few comics, and promise to return them after he'd finished reading them. When he forgot or wanted to hold onto them, Wee Boon did not say anything or remind him to return them.

In class, Wee Boon was the kind of student that the teachers liked: obedient, quiet, giving all his attention to what was said or written on the chalkboard. He handed up his homework on time and his name was always among the top when the teachers announced the results of a test or examination. He was the form teacher's pet student, the one she could count on to be reliable and submissive. This naturally meant that he was intensely disliked by the other students in the class, especially the boys, who would ransack his school bag and hide his textbooks. But Wee Boon never told on anyone, and would bite his lips and smile away any discomfort or annoyance. Some of the girls would tease him for his shyness, but most of them would befriend him and invite him to join them for zero-point or hopscotch. Because Cody sat beside him in class, he would often copy Wee Boon's homework; his parents had hired two tuition teachers, one to teach only Chinese, and the other English, maths and science. Cody had to seek help for his homework from his two sisters, who were less than helpful, being too impatient or busy. When Cody was ill-prepared for a test, Wee Boon would tilt his test papers in such a way that made it easy for him to see, and in this way, and many others, they became fast friends, with a hoard of each other's secrets.

On weekends, after tuition classes, and if Wee Boon's parents allowed, they would play at the void deck under his block, kicking a ball or taking turns on Wee Boon's new bicycle, which he had received as a present for getting the highest marks in the mid-year examinations. They rarely ventured farther than the void deck or the playground in front of the block of flats, coming up with imaginary battles and using the playground as the battlefield, dividing it up into different lands, fighting against each other, the hero against his enemy. Once, Wee Boon clamoured to be the hero, and Cody pushed him to the ground, telling him that he was too weak to be one, and Wee Boon turned away, his eyes brimming with tears. Sometimes, Cody would let him win the battle, only because he had pitied him. When it was time for dinner, Wee Boon's grandmother would come down to fetch him, and he would shout at her to leave them alone. Cody would never have dared to raise his voice at any adult, especially his elders; the few times he had done so, he was punished with strokes of the cane. Wee Boon's grandmother would wait patiently for their game to end, and when they were done, she would draw out a handkerchief from her pocket and wipe down Wee Boon's reddened face and damp hair, which he would shake off with a brusque shrug.

Their friendship was never a balanced or fair one. While Cody often sought peer approval from the more popular boys in class, joining them whenever they asked him to play football or other games on the school pitch, Wee Boon would seek out only him when he wanted someone to play with. Even at that age, Cody knew better than to be seen playing with him all the time in school, and from time to time he would shun Wee Boon deliberately, or push him away whenever he saw the other boys glancing in their direction. They would make jokes about Wee Boon behind his back and tease him to his face, and even if Cody were standing there, he would pretend not to see or hear anything, and let their laughter run their course and die off. While he was sometimes angry with himself for not doing anything, he was angrier at Wee Boon for being such a pushover, a weakling with no backbone. During these times, in Cody's dark moods, Wee Boon would stare at him, a look of hurt and incomprehension in his eyes. But

Cody learnt soon enough to ignore these looks, pushing them into the background.

It was Cody's idea to take up swimming as their extra-curricular activity in Primary Six. The swimming lessons were held twice a week after school, at a swimming pool only five minutes' walk away. After lunch at the school canteen, Wee Boon and Cody would walk there and flash their school passes to gain free entry to the pool. They would change into their trunks at the changing room, and head for the main pool where the coach, a pot-bellied man with leathery skin, would be waiting, along with other students of the school's swimming club. While Cody learnt to swim the breaststroke adequately after only three lessons, able to complete a lap without panicking, Wee Boon was still struggling to keep his body afloat and to regulate his breathing. After each lesson, he threatened to quit, though he never did. The boys were taught other strokes—freestyle, butterfly, backstroke—and practised these by swimming a few laps. While they swam, the coach would bark out instructions from the side of the pool, correcting arm or leg posture, or telling them not to slow down. When they finished their assigned laps, they would hang onto the edge of the pool, splashing water at each other or competing to see who could hold his breath underwater the longest. Sometimes they would tickle or punch each other in the water to make the other person give up, to let go of his breath. In most cases, Cody was the winner, but during those times, when they really wanted to know who could hold his breath the longest, without any trick or disturbance, Wee Boon would emerge the winner; his longest record: two minutes and fifty-one seconds.

After the lessons ended, Wee Boon and Cody would continue to swim or wait inside the pool, since the changing room would be crowded with their classmates and there were only a few showerheads. They would linger until most of the boys had left before they came out of the pool.

One day, after a long and strenuous lesson, Wee Boon and Cody decided to forego the waiting and brave the crowd in the changing room. By the time they entered, all the stalls were occupied, and they had to wait, sitting on the damp wooden benches in front of the stalls. Wee Boon turned suddenly quiet, tapping his feet on the wet floor, his body radiating tension. The boy who was showering in the nearest stall, a fellow classmate, turned his body slightly towards them, and in a glimpse, Cody saw a neat turf of black, curly hair above the boy's penis. He was not surprised, since he had seen other grown men showering in the changing room, and knew what their bodies had looked like. Around him, in school, he was vaguely aware of the changes that were taking place in the bodies of his classmates: the breaking of their voices, the growth of hair in their armpits and on their arms and legs. While it would be another year or two before these changes occurred to Cody, he knew that he was heading for some sort of a transformation, though the thought itself was not comforting in any way.

When the classmate was done showering, Cody told Wee Boon to go ahead, but he shook his head, telling Cody to go first, that he would wait for another available stall. Cody rinsed himself off; his skin felt sticky even after the shower. He quickly towelled off. Later, when he was busy packing his wet swimming trunk and goggles into his school bag, he did not notice Wee Boon coming out of the shower. It was only when he heard laughter coming from some of the classmates at the other benches that he turned to see what they were snickering at. Wee Boon, naked, was frantically searching through his bag for his towel, and even though he tried to hide it as best as he could, there was something odd about his penis at first glance. At first, Cody was surprised that Wee Boon too had grown some pubic hair, since they were the same age, but what was more surprising was that he was sporting a hard-on. It was a new sight to Cody's eyes, and looked painful. Wee Boon's dick was bent upwards, red, angry-looking. In his distress, and amidst the boisterous jeering, Wee Boon's dick got even harder, stretching out of the foreskin, like a turtle's head peeking out from its wrinkly neck.

The classmates' taunting grew louder and more explicit, and Wee Boon snatched up his bag and ran to one of the toilet stalls, slamming the door. Even as they left the changing room, the boys continued to chant names at him; one of them even kicked the toilet door hard as a parting gesture. It was only when all of them had left that Cody offered his wet towel to Wee Boon and coaxed him out of the toilet stall. His face was livid with shame, and he did not look at Cody once while they were making their way home, not even stopping at the snack-food stall where they would usually buy a stick of fish balls or a curry puff to share between them. When Wee Boon reached his block of flats, he ran up the staircase without saying anything.

For the next few days, Wee Boon had to endure a battery of merciless teasing from the classmates who had witnessed his episode at the swimming pool. The news took less time to spread than a match catching fire; before the morning assembly was over, it seemed that everyone, including the girls in their class, was aware of what had happened. The girls giggled and whispered loudly among themselves, about how disgusting it was, how gross, so like him to do it, how dirty, how shameless; their taunting, unlike the boys', was relentless and vicious. Wee Boon, on the other hand, kept up his composure and silence; the only sign that betrayed his distress was his lips, which were tightly pressed into a thin, quivering line. Sitting beside him those few days was like being near a seemingly calm dog with a muzzle over its jaws, contained and subdued, but only barely. He and Cody did not talk about what had happened; they hoped, separately, for all this to pass, which it did, after another episode of embarrassment from a different classmate, who was caught staring up some girls' school skirts.

Yet the whole incident shifted something imperceptibly between Wee Boon and Cody, as subtle and permanent as a fissure left behind after an earthquake. They still talked, and still played whatever games they had played before, but there was a distinct, though unvoiced, divide that held them apart. It was as if, now that Cody was aware of Wee Boon's undeniable transition into a different person, he could not *not* see who he was: a person who was no longer someone Cody could say he knew well, a stranger who had taken the place of a friend. Even in their closeness, they held a respective distance. It was only much later, when Cody discovered his own inclination towards other boys that he knew what he had been afraid of acknowledging then: attraction. Raw, open-faced desire.

Even after the incident, they did not stop attending the swimming lessons, though they had learnt to wait until all the classmates left before getting out of the pool and showering at the changing room. In their separate stalls, they showered and changed quickly, and avoided looking at each other's bodies.

Even though the swimming lessons ended after the June school holidays, Wee Boon and Cody continued to swim whenever they could, on weekends and on days free from remedial classes or other school activities. Most of the time, they went together, but sometimes Wee Boon went by himself. At that stage, he had become a more consistent swimmer than Cody, and could easily beat him at freestyle. His body too had taken on a different proportion, lean and broad-shouldered, with hair growing intermittently on his lower calves; his voice had cracked in the midst of their final year in primary school.

One Saturday afternoon, Cody was at the swimming complex early and waited for twenty minutes at the entrance before deciding to go ahead without Wee Boon, thinking he must have forgotten about the appointment. After changing, Cody walked to a corner of the seating area, where there were fewer people, put down his bag and began his warm-up. Scanning the pool, he noticed someone getting out at the far end and stretching his legs. Wee Boon. Cody wanted to shout to him, to let him know he was there, but stopped when he saw Wee Boon staring at a man who had also got out of the pool and was walking towards the changing room. The man turned to glance at Wee Boon when he walked past, and from where Cody was standing, he could sense something between them, a sort of tacit agreement, conveyed only by the briefest of looks. Wee Boon paused for a few seconds, and then stepped into the changing room. Cody followed them.

The changing room was quiet except for an occupied shower stall; Cody crept over and saw two pairs of feet in the gap of the stall door. A stream of chatter came from inside, and then there was a long period of silence, followed by some other unfamiliar sounds, as if someone were trying to steady his breathing—sharp exhalations, feral and animal-like. Cody stood there, unable to move, time measured only by the growing lump of bile in his throat that he had to force down.

And suddenly the toilet door burst open. Before Cody could think, his feet were already edging towards the exit. In his haste, he slipped and fell onto the wet floor. He looked back; the man and Wee Boon were staring down at him, a mutual look of alarm and panic on their faces. The man came towards Cody, offering his hand, as he struggled to his feet. Wee Boon stood absolutely still, and even as Cody avoided his look, in that brief moment he saw something in Wee Boon's eyes that he could only interpret at that instance as: *Please, no, don't.* Cody changed into his clothes at the seating area, grabbed his bag and left the pool.

Back in school on Monday, Cody and Wee Boon pretended nothing had happened, even as they went through the usual routines. But nothing was the same again after that. They plunged headlong into their studies, revisions and remedial classes—the PSLE was less than three months away—and left things as they were, unasked and unquestioned. Cody studied with some of the boys from the class, and spent more time playing with them, which meant seeing Wee Boon less.

They took the PSLE, and after the results were announced—Cody and Wee Boon got accepted to different secondary schools—they never contacted each other again. They sheared themselves clean of their past, their childhoods, and moved on. The friendship they had was cast aside quickly, heedlessly, as they began their new lives in their new schools.

15

Wei Xiang

For the past twenty minutes, Wei Xiang has followed a local man carrying a young girl in his arms—small in her pink Hello Kitty pyjamas, her limbs loose by her sides, blood flowing from an unseen wound on her head—as it is clear, even through the man's visible grief, that he knows where he is going. The man's face is tormented, his gaze far away, and the last two fingers on his left hand are missing and bleeding freely. His open anguish singles him out in the crowd, and Wei Xiang was drawn to him at first sight. They now approach the compound of a school cum emergency medical centre, circumscribed by a chain link fence crowded by adults and street kids, and a gate attended to by a guard, who lets the man through. Wei Xiang stands by a muddy puddle near the gate. In the courtyard are a number of dead bodies, and several volunteers are constructing a shelter with metal poles and tarps. A group of street kids lingers at the fence, whispering to one another; one of them stares at him with an undisguised curiosity, before his companion distracts him, pointing

to something in the weedy shrubs at the edge of the
school field. The growing crowd gawks at the commotion,
sometimes letting out a collective cry or yell when
another body is carried into the school, clearing a path for
the procession.

Wei Xiang steps up to the school gate, and the guard
stops him, jabbering at him in Thai. Wei Xiang points to the
school assembly hall and, with a loud voice and a series of
wild gestures, tries his best to convey his intentions. The guard
stares at him, and Wei Xiang, exasperated, raises his voice.
"My wife!" he screams into the guard's face, finally losing his
calm. He is aware of the attention he's getting, the numerous
pairs of eyes watching his outburst, but he ignores them. The
guard finally backs down, moves aside and allows Wei Xiang
to enter the school compound. When he looks back, the street
kids are still staring at him from behind the fence.

Wei Xiang quickly makes his way through the entrance of
the low-ceilinged hall, careful not to trip over any of the dead
bodies lying on the sediment-encrusted floor, moving aside
for the helpers making their rounds, scribbling on pieces of
paper or separating the bodies according to gender and size.
He passes through the men's section, a marked-out area near
the entrance, with most of the bodies left uncovered; only
the worst cases are occluded by torn sections of cardboard,
pieces of clothing or newspapers over their faces or severed
limbs. Wei Xiang catches a glimpse of a man with a deep
gash that has split open his chest, his face covered by a flimsy
rag soaked through with blood, with a stone on top to weigh
it down. He moves to the women's section, near the raised
platform at one end of the hall; a wood-and-copper plaque

featuring the school insignia—branches of laurel and a yellow lamp—hangs on the peeling wall above the platform. Dead children have been placed on the platform, lined up in neat rows, with white plastic sheets and blankets covering their bodies.

Wei Xiang preps himself mentally as he starts to examine the first row of dead women's bodies. The faces of the women—ashen, grim, distorted—imprint themselves like a hot branding iron into his frayed, exhausted mind. Every face is a torture, and every anticipation of possible recognition raised and thwarted leaves him stricken with a deepening sense of futility. After the fifth body, Wei Xiang blanks out unwittingly. For a fleeting moment, he can't remember anything about Ai Ling—her face or any of her features; she has become a phantasm, a figure made up of a multitude of disembodied, indistinguishable parts. What kind of ears or eyebrows or lips does she have? Does she have a scar or a mole? Nothing comes to mind. All the faces he sees are the same to him, each possessing a similar death mask. He closes his eyes to pull himself together, to let the images of the faces fall away. Then, hardening his resolve, Wei Xiang continues down the line to the next row of bodies, lifting the coverings and taking quick glances. He holds his breath; the air in the hall has thickened, and the helpers who wear improvised face masks made of dirty rags and handkerchiefs are fanning themselves with cut-outs made of cardboard.

Wei Xiang pauses beside a body, the face concealed by strands of long hair but clearly missing both eyes and nose; his gaze glides down the body, to check its shape and proportions for any recognisable traits or features—does Ai Ling have a mole near her right breast? Or a pale crescent scar on her hip? He covers the body and catches his breath, emptying his mind of the image of the woman's face. From somewhere, he hears a shout and sees men bringing in another dead body, dropping it on the floor with a dull thud. Two women rush to identify it, pointing to the platform; one of them speaks in a firm voice to a helper who is propping himself up with both hands on his thighs, panting visibly.

Wei Xiang presses on. Nobody has stopped him so far from looking at the bodies, though he notices one or two helpers giving him strange, puzzled glances. After examining the last body in the section—a heavyset woman in her late forties with half-shut eyes, white-purplish lips and a stunned scowl on her face—Wei Xiang stretches, feeling the tension in his neck and waist, the nagging ache in his lower back.

He looks back towards the entrance of the assembly hall and sees the silhouette of a young boy standing there alone, his small form dark against the harsh sunlight from outside. By the time Wei Xiang blinks and clears his vision, the boy is gone. He wonders how a kid could have sneaked into the school compound, with the guard at the gate.

Wei Xiang notes the time on his watch: already half past four in the afternoon. He has spent more than two hours searching the assembly hall for Ai Ling. The stale air barely stirs, permeated with a strong, unbearable stench; Wei Xiang feels his nausea getting worse, so he steps outside. The helpers have finished constructing the makeshift tent in the courtyard and have placed Red Cross signs on the dark green canvas. Several people carry bundles of blankets and large boxes of medical supplies into the tent, the flaps tied as wide as possible to allow unobstructed entry. A few wooden tables sit at the entrance, with a radio crackling with alternating bursts of static and voices. From where he stands, Wei Xiang can hear muffled voices. A blue pickup truck pulls into the school's driveway and disgorges a few young men in uniforms, who move in swift strides to the tent, led by a stout man with a severe buzzcut. A young woman with dishevelled hair and tired features stands up nervously to speak to the soldier, and passes him a handful of documents.

Wei Xiang turns towards a covered pathway that leads to the back of the school, where there are three blocks of classrooms each two-storey high, a garden gone riotous, a scummy pond filled with floating aquatic plants, and a cobblestoned quadrangle. Along the corridors, a few men, thickly bandaged about the head and torso, are groaning and futilely swatting the flies from their bleeding wounds. Wei Xiang looks into the classrooms, giving them a thorough scan; most of the rooms are packed to capacity, and the walls and floors filthy, reeking with a fetid odour. The women's and children's quarters on the second floor are not any better; outside one of the classrooms, a woman carries a child swathed in rags on her back—a girl or a boy? sleeping or dead?—undecided over whether to place the child on the cramped floor inside. In another room, a young woman is weeping over a naked boy, her cries echoing off the walls. The bodies of those who have just died are dragged out of the rooms and stacked along the corridors, to make way for the incoming injured. After checking every classroom, Wei

Xiang sits on the cement steps in a stairwell and rests his face in his palms. His head is starting to throb with a vicious intensity. He needs to head back to the school hall, he's not done yet; there are bound to be more bodies now. He steels himself against the thought of this endless task, and then pushes himself to move.

Back in the assembly hall, the stench has become overwhelming, rushing out to hit Wei Xiang in the face before he has even stepped inside. Four standing oscillating fans have been set up to alleviate the situation, but they do nothing more than stir the miasma into a thick, putrid stew. Wei Xiang holds his shirtsleeve to his nose, trying to block out the smell, but it's useless. Everywhere he turns, he is overcome by the corporeality of death. The helpers are still carrying in new bodies, forming additional lines that come up all the way to the entrance of the hall. A group of men with pens and clipboards and cameras is examining the corpses, taking snapshots and jotting down notes. On the concrete walls, beside the broken-paned windows, a woman is taping up sheets of paper, some of them showing grainy photographs.

Wei Xiang looks around, unsure where he has left off before. A pair of bloated legs with patches of dark bruises sticking out of a thin blanket catches his eye. He lifts the cover and recoils backward when he sees that a part of the head has been sheared away, revealing the mushy, wrinkled surface of the brain. Wei Xiang feels the bile rising at the back of his throat, and before he can take another step, the vomit gushes out of him and onto his shirt, his hands, the dead woman on the floor. He stumbles outside and squats at the clogged drain, puking and shaking in violent spasms, as if his body were trying to purge itself of something horrible inside him. He retches for a long time, then wipes his mouth on his sleeve, and sinks to the ground. It's impossible. There is no way he can go back in. Fighting his growing despondency, Wei Xiang stares at the faces of the curious onlookers peeking through the chain link fence. Then he sees the boy again.

Standing next to two middle-aged local women dressed in floral-print blouses and dark pants, the boy is staring at him. The look on his scarred face is not hostile, but hovers in a state of neutrality and blankness. Standing motionless amongst the crowd at the fence, the boy seems composed, unruffled by the tide of noises and commotion around him. Wearing a dirty white singlet and a pair of drawstring khaki shorts, he looks like any other street kid in Phuket, who might be playing beside the busy lanes of traffic, or panhandling the passers-by for money or sweets or pens. Getting up from the ground, Wei Xiang moves towards the school gate, brushing past incoming stretchers and scores of arm-banded helpers shouting instructions at one another. He bumps into a bony young girl with jutting shoulders and elbows, barely a teenager but carrying a baby slung across her back, and sends her toppling to the muddy ground. She shows no sign of annoyance, but simply gets back to her feet and makes her way to the Red Cross tent. By the time he makes his way through the crowd and out the gate, the boy is no longer standing at the fence. Frantically, Wei Xiang scans the area and again spots the boy walking away at a brisk pace towards the main road. He trains his eyes on the boy's retreating back as he manoeuvres through the crowd. When he thinks he has almost lost him again, Wei Xiang cries out and the boy stops in his tracks, turning to look at him. At a road junction, the boy stands against the flow of human traffic, as if waiting for Wei Xiang to catch up.

But no matter how fast Wei Xiang pursues him, he can never reach the boy, who disappears momentarily and materialises somewhere farther ahead of him, always drawing Wei Xiang to him with his presence. Wei Xiang chases him down a network of lanes and alleyways across town, determined to reach him no matter what it takes, his feverish mind fired up by this all-consuming task.

16

AI LING

As the sun begins to set on the third day after the tsunami, the tiny island falls into shadows, steeped in silence. Across the iridescent spread of the sea, the waves ripple, a skin of shimmering light. The breeze, blowing from the northeast, has turned a few degrees cooler, stirring the tufts of grass on the island, caressing the topography of the sand dunes.

A fine layer of condensation has formed over the woman, cooling the body that has been baking under the sun for days. In the soft, forgiving dusk light, the woman's body exudes a frail, otherworldly beauty, as if released from its struggle. Along the stretch of beach, more things have been deposited by the waves: a few broken planks, pockmarked with decay and tiny holes where the screws used to be; a rutted car tyre; half-filled soft drink bottles; a decapitated plastic doll head with half-closed eyes.

With her head tilted westward, facing the horizon, the woman seems to be contemplating the sunset, and the trembling lights pirouetting on the surface of the sea. With her lips parted, as if in mid-sentence, the unspoken words that have pooled in her

mouth slowly leak out in dark, viscous drips. The wind carries
her silenced words out into the sea, scattering them like dust.

∞

"Look at this," Ai Ling said on the evening of Christmas
Day. "It looks amazing, right?"

The quartet of friends had just settled into their seats at
the seafront restaurant, and the waiter had left them with
the menus. The view from where they were seated opened
out to a commanding, picturesque vista of Patong Bay, with
the sun sinking down to the horizon. It had taken them
nearly twenty minutes to find the restaurant, following the
poor directions given by the hotel bellhop, and using the
grainy map that Ai Ling had photocopied from the Lonely
Planet guidebook, which only showed the main roads of
Phuket, inconveniently leaving out the many arteries that
branched out into every perceivable nook and cranny of the
city. Ai Ling had insisted that they walk instead of taking a
taxi or tuk tuk, and by the time they found the restaurant
along the stretch of Prabaramee Road, they were all covered
with a thin coat of dust and perspiration, the collars and
armpits of their clothes stained dark.

Wei Xiang turned to take in the view of the sea, while
Cody and Chee Seng studied the menu and scanned the
drinks list. The waiter, a waifish teenager with a gaunt,
acne-ridden face, came over and filled up the stain-spotted
glasses with ice water, leaving the almost-empty pitcher on
the table, and waited with a pen and a dog-eared notepad,
smiling awkwardly. Chee Seng dismissed her with a request

for more time. Ai Ling allowed her vision to follow the vanishing line of the horizon from one end to the other, noting the gold-and-red swathes of light piercing through the heavy, low-lying clouds. From somewhere, hidden out of view, Ai Ling could hear the gentle bobbing of longtail boats and the occasional cawing of seagulls.

"What do you feel like having?" Wei Xiang spoke up, drawing her attention.

"You order. I'll eat anything," Ai Ling said, turning back to the sea.

Wei Xiang, in turn, deferred to Cody and Chee Seng when the waiter came around to take their orders for dinner. They picked papaya salad and fried spring rolls for starters; green curry, minced pork with basil leaves and sweet-and-sour tilapia for entreés; and held back on dessert, unsure whether they could finish what they had already ordered. The restaurant was sparsely decorated: a few old-looking tribal masks hung up on the wall, a Chinese scroll of unintelligible scribbling, and a bland painting of an island sunset. Couples and small groups trickled into the restaurant from time to time, and the din of chatter soon filled the room. The sun had submerged halfway into the sea, sending out its last rays of the day.

"Nice little place, great view," Chee Seng said, taking out his Motorola phone from his pocket to snap a few pictures of the scenery. "You can never take a bad picture with such a view, it's just impossible." He previewed the pictures and showed them to Cody.

"Yes, you're right. I don't think I'll ever get tired of seeing this," Ai Ling said, and held Wei Xiang's hand on the tabletop, giving it a gentle squeeze. She sipped from her glass of water. "See, I made the right choice in picking this place, right?" The guys chorused their approval in unison.

The food soon arrived, and the conversation turned to past relationships.

"You wouldn't believe the kind of guys Cody dated before," Ai Ling said. "Some of them were plain creepy."

"Just one of them," said Cody. "You make it seem like I dated so many guys, which I didn't."

Ai Ling went on: "Remember that one guy, the one who worked in the bank? He locked you out of his place one night when you came home late and refused to let you in, all because you forgot to tell him you would be late. You called me after that, so pissed off, and didn't know what to do. I had to calm you down."

"You're just being overly dramatic with your storytelling. It didn't happen that way. I just panicked, for no good reason. Okay, enough about him," Cody said, noticing Chee Seng looking at him.

"You never told me this before," Chee Seng said.

"There's nothing to say. It all happened in the past, water under the bridge," Cody said, and quickly changed the subject. "Wah, so much food left."

"What I could not understand was why you stayed with him for another two months before you finally broke up with him," Ai Ling said. "He was such an asshole, so overbearing, possessive and demanding. He bullied you into submission all the time."

"But you're seeing it from just one point of view. You don't know unless you're in my shoes. It's hard to understand, even for me. He had a nice side to him, and he treated me well."

"He pestered you for months after the break-up," Ai Ling said, unable to stop herself. Cody glared at her, but was silent.

"Hey, why are we talking about all this?" Wei Xiang said.

"Ask your wife. She brought it up first. She always likes to make a big production out of my past," Cody said.

"But your life is always filled with drama, and anyway, it's way more exciting than mine. I live vicariously through you, you know that, right?" Ai Ling said, and Cody rolled his eyes.

"Well, you guys seem to be quite stable," she said, nodding at Chee Seng. "How long have you been together now? Eight, nine years? You guys are doing well."

"Ten years, come April next year," Cody said, looking over at Chee Seng.

"You guys are like practically married, anyway. Ten years, that's long, that's like a lifetime," Ai Ling said. The men laughed.

"Yup, and it feels like it, too," Chee Seng said. Cody punched him lightly on the arm and creased his face into a mock-wounded expression.

"Maybe you should consider, you know, getting married. Maybe move somewhere, like Canada, to get hitched."

"No lah, don't be ridiculous. It's not for us. Remember we are Singaporeans. We are too risk-averse," Cody said. "I'm happy where we are now, with what we have. What's the point of getting married, anyway?"

"Don't you want your commitment to each other to be recognised, in one way or another?"

"In Singapore? Gays getting married and being lawfully

recognised? Who are you kidding? You must be joking. It'll never happen in a hundred years. And what's the use of getting married overseas, and then coming back with a meaningless certificate that's worth nothing here?"

A loud crash suddenly erupted from the entrance of the kitchen, where two waiters had collided into each other, sending a tray of empty glasses and a plate of fried chilli fish to the ground. The manager of the restaurant hurried over from the cash register and scolded the waiters loudly.

"I'm just saying, that's all," Ai Ling said. Wei Xiang waved a waiter over to refill the drinks.

"How about you two? How long have you been married now?" Chee Seng asked, taking a sip of water.

"Seven years. We dated for three years before getting married," Wei Xiang said.

"That's long too," Chee Seng said.

"You know how it is with a woman like Ai Ling, the moment she set her eyes on me, she was head over heels in love and pursued me until she got me," Wei Xiang said with a smirk.

"Says who? You bloody liar," Ai Ling said, slapping Wei Xiang's hand. "You're the one who had to chase after me, okay? I didn't make any move on you, just for the record."

"I don't believe you," Cody said, grinning. "You were always so daring during university days, soliciting numbers from boys and asking them out."

"Hey, you're supposed to be on my side. Don't badmouth me. When did I ever do that? You must be talking about yourself." Ai Ling scowled at Cody, who reacted on cue, frowning in shocked amusement. "Cody was the real flirt at university. You would not believe all the things he did, even if I told you."

"I want to hear," Chee Seng said.

"Some things are best left in the past. No point dragging them out again," Cody said, laughing. Under the table, he slipped his hand onto Chee Seng's thigh, stroking it.

"Okay okay, I let you off this time," Ai Ling said. "I'm sure everyone has a part of their past that they're not proud of. God, I know I've done so many things in the past that I wish I could forget. Why is it that we always remember so much about this bad stuff, and so little of the good in our lives? It's almost like we're punishing ourselves for every single thing that we've screwed up." She turned to stare out at the sea again. The sky had deepened from a deep blue to a deeper purple. She could feel Wei Xiang's eyes on her.

"Now you're just being morose," Cody said. Ai Ling turned to smile at him. The loud cawing of the squabbling seagulls in the distance reached their table.

"But you know what I'm talking about, right? This fixation on the past that all of us have," Ai Ling said. Around them, the restaurant, now full, bustled with a hum of voices, laughter and the soft soundtrack of Thai pop songs playing over the audio system.

"Shall we order some Singha beer? I'm suddenly in the mood to drink," Wei Xiang said. "Do you want one?" Ai Ling shook her head without looking at him. Cody and Chee Seng took Wei Xiang up on the suggestion, and Wei Xiang placed the order with the waiter.

When the beer came and they had taken swigs straight from the bottles—Wei Xiang had declined drinking glasses and a bucket of ice—Ai Ling spoke again: "Actually it doesn't matter how long a couple has been together, to show the kind of love they have. Though of course, the longer you know someone, the more you know about him, what makes him tick, what makes him happy. But is that all we can know about him? How can we claim to know anyone, a lover, a husband or a boyfriend, fully, completely, when there's always a part that is hidden from us, maybe a side of him that even he is not aware of? Every man is a mystery, to himself, to others.

"Maybe that's why we can continue to love someone after so many years, because we can never get to the end of this mystery. But I don't want to pretend to know anything about love, when it's hardly the case, when I'm still trying to understand what it's all about. Don't laugh at me, I know I sound silly, but seriously, what do we actually know about love? What is it exactly about this person we profess to love that we actually love? What, really?"

"Are you drunk? What's in that calamansi lime drink you had? Did they spike it with something?" Cody said.

"Don't pretend you don't understand what I'm saying," Ai Ling said, keeping her voice level, before continuing. "Just hear me out. I have this aunt, my mother's younger sister, who lost her husband to a heart attack while he was driving. One moment he was signalling to turn right at a junction, talking to my aunt, and the next moment he was clutching his chest. The car was still moving and slammed right into the back of a truck. He was dead before he reached the hospital."

Cody sneaked a look at Chee Seng, and then back at Ai Ling and Wei Xiang. Nobody spoke.

Ai Ling tapped her fingers on the red-checked tablecloth and took in a long breath.

"I'm very close to my aunt. My mum used to ask her to babysit me when I was much younger, when she had to work an extra shift at the factory. Maybe because they were childless, my uncle and aunt doted on me a lot, always giving in to my requests for anything: snacks, toys, colouring books. They treated me as if I were their own daughter.

"Right after the accident, I rushed to the hospital. My aunt had suffered a few broken ribs and some bruises, and was in a coma for a few days, but otherwise she was okay. I can still remember when she finally woke up, the look on her face, this raw, open confusion, like an exposed wound. Nobody wanted to tell her about the death of my uncle at first, but I think somehow she knew, from the way we were keeping a guilty silence around her. We thought we could spare her the pain for as long as we could."

Ai Ling caught her breath, brought Wei Xiang's beer to her lips and took a long swig. Wei Xiang covered her hand with his and held it. Ai Ling smiled at him.

"This tastes great, I should order one," she said. Her eyes shone in the semi-darkness of the restaurant. The waiters were flitting about, lighting the tea light in the flask-lamp on every table. Tiny buds of flame came to life from every part of the room, a field of hovering fireflies. Outside, the waves fell and crashed in gentle, lulling succession; moonlight dappled across the inky surface of the sea, tracing the outline of each wave as it pushed onto the shore.

"So what happened to your aunt after she knew? I mean, she would have known everything later on, right?" Chee Seng said.

"Of course she knew everything, my parents had to tell her. My aunt took in the news with composure, but underneath you could tell she was not herself at all. She seemed so lost and helpless then, stuck in her grief. The doctor said it was only natural, and that we should be patient and just let her take her time to come around."

Ai Ling paused to take another sip of the beer, to clear her throat.

"I'm not sure she will ever get over it. She was married to my uncle for over forty years. How can anyone survive that kind of loss? How can anyone get over this? It's like having two arms chopped off and someone telling you to get over it, move on, live a normal life, go back to the life you used to have? It's ridiculous."

"But people do get over these things, and move on," Cody said.

"No, not entirely. All this nice talk about getting over death and moving on is just bullshit. If you're truly frank with yourself, you won't get over these things so easily. It will hit you again and again, and you won't know what to do with it, this terrible grief that's inside you, that's fucking you up inside out. How can you stop loving someone just because he's dead?"

"Now, who's the one being melodramatic?" Cody said.

"Anyway, let me finish the story. Shortly after my aunt went back home, I got a call from her in the middle of the night. She was distraught over the phone, trying to say something to me. I rushed over to her place and found her on the floor, clenching my uncle's reading spectacles. I had to pry her off the floor and coax her back into bed. The spectacles were crushed in her grip and the broken glass had cut deep into her palm. I bandaged the cut and stayed with her until she finally calmed down. It was a long time before she returned to herself. That was the only time it happened, and we never talked about it." Ai Ling stopped and shook her head.

"Dear, don't…" Wei Xiang said.

Ai Ling continued: "Some nights, I dreamt that I was my aunt, sitting in the car, watching my uncle die before my eyes. The car still moving, just about to crash into the other vehicle, my uncle with a fist to his chest, head on the steering wheel, losing control of the car. I could not move a single muscle while watching all this unfold before me. I could not understand a single thing of what was happening. The whole event took only a split second, everything flashing forward and playing out in slow motion. And then the crash finally came, and in my head, or maybe my aunt's, all I could hear was just: Why didn't I die with him?"

"Ai Ling…" Wei Xiang brought his arm around Ai Ling's shoulders. Under the table, Cody felt Chee Seng's hand tighten on his, fingernails digging into his flesh.

"Okay," Ai Ling said. "I'm just being incoherent now. I've talked too much. I'll shut up now."

The waiter came over to suggest some desserts, but nobody was in the mood for any. Wei Xiang asked for the bill and took out his wallet. Chee Seng offered to pay but Wei Xiang declined. "You can pay tomorrow," Wei Xiang said.

Cody brought up his bottle of beer and proposed a toast. "For our trip, for the next few days. And also, Merry Christmas!"

"Yes, to us, to what we have now," Ai Ling said, tapping her glass against Cody's bottle.

When the waiter came and put Wei Xiang's change on their table, he barely looked at it. Even when everyone had finished their drinks, nobody made a move to go. A silence had settled between them.

"Where shall we go next?" Wei Xiang said, eventually.

Ai Ling looked at him, not registering anything, her eyes blank. She held Wei Xiang's gaze. Chee Seng turned to look at the dark sea; Cody closed his eyes for a moment, stifling a yawn. Sitting in the noisy restaurant, separated from the other patrons, none of them wanted to make the first move to leave.

17

CHEE SENG

We leave the burial mound and head back to the hut in silence, treading through the dark, the night air chilly on my skin. The old woman has taken the lead, and I try to stay in step with her, not wanting to lose sight. She moves with the certainty of a person who knows her way through the forest—a dark maze of rocky, dirt paths—even with her eyes closed. Around us, the forest is a discordant chorus of nocturnal sounds: buzzing, clicking, and the occasional throaty drone of an unseen bird that sounds like a prolonged burst of pellets shot from a pistol. Even with my eyes open, I can't see much, except for the dark moving form of the old woman before me; the darkness is full and material, a presence that envelops me from all sides. My legs are covered with scratches, my arms and neck dotted with mosquito bites.

When I look up, I see the silhouettes of trees against the satin deep-blue sky, glittering with stars. The hue of the sky is like nothing I have ever seen before—rich and velvety. I crane my neck to see what lies ahead of the old woman; the small hut slowly materialises. I sense the old woman hastening her steps, her footfalls light, almost soundless. We stop at the well and she draws up a pail of water and splashes both our feet, a biting relief. I plunge my hands into the pail and splash the water all over my face, feeling my sweaty skin bristle.

After crossing the threshold and entering the hut, it takes me a few moments to adjust to the dimness of the room. The smell of paraffin oil fumes from the lamp hangs heavily in the air, and, along with it, I detect the faint burning of dry wood. The old woman is at the brick stove, setting a kettle to boil, fanning the flames. The red-orange glow casts a halo of soft amber light around her, agitating her shadows on the wall. She takes up a flask and puts some dry leaves—tea? herbs?—into it.

I sit on the wooden bench and lower my head onto the table, burying my face in the crook of my arm. I can feel my body losing its tension, unwinding; a numbing fatigue soon takes hold, spreading across my body. Draining slowly of energy, I can't keep my eyes open, though my thoughts are creating a racket in my head. The old woman sets a bowl before me. The soothing scent of jasmine fills my nose, and I take a few sips. She sits beside me and watches me drink. With the shadows flickering on her face, her eyes seem like empty pits that draw me into them—a deathly calm, the gravity of darkness.

It would be easier to stay where I am, somewhere up in the hills with the old woman, distanced from the rest of the world. Nobody knows whether I'm dead or alive, and this realisation is harsh but sobering. I could live like this for as long as I want. Maybe in some ways, I'm avoiding the need to take the next step; maybe I'm hoping to delay the decision to head back, to return to where I'm expected. Nobody can stay still, or hidden, for long; life always demands action, movement, choices, a nudge to take the next step.

In the days I have spent in the hut, recovering under the care of the old woman, I think about the life I used to have, about Ai Ling and Wei Xiang, and of course Cody. They are the people I care about and love the most, but now, after all that has happened, I can't summon anything in me to feel for them. They have become, over the last few days, immaterial, mere shadows from the past, stripped of any history or connection to the reality of my current existence. It's as if I have conjured them up from my own imagination, from different fragments of other people I have known— wisps of smoke rising into the air, fading into nothing. I have almost no desire to return to them, or to whatever is waiting for me.

The old woman, on the other hand, is already preparing for my eventual departure. She feeds me another round of the bitter brew, changes the wound dressings, and mends the rips in my clothes, going about these tasks with her usual efficiency and silence. From time to time, she checks on me, putting her hand to my forehead or applying a lotion to my bruises. She takes out a cloth bag from the larder and puts in a few vegetable buns that she has prepared, a bottle of water and a small jar of medicinal lotion. She secures the opening of the cloth bag with a piece of rattan string and leaves it at the foot of the bed.

Watching her move about in the small, dimly lit hut with

a single-minded focus stirs up memories of my maternal grandmother who passed away six years ago. She was the one who took care of my siblings and me when my mother was holding down two jobs, after she and my father were divorced. Every day after school, my grandmother would keep me in the kitchen for hours, seated at the dining table to have my meals or work on my homework, as she busied herself with the scrubbing of pots and pans, preparing the spices for her special bak kut teh soup, or cleaning out the fridge, which was always packed to the gills with plastic bags of varying size and colour, the contents known only by my grandmother. She never wasted or threw away food, even when it was past the expiry date. For snacks, she would give me stale cream crackers that tasted like dry cardboard, which she kept in a large tin can. The day after she died of a sudden stroke, I peeked into the fridge and saw that it was as full as it had always been.

In my dreams—sleeping and waking in an unending cycle—I sometimes confuse what is there with what isn't— my long-gone past and the elusive present, the old woman and my dead grandmother. At one point, when the old woman put her hand on my forehead, and I opened my eyes, I could see my grandmother's features superimposed on her face—the scattering of age spots on her cheeks, the sharp creases around her eyes and mouth like knife cuts, her perceptive stare. Words came pouring from me in a jumble of hard consonants as if I were learning to speak in tongues, harsh and guttural. And always, a presence hovering near me, a shadow cast over the wavy landscape of my dreams.

Towards evening, when the light outside the hut has

gradually turned mellow, easing from a fiery red to a deepening shade of blue, I finally wake up from my spot at the table. My mind feels empty, my body light and incorporeal. From where I sit, I watch the changing sky through the doorway, and beyond the sweep of the trees, the satiny cloak of the dark sea. When dinner is ready, the old woman motions to me to join her. We eat in silence, and by the time we are done, night has fully descended, the lamps in the hut providing our only illumination.

Once the old woman has washed the dishes and put them away, she comes over to me, reaching into the side pocket of her threadbare shirt to pull out a ring. It catches the light from the lamp. It's a simple, unadorned ring, perhaps a wedding band—where did she find it? Putting it in my palm, the old woman looks at me, pats my wrist once, and turns away. I try on the ring, but it can't fit any of my fingers except the last one on my right hand. Whoever owned the ring must have had slim fingers, and it occurs to me that perhaps it belonged to a woman. I wrap it in a torn rag and put it in the pocket of my jeans.

∞

For our fifth anniversary, Cody bought me a ring and hid it between the pages of a book that I was reading. That night, as I was picking up the book, a collection of stories by Alice Munro, the ring fell into my lap. For a while, holding the ring between my fingers, I wondered whether the ring was Cody's, that perhaps he had misplaced it. From across the bed, Cody grabbed my hand.

"Happy anniversary," he said.

"Happy anniversary. What is this?"

"A ring."

"Yes, I know that. Why did you buy me a ring? So tacky."

"No, it's actually quite nice. Don't you like it?"

"Yes, but still. A ring. You want to propose to me?"

"Yes, but only if you want to marry me."

"No, take it back. I don't want to marry you."

"Why not? I know you want to." Cody pressed closer to me, took the ring and slipped it on my index finger.

"Okay, now you are married. To me," he said. "You can kiss the groom."

I wore the ring whenever I was with Cody, so he could see it. But I was never interested in accessories; maybe a watch, but only because I needed it to time my regular runs, and even then it was a cheap, plastic Casio. And if I received gifts from friends—a chain, bracelet, leather wristband—I would put them aside for re-gifting, and if they started to clutter up the drawer, I would put them all in a box and give them away to the Salvation Army. Occasionally, when Cody saw a piece he liked, I would give it to him.

But the ring that Cody bought was a different thing altogether. It had meant something, at least to Cody, a commitment of sorts, a symbol of the years we had been together; but for me, it was nothing more than an inanimate object made to embody some significance that existed only in the mind of the giver, and divorced from this, it was nothing more than a piece of metal. So to counter my initial reluctance, and mostly for Cody's sake, I wore it as if it really mattered, as if it were something that carried the weight of importance for both of us. I wore it when I went to bed, when we had breakfast, when we went out with friends, when we had sex. But when Cody was not around, or when I had to go for my runs, I would take it off and leave it in the drawer. By then the ring had already left its mark on me, the slight indent that went around the base of my finger, the skin a tone lighter as if drained of blood.

When Ai Ling saw the ring during one of our dinners, she looked puzzled.

"Thought you didn't like to wear accessories?" she said, holding up my hand to examine the ring.

"No, but Cody bought this for me. I would never buy it myself."

"Does it mean what I think it means?"

"No, it's just an anniversary gift."

"Can't be that simple."

"It is, don't overthink it. You women are so drama, always imagining things."

"I don't think so. The ring has to mean something. You don't buy a ring for someone without a reason." Ai Ling looked at me, widening her eyes in feigned surprise. "Oh my god, he proposed to you, didn't he?"

"No, don't be crazy!" I protested, and laughed, and pushed our conversation in another direction.

∞

I'm the eldest son in my family—my father was a car mechanic, and my mother a coffee-shop assistant—and I have three younger brothers. My parents were divorced when I was in primary school, but they kept this from us for a long time. My father continued to stay with us even after, and when he moved out, he took only what he needed, leaving behind many personal items. Because of this, we did not feel his dwindling absence in the house, and subsequent abandonment, for some time. Because my father stayed out late most nights, drinking with his friends, my brothers and I never thought anything was amiss. Only the look on my mother's face told a different story, but we did not know how to read it. She held back, and carried on: a cycle of housework and chores, taking care of us, cooking our meals. We would not see our father for a day, and we would think nothing of it, perhaps he was busy and had spent the night at the car repair shop. Then it became two nights, but still we held up the illusion; we looked to our mother for a word or some sign, but she did not let on. My father's absence stretched to a week, and then a month. My brothers and I did not hear from him after that, and whenever the house phone rang, it was usually my mother who picked it up and spoke into it with a moderated tone, turning her back to us. When she hung up, she would avoid our stares, her expression inscrutable.

When we were alone, my brothers and I would speculate about the disappearance of my father—it was the early eighties, and divorce was a rare thing, something nobody talked about, and we did not know anyone in school whose parents were divorced—and came up with many reasons: he had killed someone and was on the run, or worse, in jail; he was suffering from some hideous disease and had to stay away because he did not want to infect us. Not once, in all our speculations over the months and years, did we think that our father had deserted us. It was only years later that we found out that he had returned to Malaysia, to his hometown of Ipoh, with another woman, to start another family. By then, we had not heard from him for so long that he no longer mattered in our lives, a marginal figure that hovered in a corner of our memories. We did not even know he had died from prostate cancer until my mother told us and asked one of us to accompany her to Ipoh to attend his funeral; none of us wanted to go until my youngest brother relented. For me, it was a matter of pride: he had abandoned us, and I did not want anything to do with him, even when he was dead. I had banished him to the farthest reach of my mind, but the act of forgetting was never an easy task.

For many years, I could not understand my mother's actions, how she had behaved so civilly to someone who had cheated on her and deserted the family. She never felt the need to explain her actions or feelings to us. Perhaps she had thought it was better to maintain a link with my father for our sake, or because of their past and the ties that went beyond what we could see. How she had kept up the correspondence with my father over the years was something she did behind our backs, without our knowledge. She never remarried, and led a quiet life that hardly stepped out of the boundaries of my brothers' lives and mine. In a stolid, unwavering way, she led her life for our sake, and growing up, we could not get away fast enough from the different ways she was smothering us, keeping us under her fierce watch. Our little acts of rebellion were forms of betrayal to her, manifested in the cold wars that raged between us and her, the long silences broken only when one of us finally gave in, or gave up. Even my coming out was a sign of aggravation towards her, another telltale mark of how she had, once again, failed as a mother. Whatever secret pains she nursed were invisible to us, a self-serving defence, an impenetrable fortress she put up against her own children.

So, whenever I held up the ring, my mind would dredge up these thoughts about my parents and their failed marriage, and I would have to resist the urge to associate the ring with something I had never truly believed in, an object meant to represent the fragile, breakable bonds between the ones you loved. What was the point of it, after all? I would have given it more credit if it were purely decorative; at least then it would have served a particular function. I wore it less and less, if I could help it, and Cody did not seem to notice.

One time, I lost the ring at the gym. I was not aware of the loss at the time, and it was only when I was on the train heading home that I felt its absence on my finger. I had picked up the habit of twirling the ring whenever I was deep in thought, an absent-minded gesture that had become second nature to me. So when I could not feel it on my finger, I panicked. Rushing back to the gym, I tore through the changing area, heading for the showers; the ring was where I had left it, on the ledge between the shower stalls. Days after this, when I thought about how I had felt then, I found myself embarrassed at the excessive display of feelings, which ran counter to how I had felt about wearing the ring in the first place. So what if I had lost the ring? Would it have mattered? Cody might chide me for my carelessness, but at least the whole issue would be off my mind, something I would not have to struggle with anymore. This, too, could be a form of immense relief. But I never did find the courage to do what felt like the right thing to do.

"Do you want me to get a ring for you, too?" I asked, around eight months after he had given me the ring.

"No," Cody replied, looking at me to see where I was going with the question.

"Why not? You bought one for me."

"Because if you wanted to, you would have done it a long time ago."

"It didn't cross my mind then. Maybe I can get one for you, if you want."

"I don't need one."

"Seems kind of pointless if I'm the only one wearing it, right?"

"It suits you better."

"Nonsense. You know exactly how I feel about accessories."

"Anyway, you have got used to the ring now, haven't you?"

"It's just weird for me to wear it if you are not wearing one."

"So it would make you feel better if I get one too?"

"Yes."

"Then get me one."

"But do you really want one?"

"Not really."

After this, we never brought up the issue of the ring again.

∞

Lying on the mat in the darkened hut, I can't sleep, my eyes glued to the ceiling. Light from the table lamp throws long shaky shadows across the floor of the hut. The lonesome moth that has flown in remains stock-still on the wall near the stove, the pattern on its wings like the unblinking eyes of a nocturnal beast. Toads drone mechanically, along with the insistent chirping of the cicadas. Darkness lurks like a predator outside the hut.

The old woman sits on a wooden stool at the threshold of the hut, fanning herself with a straw fan, looking out into the courtyard, into the dark forest. From where I'm lying, looking at her arched back, she seems vulnerable. Under her breath, she mutters something rhythmic to herself, perhaps a song. The sound comes to me, in a mellifluous cadence, and I strain to catch the notes. In my mind, I play out memories of my dead grandmother, my head on her lap on warm, lazy afternoons, her hand patting me gently on my back, coaxing me to sleep. She would always sing to me in Hokkien, always a song about a lonely, tragic woman pining for her faraway lover, and waiting for him to come back to her. I would tried my best to decipher the lyrics with my limited knowledge of the dialect, waiting for the song to end before asking my grandmother about the things I did not understand. Why couldn't the woman in the song go and find her lover? How could she not have eaten for so many days, wasn't she hungry at all? Why did she drink the poisonous potion? My grandmother would answer some of my questions, and then tell me to hush and close my eyes. I would try to think of the ways I could save the woman from her misery.

Now, with the night sounds pressing in on us, I wonder about the old woman's life in the middle of this deep forest, high up in the hills, surviving all on her own. How can she live the way she does, with nothing except for the barest of necessities? Yet, she can, and she has, for god knows how long. Does she have a family, or someone who's aware of her existence? Over the past few days, I have seen no other person in the vicinity. For all I know, she might have lived this way for a very long time, without the need for anyone, or anything else.

And in imagining her life, I recall my grandmother's, who lived alone for twenty-two years after my grandfather passed away. While she had taken care of my brothers and me on days that my mother was at work, she was often alone, occupied with her own life. She did not trouble my mother, her second daughter, with anything, even on occasions when she was sick; one time she even admitted herself into the hospital after she had a bad fall, and did not inform my mother until the day she was checking out. She claimed she did not want to inconvenience anyone, to make my mother take time off from her job, seeing how busy she already was with us four boys. She did not say much when my parents got divorced, and it was hard to tell how she felt over the whole thing, given the stoic front she put up before us. She kept our lives going on track, and did not let up her tough discipline and punishment whenever one of us misbehaved. In a way, my grandmother had taken the role of our missing father, writ large by her actions and influence over us. She died when she was eighty-five.

The old woman gets up from where she is sitting and closes the wooden door. She steps towards me, and with the weak light behind her, I can't see her face clearly. Again, she places her palm on my forehead and utters something. Then she moves to turn off the lamp, reducing the hut to a near-complete darkness. I hear her getting into her bed—a structure made of long wooden planks tied together with ropes—and within minutes she is asleep, her breaths light and even. In the dark, I listen to her breathing and measure it against mine. I stay up for as long as I can, trying to stay afloat against the irresistible pull of the unknown.

18

WEI XIANG

Wei Xiang wakes with a start, the memory of a hand brushing across his face lingering on his skin, and looks around the hotel room. He has slept in the clothes he wore yesterday, which reek of sour perspiration, and have hardened with dirt stains. He feels disoriented; he can't remember how he managed to get himself back to the hotel and into bed the night before. He lifts his heavy head from the sticky, stale-smelling bedsheet, before letting it fall back again. Wrecked with exhaustion, he rubs his temples, feeling the start of a low-grade headache.

In his half-awake state, his thoughts run immediately to the strange boy who eluded him the day before in the streets of Phuket. Wei Xiang can't remember how long he trailed him, always just missing him. Sometimes the boy was right in front of him, and at other times appearing far away, a lonesome figure amidst the thronging, agitated crowd. It was as if the boy were playing a game of cat-and-mouse, teasing and frustrating Wei Xiang at the same time.

Yet, as he tries to recall what the boy looks like, his

mind draws up only fractured images—a mop of wild hair, small seashell ears, skinny legs, dirty unshod feet, a deep scar across his left eye—an incomplete picture. Even when he attempts to put the different parts of the boy together, the resulting image is incoherent, indistinct, an out-of-focus photograph.

Wiping the dried saliva from his cheek, Wei Xiang checks the time on his watch. 10.45am. The morning is almost over. He rolls out of bed, shocking his body into action. In the toilet, looking into the mirror, he sees his reflection: days-old stubble, dark eye-bags, deeply creased lines across his forehead. His eyes are dull, the light gone out of them. He slaps his cheeks hard, trying to wake himself up fully, his body still steeped in lethargy. He notices Ai Ling's barrette lying beside the bottles of hand cream and body lotion, and sweeps everything into her toiletries bag on the counter, putting them out of sight. Then he wets a hand towel, rubs his face roughly with it, and steps back into the bedroom to change his clothes.

At the hotel lobby, Wei Xiang notes that the level of water has dropped significantly, barely at ankle-height now, and a coarse layer of sediment has settled on the exposed surfaces. There is a water-level stain on the walls; the wallpaper has peeled and curled into long stiffened strips. Large flakes of paint have fallen off as well, floating on the water like wood shavings. The furniture has been arranged back to its original layout, though there is something amiss about the placement, as if nothing fits the scene any longer, incorrect props in a stage setup. Stripped of the usual accoutrements—flower vases, throw pillows, travel magazines, mural paintings—the lobby looks like a shell of a room. Nobody seems to be around, not even behind the front desk, a sharp contrast to the commotion the day before, when the noisy hotel guests hounded the staff for updates and whereabouts and flight changes.

As Wei Xiang walks through the lobby, a man appears from a walkway, carrying a metal pail. Wearing a dirty uniform, he seems surprised to find Wei Xiang standing there, his brows coming together in a crease. It's the same porter who advised him to stay in the hotel yesterday, to wait till things were better.

"Morning, sir. How are you today?" the man says, hiding the pail behind him.

"Okay. How come there's nobody around? Where are the other guests?" Wei Xiang asks. A face pops out from behind the reception, a sleepy-looking girl with frizzy hair, and looks around nervously. She gives Wei Xiang a wan smile and ducks her head under the countertop.

"Many people gone yesterday. Only few left." He hesitates, darting glances to his side, before saying, "Do sir want breakfast? I can get."

"No, no, I'm heading out now."

"Where sir go today? Outside messy, no good to go out today."

"I don't know. I don't know where I'll go."

"Then stay in hotel. I bring sir breakfast."

"No, no need. I have to find someone."

Wei Xiang moves away, his eyes already on the exit. The shattered glass panes and metal frame of the doors have been removed, leaving only a gaping entryway, through which the late-morning sunlight pours in mercilessly, blinding Wei Xiang temporarily to the outside.

"Wait, sir." The porter runs off and returns with a bottle of water, handing it to Wei Xiang. He thanks the man, takes the bottle and leaves.

Out on the street, he feels an uncanny sense of déjà vu, with the crush of people pushing in opposite directions, the scene before him familiar, and Wei Xiang can't tell whether he is reliving the same day again. The only difference is that the sea water in the street has largely subsided overnight, though many side lanes are still impassable. The salty air holds a rank fetidness—is it the sea? or the smell of rotting flesh? Instantly the images of the dead bodies he saw yesterday flash through his mind, and he has to fight off a sudden urge to retch. He spins the cap off the bottle and gulps down several mouthfuls of water. In the humid heat, Wei Xiang has already started to perspire, his armpits and forehead damp. He assesses the scene before him: an elderly man driving a bullock cart on which sits a family of six; a trio of shirtless street kids—the boy he has been following is not one of them—nosily dousing one another with toy pails of water; and a young woman sitting on a high stool opposite the hotel, staring blankly into space, biting her nails.

From somewhere across the town, a high-pitched siren blares. Wei Xiang swivels his head in the direction of the sea and holds his breath. Except for the wreckage of collapsed buildings, telephone poles and uprooted trees, there is only stagnant water all around. Lumpy clouds hang low in the azure sky. He waits for a few seconds, anticipating a sudden change in the density of the air, or for something ominous to appear on the horizon. Nothing but the stream of people dispersing into the alleyways and lanes, each moving with a sense of purpose.

Then he hears the words in his head: *You're not really looking; you are not seeing what's there.*

Ai Ling uttered these words to him on their first day in Phuket, after they checked into the hotel and were planning to take a short stroll to Bangla Road, the main thoroughfare in Patong, before meeting Cody and Chee Seng for dinner. She pointed to something in the sky, but Wei Xiang could not see what it was at first. Then she told him: a flock of seagulls gliding back and forth in the distance, over a patch of sea. The sharpness of the memory causes his insides to tighten: *You are not seeing what's there.*

Shaking off his thoughts, Wei Xiang heads back to the school, where he can check for updates. He refuses to entertain any thoughts that might pull him asunder; as long as he acts decisively, things will come around or take a fortuitous turn. Everything will be all right in the end. Life is unpredictable this way, he reasons, and it's no excuse to lose hope and despair. He only needs to press on, and to have faith in his own actions.

At a bend along Sai Nam Yen Road, near a row of boarded-up restaurants, Wei Xiang feels an odd sensation rippling under his skin, of being observed. He whips his head around, and comes eye to eye with the boy with the scar, who is standing several metres away from him beside a pile of fallen bricks. The boy tilts his head as though he's hearing something interesting in the commotion around him. His feet are coal-dark with dirt and grime, and his skinny arms hang from his body like the long limbs of a marionette doll. Despite his shoddy appearance, he is calm and composed. Not wanting to scare him off, Wei Xiang crosses the street without any visible hurry, and walks up to him. The boy does not run away this time, but remains where he is, looking up at Wei Xiang with a steady gaze.

The previous day, he was plagued with questions about the boy—who is he? where has he come from? why isn't he accompanied by an adult?—but now, standing close enough to touch him, Wei Xiang finds himself dumbstruck, unable to speak. He mutters a simple greeting in Thai, but it does not elicit any response from the boy. He utters another phrase, but still nothing. Apart from these pleasantries, Wei Xiang does not know how to break the silence between them. Looking around, he hopes to find someone who might be able to interpret on his behalf, but the stricken looks on the passers-by hold him back.

The thoroughfare where they are standing has been closed off to traffic, with roadblocks on both ends, only allowing in medical supply trucks and ambulances. The media has descended on Phuket—Wei Xiang notices a small television crew setting up their equipment near a toppled two-storey shophouse, and a swarm of photographers, wearing vests with many pockets and carrying bulky bags, aiming their long-lens cameras at every sign of destruction—and for a moment he imagines himself watching these captured images and videos on the nine o'clock news back at home in Singapore, with Ai Ling beside him. Then the spell breaks: he's still here and Ai Ling's still missing. The present moment sucks him right back in, demanding his full attention: the noise, the heat, and the water that is everywhere he walks.

And the boy still stands before him, motionless, waiting.

Wei Xiang offers the bottle of water, but the boy only stares at it, not moving to take it. Houseflies whir about the boy's head, but he does not swat them away. Wei Xiang studies the face in detail; unlike the other street kids he has seen over the past few days, with their flat noses and wide-set eyes, the boy has a sharper set of features and a fair complexion. Perhaps he's of mixed ethnicity, Thai-Chinese. And the deep scar across his left eye. Wei Xiang can't shake off the impression that he finds the boy familiar, that there's something about him that triggers a vague recognition. Maybe he has got the boy's face mixed up with the numerous faces of the dead children he has seen. Yes, he must have been confused by all those faces. Yet when he looks into the boy's face, Wei Xiang is very certain that he has seen him before—in a different place or time.

The boy regards Wei Xiang with the same interest, a smile raising the corners of his mouth. It's a strange, knowing smile, one that holds a deeper meaning unknown to Wei Xiang. He returns the smile. The noises in the background come and go—the sporadic shouting, the honking of trucks, and the desolate blast of the siren. Wei Xiang and the boy seem to be in their own bubble, surrounded but untouched by the sea of people around them.

"Who are you?" Wei Xiang finally blurts out in English. The question hangs in the air, an invisible buffer between them, before fading away.

The boy remains silent. Then suddenly he extends his left hand and slips it into Wei Xiang's. It's small, light and bony, like a tiny sparrow, frail and vulnerable in his hand. He could easily crush it with little effort. The boy glances down the crowded road, turns on his heel, and steps in the direction opposite from where Wei Xiang was planning to go, towards the southern end of Phuket. The boy's gentle tug breaks Wei Xiang's flow of thoughts, overcoming his hesitation. He quickly follows the boy's lead, a small seed of hope sprouting inside him.

19

AI LING

Back in 2002, Ai Ling visited her aunt in the hospital daily after the car accident. She knew it was not required or expected, but the act of visiting made her feel useful, as if she were helping in her aunt's recovery through her presence. While her aunt slept, comatose, Ai Ling would keep up a steady one-sided conversation, careful to enunciate each word slowly, keeping the topics light. With plastic tubes running to the machines that stood to the side of the bed, beeping with stubborn regularity, her aunt looked like a creature entangled in its own mess of tentacles. Ai Ling would study the numbers displayed on these machines, trying to understand what they indicated.

No matter how she was feeling on any day, upon entering the hospital room where her aunt was staying, Ai Ling would feel a quickening sense of calm, as if she were entering a temporal state where things stood still, unchanging. She had never felt this way—whether at the childcare centre or at home with Wei Xiang—and the sense of serenity had continued to stay with her, deepening with each visit.

Sitting on the bus on the way to the hospital, surrounded by other commuters, she could sense her body readying itself in anticipation, like someone preparing for an underwater dive. When she closed her eyes, she could imagine her aunt on the other side of where she was going, and if Ai Ling continued to stay very still, she could get a glimpse of her late uncle—a lonely figure in her mind's eye, staring absently at her. These daydreams, Ai Ling told herself, were nothing more than illusions, mere flights of fancy. Yet the memory of her uncle was always at the back of her mind, a shadow hovering behind her consciousness; at times, she was afraid of confusing it with the other memories she had hoarded. Whenever she thought of her uncle or aunt, Ai Ling had to suppress the sadness, the sly encroachment of grief. She felt divided, like having many different selves working in tandem inside her, directing her down different paths. Still she was able to find the middle ground to exist, without breaking up over every stirred-up recollection. To her parents, who seemed to be having a worse time over her uncle's death, Ai Ling was the embodiment of steadfastness. Yet, inwardly, Ai Ling knew she was barely holding everything together, always fearful of her moods running awry despite her self-control.

After the accident, Ai Ling had tried to distract herself with reading books and articles that dealt with situations like this, and picking up pointers on how to help a person in times of trauma, though she was still unsure how she could help her aunt when she would finally wake up. Looking at her aunt's face—placid and peaceful in sleep—Ai Ling could hardly imagine what her response would be when she later heard the news about her husband's death. In her darker moods, Ai Ling wished her aunt would remain in her slumber and never wake up, or if her memories were all wiped clean so that she would never even know who her husband was.

Unlike Ai Ling, her parents were industrious, keeping themselves busy with tasks and follow-ups. They would consult the doctors and nurses, arrange for further checks and scans and medication, and bring the necessary items to the hospital: a blanket, a change of clothes, packets of Milo, body and hand lotion. They barely stayed in place for more than a few minutes, before they were onto their next task, keeping themselves occupied. Only once did Ai Ling see her mother standing quietly by the bed and looking down at her sister, but when she heard Ai Ling entering the room, she quickly excused herself, muttering about something she had forgotten to pick up on her way to the hospital. Ai Ling tried not to notice that her mother's eyes were red and puffy when she picked up her shoulder bag and left the room.

Her parents wanted to hold the funeral without any delay. Ai Ling protested, but later dropped it when she knew it would not change her parents' minds or decision. During the entire period of the wake—three long, seamless days—Ai Ling prayed for her aunt not to wake up from her coma, to remain in her blissfully undisturbed dream. For three days, Ai Ling was a bundle of tired nerves and fraught emotions, moving from the hospital to the funeral parlour, and vice versa, several times a day. She felt strangely disembodied, cut out of time.

It was during those days—Ai Ling had taken a week of compassionate leave, and gone home only to sleep and shower—that she sometimes imagined the kind of conversations she would have with her aunt when she woke up. Her aunt had a measured manner of speaking, as if she were always weighing her words for the correct tone or delivery. She never seemed to hurry when she talked, and it was this particular trait of hers that Ai Ling was drawn to. She could tell her aunt anything about her life, and she would listen patiently, never once jumping in to interrupt her with her opinions or views. Though her aunt's replies were occasionally clichéd—"You have to be more patient with him…" "A married life is full of ups and downs…" "Give him time and his own space, and he will come back to himself…"—Ai Ling had never felt patronised or brushed over by her aunt's advice or encouragement.

On the last day of her uncle's funeral, after they had cremated him, Ai Ling went straight home with Wei Xiang. When they were alone in the bedroom, Ai Ling laid her head on Wei Xiang's chest and wrapped her arms around him. The warmth of Wei Xiang's skin brought tears to her eyes. When she kissed Wei Xiang and started to take off her clothes, he was taken aback.

"Are you sure? Don't you want to rest?" he asked.

"No, no need."

"You sure?"

"Yes."

Ai Ling then led Wei Xiang to the bed, holding her body to his, reaching for his physical presence—a weight to hold her down when all she could feel was a benumbing sense of lightness, of being unmoored from everything around her. She felt lost, and had a terrifying desire to regain what was missing from her, to seize it back for herself. She needed Wei Xiang's body, his physicality, to make her feel she was still alive.

"Please, I want this," Ai Ling said, breathlessly.

In their lovemaking, Wei Xiang was gentle, almost too careful, with her. But Ai Ling wanted it rougher. She clamped her legs tightly around his waist, forcing him to thrust deeper into her. Still Wei Xiang remained cautious. At one point, she saw his face registering signs of held-back pain.

"I'm sorry, I'm so sorry," she whispered, when Wei Xiang finally came inside her.

"No, it's okay," he said, his breath warm on her chest.

Ai Ling held onto him until he fell asleep. In the dark, she listened to his light snoring and watched his body move through the quiet stages of sleep.

∞

It was easy to forget that other people existed outside one's own realm of existence. In her preoccupation with her own thoughts, Ai Ling sometimes failed to see how her aunt's current state was also affecting her parents, especially her mother. It did not help that her mother was never one to wear her emotions on her sleeve, unlike her father, who was much more open to expressing his feelings. Ai Ling had often wondered whether the trait—the reticence—ran in her mother's side of the family, and in her too.

Whenever she was in the hospital, her mother tended to her aunt with minimum fuss—covering her with another blanket, dabbing her dry lips with lip balm, changing the socks on her feet, combing her hair—and mostly when Ai Ling was out of the room, so when Ai Ling returned to the bedside, she would always notice something different about her aunt. One time, behind the closed door of the hospital room's toilet, Ai Ling heard her mother crying, though she had tried to mask it by running the sink tap.

A day before her aunt woke up, Ai Ling and her mother were in the hospital room—her father had returned home to rest, after a night of keeping watch—and in the midst of wiping down the mobile side table, her mother looked out of the window, staring into the distance.

"Your aunt loves the outdoors. She would have loved the weather today."

Ai Ling glanced out the window and saw the leaves of the trees fluttering in the breeze, lusciously green, the sky full of clouds.

"I'm sure she would."

"When she was younger, when we were still living in the kampong, she never wanted to stay indoors for long, always clamouring to go out, to the vegetable fields where my father and uncles worked, to the stream where she would catch tadpoles and small fish. Nobody could stop her. She was very stubborn."

"Really? But she always seems so agreeable."

"Don't be fooled." Ai Ling's mother smiled and glanced at her sister before turning back to what was outside the window. "She hurt herself badly one time, but never told anyone. Got her foot cut by a nail. Didn't once mention it to anyone, until she started limping the next day. The infection was really bad, took almost a week to heal properly. It was just like her to keep everything to herself until it got worse."

Ai Ling's mother moved nearer to the bed. She tucked

her sister's hand under the blanket, patted it over the covers. "Why are hospitals always so cold?"

"I'll raise the temperature."

Ai Ling got up from her chair and adjusted the thermostat with the remote control. The air-con, perched over the bed, beeped once and lowered its louvres. Silence descended on the room, making it feel more confined.

"She will come around soon."

The crack in Ai Ling's mother's voice was magnified in the quietness of the room, and Ai Ling started to cry, holding her hands up to her face, unable to halt the rapid transition from sobbing to wailing. She could feel her mother's hand on her shoulder, light and steady, an anchor keeping her still. Her mother did not say anything, but waited till Ai Ling had finally finished before withdrawing her hand. She then left the room, leaving Ai Ling alone with her aunt.

∞

"Let's go home," Wei Xiang said later that day. He had stayed by Ai Ling's side from the moment he stepped into the room. From time to time, he would bring Ai Ling a cup of coffee or massage her shoulders or go to the nurses with minor requests. Ai Ling would smile at him, to acknowledge what he was doing.

"Yes, go home and rest, I'm here," Ai Ling's mother said. "If there's anything, I'll call you."

While walking through the hospital ward, Ai Ling peeked into some of the rooms and glanced at the faces of the relatives of the other patients. While most were serious and glum, there was sometimes laughter from a few, a snatch of cheerful dialogue or conversation. Evening was approaching fast, as the exhausted daylight slowly extinguished over the horizon. Crossing the garden compound to the hospital entrance, Ai Ling could smell the sweet leafy scent coming from the recently watered patch of grass. She found herself taking deep, long breaths, as if she had been barely able to breathe while she was in the room with her aunt.

"She'll be all right, the doctor said so," said Wei Xiang.

"I don't know. What will she do when she hears the news, when she wakes up?"

"One step at a time. First she needs to recover, and then you can break the news to her. It'll take a long time for her to accept this." In his voice, Ai Ling could sense Wei Xiang's optimism. He had always believed in keeping his hopes up, especially when things were going wrong. Ai Ling had never had what came so naturally to Wei Xiang: an easy, buoyant sanguinity.

"What would you do if I died?" Ai Ling asked.

"Statistically, I'll die before you, husbands going before wives…"

"No, I'm serious. What would you do?"

Wei Xiang stopped in his tracks and turned to Ai Ling.

"I wouldn't know what to do," he finally said.

That night, Ai Ling woke from a long dream in a state of panic, gripping the sheet in fistfuls. In the dream, she had been held down by something huge that loomed darkly over her, a force that broke down all her defences, despite her fight to break through. The stretch of thin light that arched over her, hovering above the darkness, was out of reach,

holding out a promise—of what? salvation? survival?—
something she could never come near to. When the fingers
of surrounding cold crept into her, she had let go—and only
then was she able to break out of her dream and wake in
her bed. She steadied her breathing until it was manageable,
then got up, went to the wardrobe and changed into a new
T-shirt, throwing aside the drenched one. In the kitchen,
she drank two full glasses of cold water. Her mind was alert
to her surroundings; the milky shafts of moonlight coming
through the windows offered some illumination. Ai Ling felt
a deep relief, as if she had survived some sort of test.

Finding herself unable to sleep, Ai Ling sat on the sofa
in the living room for some time. Then she went into the
study and searched through the cabinet where she kept
all the important documents; near the bottom, she found
what she was looking for: the marriage certificate, in a
cylindrical container. Unrolling the certificate, stiff and
resistant with age, she noted the date and signatures,
before putting it back.

Ai Ling thought about her marriage to Wei Xiang and
was reminded again by how short it was compared to her
aunt's—how little she knew about living with Wei Xiang,
despite their similarities and compromises. She knew, of
course, that life was fickle and irrational, that whatever one
built was subject to the pulverizing effects of time. Yet the
knowledge brought little comfort. No matter how much she
fretted about the future—about Wei Xiang, or her aunt—
she could only live one moment at a time, one day followed
by another. And Ai Ling suddenly felt terribly weighed down
by it all.

She knew there was no comparison between her marriage and her aunt's. She and Wei Xiang had only been married for five years, while her aunt and her late uncle had spent over forty years together. Those decades made all the difference: their history, seasoned with joys and miseries, hopes and wasted opportunities; the years had borne them along, carried them through, and now this, a rupture, a death. How was one supposed to deal with the fact of death? It cast a long, unwavering shadow over everything, and Ai Ling had felt its hand on her in her dream, scorching the edges of her self.

She looked at the framed portrait of their wedding photograph on a long wooden shelf beside the study table. For the shoot, they had opted for a dressed-down, everyday look: a light blue tailored shirt and dark pleated pants for Wei Xiang, and a red floral dress with an empire waistline for Ai Ling. Their faces were beaming with happiness. Ai Ling stared at her own face in the photograph, trying to bridge who she was at that moment with the woman she was now, the divide invisible but deep. What had she been thinking then? She tried to extract the memory, but could only recall the flashes of the camera, the encouraging instructions of the photographer to smile brighter. *Remember, you're happy, so must smile more!* She had quietly and obediently done what she was told.

Standing in the study, Ai Ling did not know how to make sense of the happiness she had once felt. She shook her head, then turned off the light and stood in the dark for a long time.

∞

The next morning, Ai Ling was reading a magazine in her aunt's hospital room, seated on a chair facing the room's entrance, and when she glanced up, she saw her aunt's eyes wide open, staring at her. Ai Ling jolted up out of the chair, tossed down the magazine, and rushed to the bed, careful not to touch any tubes when she held her aunt's hands. Her aunt smiled weakly, but did not say anything.

Barely an hour after she called her parents to inform them about the news, they were there beside her aunt's bed, attending to her needs, and skirting the growing puzzlement gnawing at her features. Ai Ling's mother gently hushed her with admonishment to rest, to have some food, a hot Milo drink. A few times, her aunt looked at Ai Ling for answers, but she was quick to avert her gaze. The following afternoon, Ai Ling's mother told her aunt about the death of her husband in a truncated account of the accident. By the end of that day, her aunt was ready to be discharged from the hospital. Ai Ling and her mother made the arrangements to take her back to her parents' place, where she would stay until she was well enough to return home. Her aunt did not offer any protest. "She's still in shock," her mother said.

At her parents' flat, Ai Ling watched her aunt even more intently, as if observing a trapped, terrified animal, though she kept an appropriate distance, not wanting to draw attention to herself, even as she stayed alert to her aunt's presence whenever she paid a visit, every night after work. Her aunt showed little emotion. Once, when Ai Ling saw her aunt standing by the window, staring into space, she approached her and stood by her side, waiting for her aunt to notice her. When she did not, Ai Ling spoke up.

"Are you okay?" Ai Ling said. Her aunt, startled, turned to look at her, rearranging the expression on her face to something less fearful.

"Yes, I am, of course," her aunt answered.

With the bruises on her face and arms slowly fading, her aunt convinced Ai Ling's parents that she had recovered and wanted to go back home. After thanking all of them for their caregiving and also for helping to arrange her late husband's funeral, her aunt packed her things and made a quiet departure. Ai Ling offered to help her aunt settle back in. She swept and cleaned and put everything back in place, while her aunt glanced at every item in the flat with a detached gaze, as if she did not know how they had got there in the first place. She left Ai Ling to the tidying up and went to lie down in the spare bedroom, which had a single bed for visiting relatives or friends, closing the door behind her. When she had finished her tasks—the day had slipped into a dusky, warm evening—Ai Ling knocked on the bedroom door and entered when she heard no reply. Her aunt was lying on her side, facing the wall, seemingly asleep. Not wanting to wake her, Ai Ling left the flat quietly.

For a long time after her aunt had moved back home, Ai Ling lived in a state of constant anxiety, and it diverted her attention from the other things in her life that had come to somehow feel trivial and narrow, even petty. Then one night, as she was getting ready to sleep, her mobile phone rang.

"Hello, Aunt Jenny?" Ai Ling said, but there was no reply. For a brief moment, Ai Ling thought that maybe she had mistaken the caller's identity and glanced again at the screen. It was her aunt's home number.

"Hello, can you hear me? Is everything okay?" Ai Ling said, fear rising in her voice. Finally, she thought she heard something on the line, a few words, or maybe a cry—she could not tell exactly. Then there was a long, pitiable groan that seemed to reach deep inside her, clenching her in a tight, suffocating grip.

Ai Ling clung to the phone, listening, waiting for a voice to speak to her, to tell her what to do.

20

CODY

The year Cody turned sixteen, his mother was diagnosed with late-stage breast cancer and was sick for eight months before she died. He was taking his O-Level examinations that year, and his mind was distracted during the hazy period of her dying. She had known about the cancer after going for a regular check-up at the polyclinic. It was only when the cancer reached the third stage and Cody and his sisters became suspicious of the frequent hospital visits and their mother's dwindling frame and thinning hair that the parents broke the news over dinner one night. Cody lowered his chopsticks and stared at his parents, who carried on eating from their bowls of rice, seemingly unperturbed by what they had just said. His mother spoke up after a few unbearable seconds and assured them that everything was okay, and that they would talk about it in due time, after everything was settled. After this, she did not say another word.

Because he was the youngest in the family, Cody was not expected to do much except stay at home after school and study for the impending examinations, while everyone else did whatever they could for his mother. His eldest sister accompanied her to the hospital for her check-ups while his second sister helped their father out at the fish stall from time to time. When she was at home, Cody would stay by her side and talk to her about the latest Channel 8 drama serials, the actors who were in them, the gossip and the scandals, and she would sometimes ask him about school, homework, his preparation for the O-Levels, and his friends. He would skip from topic to topic with as much lightness as he could muster, not wanting to trouble her in any way. Though there were many things on his mind, Cody could not get the words out.

He often wondered how he could tell his mother about what was going on in his life then: that he was struggling with his studies, that he was failing class tests even though he had studied for them, that he had a crush on a boy in his class, that he was confused about his feelings, and how he had become fearful and anxious all the time about who he was and who he was becoming. She did not need to know all this. Even before she was diagnosed with breast cancer, his mother had a forceful and domineering personality, and raised the children with the same authority and discipline employed by her own parents. She was the disciplinarian in the family, and would watch over their comings and goings, making sure that they did not get into any trouble, that they knew exactly why they were punished, that she did not raise them to be spoilt or ungrateful children. She would mete out her punishments—ten strokes of the cane, five slaps on calves or thighs—and tell them to reflect on their actions, to think carefully about their wrongdoings. Only fools repeat their mistake, she would intone. Growing up under the unbreakable spell she cast over them, Cody's love for his mother was mired with fear and awe, spiked with thorns.

∞

The boy Cody had a crush on, Cedric, was in his form class, and they had been friends since Secondary One, though it had never gone beyond simple exchanges and basketball games and smiles-and-nods of acquaintanceship. Though they hung out together with other classmates on many occasions, he hardly knew anything about Cedric except for the fact that he had a younger sister and his father was an accountant. It was only in Secondary Three that Cody began to become aware of his attraction to boys and to Cedric specifically. It was hard to know when all this first started, and by the time he grew aware of it, it had become something that took up most of his waking thoughts, like a terrible secret had taken up residence in his head. At thirteen, his body had grown into a new one, and he was constantly conscious of its demands and urges and vanity. His first erection was a shock; he was surprised by how little he was able to control something that seemed so natural. His first wet dream when he was fourteen shamed him so thoroughly that he threw his soiled underwear and shorts into the rubbish chute. The first time he touched himself and produced an instant erection and later a quick ejaculation, he was overcome by the intense sensation and complexity of feelings that his body could generate over such a private, secret act. In the jail of his changing body, this act alone was his only constant, an escape into something that his other life, public and visible, was unable to provide.

Cody and Cedric were about the same height, though the shape and size of their bodies were at opposite ends of the spectrum. Cody was skinny, with a long torso and gangly limbs, while Cedric wore his mass of lean muscle comfortably and proudly. Like some of their classmates, Cedric would play basketball without a shirt, his pants riding low on his slender hips, the pelvic bones making a V that disappeared under the waistband of his underwear. Sitting at the side of the court, Cody would pretend to watch the game enthusiastically while, at the same time, ingraining his memory with as many images of Cedric's body as he could, which he would replay later in his head while masturbating in the school toilet or at home. He never went far with these images; they were only the means to an end, to the pleasure he wanted to extract from them, and he never considered where they could lead him, to recognise something in himself that he was evading. At fifteen, Cody was far from knowing what he wanted, or who he was, or whether there were other boys like him; yet under this murky, impenetrable surface, he was deeply aware of the burden he was carrying and the secrecy that enshrouded it, and he took great pains to hide it. He presented another self to the world to appear normal —a self that was remote and detached, yet accommodating and highly adaptive to its surroundings, changing its shape and form to survive.

Towards the end of her life, Cody's mother would lie in bed all day long, her eyes fixed on the ceiling, mumbling to herself; when he entered the room, she would turn and stare as if registering him for the first time, a person who had materialised from nowhere. It was the medicine taking effect, his father would say. Cody would bring her simple meals of sweet potato porridge or herbal chicken broth and feed her in small spoonfuls, which she would refuse after two to three mouthfuls. "Enough, enough, you eat," she would say, lying back on the bed, the exertions deepening the lines around her eyes.

On more lucid days, she would tell stories about her past, how she had wanted to be a teacher but her father's disapproval—he needed her to help out at home and at the fish stall he owned, and also to take care of her nine siblings—led to her discarding her ambition. She took great pride in her responsibilities towards her younger siblings, a no-nonsense role that had shaped her into the woman she became. Yet, when she told Cody how she and his father had met, she got more bashful. Helping her father at the fish stall in the mornings, she was always conscious of how she smelled. "The stench of fish went into everything, into my clothes, under my nails, into my skin; no matter how I cleaned or showered, it was always there."

So when Cody's father asked her out one day—he was the delivery driver for the vendor who supplied fish to her father—she was caught off-guard, though her doubt did not stop her from going out with him. She was twenty and of marriageable age, and Cody's father was the first man to ask her out; she was curious about this shy, sinewy man who had never said more than good morning when he handed her the daily invoice. They dated for four months before he proposed marriage, and then they were married for twenty-five years.

"So fast," Cody said. "How come you never considered other guys, or dated more before deciding?"

"What was the point?" she said, amused. "Waste of time. I knew he was the one I wanted to marry, a good man, stable and reliable. Unlike young people these days, talk about love and romance all the time, have so many choices but still can't make any good decision, breaking up here, divorcing there." She then closed her eyes, slipping into other thoughts.

Sometimes, after taking her afternoon medicine, Cody's mother would turn pensive while she mused. She would remind Cody that she had not got married because she loved Cody's father from the start—"none of that nonsense"—but because of the realistic, steadfast qualities that marked him as a man of conviction. The love came later, years after they were married.

"Love does not always have to be the first thing," she said. "Use your head first, and the heart will follow later."

Love was not the word Cody would use to describe how he felt about Cedric, which was something more evasive, more illicit—lust, infatuation, or something else? It only took a sneak peek in class for Cody's whole being to be wrapped up for the rest of the day in a confounding state of confusion, shame, and deep unabated longing. He felt sharply alive, and at the same time, terribly conflicted.

In school during recess, Cody would sometimes head to a deserted boys' toilet located in a quiet corner on the third floor of the Technical block where they had their weekly two-hour Design and Technology lessons. The toilet was used as a storage room for broken toilet bowls and covers, ruined tables and chairs, and cracked mirrors, the floor covered with a brown carpet of dried leaves, animal faeces, and the shrivelled carcasses of cockroaches, beetles, and even a sparrow that had flown in through the broken window slats. He had tried the taps the first time he was in there, but the water supply had been cut. He had pissed into the sink while staring at his reflection in the cracked mirror, emboldened by the little act of subversion. The toilet soon became the one place in school he escaped to whenever he needed to be alone.

Sometimes he would bring a book to read, but because the air in the toilet was stale and dusty, he could not concentrate for long. A few times he gathered the dried leaves into small piles, set fire to them with matches and watched them burn; when the smoke became too thick, he would stamp the fire out. When the mood struck, he would strip down and masturbate in front of the row of mirrors, and come very quickly onto the dirty floor.

Then one day, he heard someone outside while he was masturbating to mental images of Cedric, and ran into the nearest stall with his shorts still down. Just as he slammed the stall door closed, he heard the person enter the toilet.

"I saw you, Cody," said Cedric. "What are you doing here?"

Cody gasped, but stayed silent, his heart hammering in double-time. He was still holding onto his erection, which had become even stiffer. He willed it to subside, but no luck.

"Come out now, why are you hiding?"

"Go away, please," Cody whimpered.

"What are you doing in there?" Cedric knocked on the door, and in that sudden moment, Cody came furiously in thick, milky spurts that hit the graffitied wall of the toilet stall and slowly dripped downward. He bit his lips to suppress the cry.

"Nothing," Cody whispered. "Just go away."

Cedric laughed and slapped his palm once on the toilet door before leaving. In the ensuing silence, Cody let out a long breath, bristling with heat and shame from his own foolishness—how precariously close he had come to ruin.

After recovering, Cody left the toilet and went to one of the school administrators to report the faulty lock to the deserted toilet. In no time, the lock was changed, and, after that, he never went near the toilet again. When Cedric broached the topic later on, Cody laughed off the whole matter, brushing it aside as nothing more than a childish indiscretion, an innocuous act. Cedric cocked his eyebrows and looked doubtful, but did not inquire further.

Cody was in school the day his mother passed away. He was called out of class by the school clerk, informed of the news and excused for the rest of the day. As he made his way home, his mind was blank. There were a few relatives already present in the flat when he finally got back. His father was talking to them while his sisters went around serving tea and packet drinks. Cody slipped past them, catching snatches of words here and there, and paused at the entrance to his parents' bedroom. His mother lay on the bed, her eyes closed, hands by her sides. For a brief moment, Cody thought she was deep in sleep, her features undisturbed, but there was an absence that was palpable in its stillness. As he walked up to her, he could not look away from her face. Cody stood by her side for some time before his father entered the room with a relative, prompting him to leave quickly.

The period between the wake and the cremation was unending, an unbroken series of activities, filled with noise, smoke and condolences. People came up to Cody, took his hands and offered their words of comfort. He listened, nodded his head and returned their smiles. With his silence perceived as grief, he was able to retreat into himself, into the space where words no longer meant anything. Even when he was surrounded by people, he felt cut off, removed from whatever was happening at the moment, and the sensation that it brought was strangely comforting, as if he were slowly becoming invisible, and all he had to do was sit or kneel or stand, and nothing more was expected of him.

After they brought back his mother's ashes, Cody went into his room and did not come out for a week. At first, he thought that he was just exhausted from the frictional effect that people had on him, from an extended period of contact and proximity. He slept for eighteen hours, dead to the world, and even after he woke up, he could not bring himself to leave the bed or come out of the bedroom. His father and sisters left him alone for a while, thinking that he was a grieving, but after two days they became alarmed. His sisters came to sit beside him, patting his head and shoulders, reassuring him with their soft, cajoling words. He closed his eyes and turned to the wall, tensing his body at their touch. They brought food, leaving it on the side table beside the bed, dishes of rice and vegetables and meat that turned cold after being left untouched.

He slept for most of each day; when he could not, he would stare out the window at the narrow fragment of the sky, listening to the muffled sounds of the world outside the flat. He was not able to hold onto any thought that flitted through his mind. Occasionally, a memory would dislodge itself and force its way into his consciousness: a face, a word, a repeated montage of images. He could not shut these memories down, so he let them pass through him. When he slept, these thoughts would slip into his dreams, and in them he could see himself trying to make sense of what he could not hold on to. His mother featured in most of these dreams—standing at the stove and stirring a pot of pork ribs and lotus root soup, or listening to a radio programme on the Rediffusion. Cody would hover at the edge of these visions, observing her, unable to touch her even if he wanted to, his mother existing in a realm beyond his reach. These dreams would haunt him while he was awake, leaving him helpless in discerning the real from imagined.

Sometimes his father would come into the room. He would lay his hand on Cody's head and whisper his name, as if trying to call him back from wherever he had gone. Cody could hear his name clearly, but he did not respond, restrained by his own silence. His father would sit quietly beside Cody and stay there for a long time. Some nights, he would bring a face towel and wipe down Cody's face, arms and legs, and change his clothes. Cody did not put up any resistance as his father carried out these tasks.

One night, after waking from a recurring nightmare, his body racked with painful spasms, Cody looked over and saw his father sitting on a chair beside the bed, sleeping. In the light of the bedside lamp, he saw the sea of white hair against his scalp; how his father had aged just over a short period of time, how frail he seemed now. Looking at him asleep, Cody could feel the years that had passed between his parents, years that stretched all the way back to before he and his sisters were born, to a time that existed only between them and no one else. How this immense weight of time and history was now left to his father, who had to bear the burden all on his own.

As Cody laid his hand on his father's head, he stirred lightly in his sleep, letting out a small cry. For a long moment, Cody imagined the thoughts running through his father's mind, thoughts that followed their own logic, their own outcomes, into places only he would know—dark, oceanic places, teeming with life. He would never know what went on in there, in this secret place inside his father, but he would keep vigil over him, just as his father had done—watching over him, waiting for him to surface once again.

PART THREE

21

In late October 2004, Ai Ling had told Wei Xiang about a four-day trip she was hoping to take by herself to Cha Am, a beach resort town along the western coast of Thailand, to "get herself sorted out". When Wei Xiang asked to accompany her, Ai Ling declined, offering the answer she had prepared in advance: she needed some time on her own, to take a breather from work, to think. Ai Ling then smiled and patted his arm, brushing away his worries.

The morning she landed in Bangkok, she took a two-hour coach ride to Cha Am, and arrived at the beachfront resort tired but elated. She felt as if she had finally pulled off an impossible feat and was being rewarded with the prize she had wanted: silence and solitude. They gave her a room on the third floor, from where she could see the silver surf on the beach and hear the white noise of street sounds—snippets of Thai songs, children playing, cars driving by. Her room was simple enough, a queen-size bed with a low bedside table, a large mirror beside the door, and a small beige two-seater sofa that faced the floor-to-ceiling windows. From her luggage, she took out her toiletries bag and went for a quick shower. When she was done, she lay on the bed, hair damp, and allowed her body to sink into its silky comfort, the bedsheet cool against her skin. She fell asleep and woke up half an hour later, feeling the drag of lethargy in her body. She sat up on the edge of the bed and watched as the water swept along the coastline, the sea stretching into the far horizon.

In her half-drowsy state, Ai Ling remembered Wei Xiang's face at the airport that morning, how his eyes were alert with attention, searching hers for some sort of an answer to the questions he dared not ask. Again, Ai Ling had given him the details of her itinerary and the contact information of the hotel where she would be staying. When they parted at the departure gates, Ai Ling could not help but feel a deep sense of relief, as if she were finally freed from her obligations, her tiresome old self. The recollection of her relief brought a stab of guilt, and Ai Ling quickly let the feeling pass. She was not here to feel the same things or have the same thoughts. For the next few days, she did not want to be her usual self; she wanted to do things differently, and for her own sake. She only needed to answer to herself.

Ai Ling got up from the bed and opened every window in the room, letting the breeze in, sending ripples across the rumpled bedsheet. The greasy smell of frying oil wafted into the room, reminding her that she had not eaten since breakfast with Wei Xiang at the airport, and she could feel her stomach growling. Dusk was approaching fast, scattering stolen light across the sea; Ai Ling caught her reflection in the large mirror, suspended in this quality of light, and for a moment she felt strangely out of body.

"Light and shadow is all," she said in a self-deprecating tone to her own reflection. Then she laughed and dressed for dinner.

As Ai Ling passed through the foyer, she glanced over at the alfresco hotel bar, where a few occupants were having drinks; a television was blaring a football match with loud commentary. A face turned to her and she was surprised to recognise who the person was: a man who had taken the same coach from Bangkok to the hotel, whom she had barely acknowledged during the bus journey. He was in his late twenties, lean and bespectacled, with neatly parted hair. Ai Ling had wondered whether he was a fellow Singaporean and was apprehensive about making further contact, even with a glance.

But the man was smiling at her now, and Ai Ling felt compelled to return it. He watched as she passed through the foyer, and she was suddenly conscious of her movements and her loose, knee-length sundress. She quickly erased the thought from her mind; still she could sense the curiosity emanating from the man's stare, like a source of heat. She quickened her steps.

At thirty-five, Ai Ling knew she was already past her prime, that words like "pretty" or "attractive" no longer applied to her. She had not cared much about such things—these vacuous aesthetic labels that differ from person to person—though she was aware of the gradual fading of her looks, something beyond her control. She knew she had crossed some line, one that had separated her younger self from the current one, and often wondered how this transition had taken place, and at which point in her life. She felt centuries old in her body, in her mind.

Yet, it was times like this—a cursory glance from a man or a woman, weighing and assessing her looks—that Ai Ling was called back to her own physicality, and was reminded once again that every feature of her flesh was being calibrated and compared against different measures of beauty. She often felt shrunken by the limitations of these judgements, by the narrow-mindedness of the people who employed such measures. She did not want to be part of this, yet she somehow felt drawn in—no, unsettled—by the young man's look, which carried some sort of response to what she was unconsciously looking for. In his look, she was remade in a different light—a more attractive light—and this thought was oddly refreshing, the transformation of her self in another person's determined gaze.

She was still pondering this when she stepped outside onto the busy street, and her attention was swiftly diverted to the flow of cars and people, almost crashing into a group of children playing at a standing water tap and splashing water at each other. The hem of her dress got wet, though it did not bother her. Strolling along the long stretch of Ruamjit Road, she swung her glance from the restaurants, convenience stores, massage parlours and dingily-lit bars that lined the main street to the setting sun that was submerging itself into the dark water. The nearby crash of the waves fought its way into Ai Ling's ears, rising above the din of loud music and human chatter. After walking almost the entire length of the street, Ai Ling backtracked to the restaurant that had looked promising when she first saw it, a chalkboard outside advertising seafood phad thai and green curry. The restaurant was not much more than a large seating area made up of six tables, with an open kitchen at the entrance and living quarters behind the beaded curtains where the owner and his family supposedly lived. She was ushered to the smallest table at the front of the restaurant. Seated, Ai Ling pointed to the chalkboard, indicating what she wanted. The server, a slim girl in her late teens, wearing cut-off denim shorts, took her order and went into the kitchen. The only other two occupied tables were taken up by locals. A beat-up television hanging in a corner of the restaurant featured a drama with mostly frowning actors. Ai Ling took in her surroundings and the conversations around her with detached interest; she had always liked this sense of separateness from other people, of watching from a distance.

From the corner of her eye, she saw someone standing outside the restaurant, studying the menu on the chalkboard. It was the same young man from the hotel bar. His eyebrows arched when he saw Ai Ling sitting there, and in the next moment, he was asking whether he could join her table. Ai Ling, finding no excuse to offer, nodded her head.

"I hope you don't mind," the man said, levelling his gaze at her.

"No, it's okay," Ai Ling said, before turning to watch the show on the TV. The man, after a pause of a few seconds, began to talk.

"I saw you just now at the hotel. Are you travelling alone?"

"Yes, I'm on holiday."

"That's great. Cha Am is a great place. It's my second time here. You'll love this place."

"I hope so."

"This restaurant is one of the best here. They serve the

best phad thai, with the fish sauce they use. You won't find any place that serves better."

"I'm sure I'll like it."

Despite her best efforts, Ai Ling found herself gradually entering into a conversation with the young man, Daniel, and coming to learn certain aspects of his life. How he had quit his job recently, as a logistics engineer in a manufacturing firm, and was planning to backpack for a while before he returned home (yes, he was a Singaporean, as Ai Ling had expected), that he did not know where he would head next, planning to be spontaneous about the places he wanted to go. In return, Ai Ling told him that she too was taking a break from her work, that she had heard about Cha Am from a colleague, that she loved the hotel and the view her room offered.

When the food came, they ate in silence. Whenever Daniel's gaze strayed—when he turned to grab the tray of condiments or talk to the server—Ai Ling would glance at him. She noticed the dimples near his mouth and the slenderness of his ears. His smile was uneven, the left side of his lips tilting upwards in a slight smirk before the right side caught up. Even when Ai Ling was hesitant to talk, Daniel pressed on with questions that were never too specific or personal.

After their meal, Ai Ling decided to head back to the hotel.

"So early? The night is young," Daniel said as they stepped into the cool night air. Traffic was light at this time of the evening.

"I'm a bit tired," Ai Ling said.

"Then I'll walk you back."

"No no, it's okay."

"Nah, there's nothing to do here when it's dark. May as well head back to the hotel where I can catch a football match or something on TV, and maybe have a drink."

They walked back slowly, occasionally turning their attention to other passers-by, to the patrons that had filled the bars. They chatted about a range of topics, and before long they were back at the hotel. There, Ai Ling bade her companion a good night and climbed the stairs to her room, not turning back for another look.

In her room, Ai Ling took another shower and lay on the bed, staring up at the ceiling, thinking about the evening she just had. She could not keep hold of her own thoughts, which seemed to pull her in many directions, so she turned on the bedside lamp, took out a paperback from her bag— Toni Morrison's *Beloved*, highly recommended by Cody— and tried to focus on the words on the page. After several attempts, she switched off the light and watched the parade of shadows on the ceiling near the open windows, waiting for sleep to come.

∞

For the first time in a long while, Ai Ling woke up without a heaviness in her head, her eyes wide open with the first light of the day. She took in the silence of the room, immersed herself in it. She stayed in bed until the alarm on her Nokia phone went off, and then she forced herself to get up.

After putting on her running attire and shoes, she headed out for a run. The hotel was quiet at this hour, with only a concierge manning the reception desk and a young woman setting up continental breakfast in the hotel lounge. The morning air bristled with a slight chill, which Ai Ling shook off with a quick warm-up. The street along the beach was largely devoid of people, except for the street hawkers peddling vegetables and fish, and the housewives shopping for fresh produce. Ai Ling took off in the direction of the hill, on the western side of town, keeping a comfortable pace. A mangy stray dog with garish pink patches of skin came up to her, sniffing at her heels, and ran with her for some time before it was distracted by an old man seated on a bike who threw something—leftovers of his breakfast, some bones and rice—in its direction. Ai Ling slowed her pace, thinking the dog might catch up but it did not return to her side. When she came to the foot of the hill, she turned back, this time running on the beach. The rising sun shone across the water, causing the crests of the waves to sparkle in explosive brilliance. Ai Ling squinted.

Near the hotel, she collapsed onto the sand, her perspiration forming a dark U on the front of her grey shirt. Nearby, an elderly man with a basket in hand was combing the wet sand for crabs, while two boys played in the water, their thin torsos shiny in the morning light. Ai Ling sensed someone approaching from behind her, and she turned to see a small Thai boy walking towards her, five or six years old, wearing a dirty purple T-shirt and tattered shorts and hauling a dirty cloth bag over his shoulder, a bottle of mineral water in his hand. Closer, Ai Ling noticed the boy's large sunken eyes, turned-up nub of a nose and set of crooked brown teeth. He looked gaunt, as though he had gone for a long time without proper rest or food. His smile was hopeful, expectant.

Ai Ling raised her hands to indicate that she did not have any money with her and the boy frowned. Then, with a series of hand gestures, Ai Ling pointed to her hotel across the two-way street, indicating that she would run up to her room and grab some money, and the boy, following her gestures, smiled and handed over the bottle. Ai Ling thanked him and spoke a few short phrases in English, but the boy shook his head, waving his small hands. He sat down on the sand and opened the dirty bag, which held bottles of water and juices, and Ai Ling noted that the bag was nearly the same size as the boy. She lifted her arms in a gesture to tell the boy that he was strong, and he burst into laughter, his face brightening instantly. They sat for a while in silence, looking out at the sea.

When Ai Ling finished her water, the boy asked for the empty bottle. He put it into his bag, preparing to leave. Ai Ling told the boy to come with her to the hotel. When she offered to carry the heavy bag of drinks, the boy politely shook his head and hunched forward to counter the weight. At the entrance of the hotel, the boy stopped, his eyes on the staff inside, looking wary of trespassing into a place where he did not belong.

"Wait here," Ai Ling said. The boy nodded.

Though it took only a couple of minutes for Ai Ling to dash up to her room to get the money, by the time she returned to the hotel entrance, the boy had disappeared. Ai Ling examined the street in both directions and then at the beach, hoping to catch sight of the boy, but he was not there.

Thoughts of the boy stayed with Ai Ling as she went about her day. At breakfast, she expected to see Daniel once again, and just as she was about to grab a plate at the buffet table, he was right beside her with a morning greeting. His hair was damp from a shower, his face scrubbed pink, his cheeks unshaven. In his sleeveless shirt, he looked younger than his age, more rugged. This time, he sat at Ai Ling's table without asking. As they ate, Ai Ling brought up her encounter with the boy on the beach.

"I see those kids in the street here all the time," Daniel said, slicing a wedge out of his pancake, dripping with syrup, and forking it into his mouth. "Their earnings go back to their parents or relatives or whoever hires them, you know. I heard that some of them have been kidnapped from elsewhere and brought here to work from morning to night, sometimes surviving only on scraps."

"How come nobody is doing anything about this?" Ai Ling said.

"Maybe it's not their business to interfere. It's much easier to close your eyes to what is happening, to pretend nothing is wrong. Maybe it's just too much trouble."

"I wish more could be done for these kids somehow. To help them out of their situation."

"And then what? What happens after you've saved them? Who's going to take care of them, give them a shelter, feed them? It's not so easy."

Ai Ling said nothing; perhaps Daniel was right. She was a tourist, an outsider, after all. In two days' time, she would leave, go back to her life in Singapore, and things would remain the same here, the kids continuing to hawk their wares—drinks, cigarettes, mineral water, cut fruits—and living the only life they knew. It was foolish to think that she could befriend a boy, make him laugh, and that would be all it took to fix things.

"So what are your plans today?" Daniel said, changing the subject. He eyed her with interest.

"I think I'll do some reading, and perhaps shop around later. Maybe go for a swim if it's not too hot."

"If you want, I could rent a motorbike or a car and we can head somewhere. There's a forest park a short ride away, with limestone hills and caves we can explore. It'll be fun."

"Thanks, but I think I'll pass. I appreciate your offer though."

"Sure, anytime." Daniel shrugged, the intensity gone out of his smile.

Back in her room, Ai Ling willed herself not to think about Daniel or the boy, but her mind kept returning to them. She smiled to herself at Daniel's flirtation, at how he was trying to get her to go out with him. If she had been a different kind of woman, living a different life, she might have taken him up on his offer. In her seven years of marriage to Wei Xiang, Ai Ling might have felt unhappy at times, but she had never questioned her love for him, even as she sometimes felt drained by his dependence on her, which often left her weary.

She had to be mindful about avoiding Daniel for the next two days.

Ai Ling picked up *Beloved* and attempted to read. She had not been able to get through two pages since arriving in Cha Am, and her failure to do so again did not surprise her. It might have been the wrong book to bring along. Creeping into the bed and lying on the cool bedsheet, Ai

Ling imagined herself floating on the surface of a river, gliding away. She closed her eyes; the image of the young boy surfaced, along with the memory of the infant shoes sinking into the darkness of a pond. It had been many years since her miscarriage, but the sudden memory gripped her hard. She did not suppress it; instead she allowed it to pull others out of the pit of her subconscious. She saw herself at the hospital, standing by the roadside vomiting, the blood coming out of her that never seemed to stop. Her stomach ached now as if it, too, were recollecting the past, and she cringed from the imaginary pain.

If she'd had the child that she actually lost, would it be the same age as the boy she saw that morning? Ai Ling shook her head roughly, wanting to dislodge herself from the path that the thought was leading her towards, unwilling to know what was at the end of it. She opened her eyes and looked out the windows; the sky had changed to a dark sheet of grey, a thunderstorm breaking out in the distance, moving inland.

The heavy rain did not let up till the early evening. Ai Ling stayed in her room, dozing in and out of sleep, her mind groggy with half-remembered dreams. Her body felt dull, sluggish, as if she were swathed with several layers of heavy clothes. *Beloved* lay beside her, its pages curled from the humidity, the spine loosely holding the novel together, although one of the pages had escaped its grasp completely. She got up to drink from the tap in the toilet a few times, and to brush her hair. In the harsh light, her face looked tired, the lines around her eyes and mouth more pronounced. She put on another application of moisturiser.

Standing at the windows, Ai Ling watched the progress of

the rain, from the initial roars of the thunder to the riotous downpour, a gleaming curtain of silver needles. The sea had come to life with the arrival of the storm, roused by its own rage, the waves whipped into a frenzy, spiky white crests that pierced the surface of the water. The streets were empty. Nothing moved except for the rain and the sea.

During one of her naps, Ai Ling heard a soft knock on the door, which, in her semi-conscious state, she thought initially was the pelting of rain on the windows. She did not move to answer it. It could well have been the hotel concierge or Daniel, but Ai Ling did not care. She waited for the person behind the door to move away, for silence to return to the room.

She got out of bed when she could sleep no more. She showered, put on a loose dress, and stepped out of the room. The rain had died down to a ghostly drizzle, so faint that, as she stood under the hotel's front awning, she barely felt it on her skin, only a light tingling. The sky was a deep blue that softened in degrees as it met the horizon. The street lights stood against the dusk like solitary figures, beaming out their islands of yellow rays. Ai Ling had only taken a few steps when she felt a shadow looming over her. She turned to see Daniel, holding an umbrella.

"Where were you the whole afternoon? I couldn't find you."

"I was sleeping."

"You sleep very soundly. Maybe that's why you didn't hear the knocking."

They laughed, and started to walk in the direction of the restaurant where they'd had dinner the night before. With

Ai Ling's assent, Daniel ordered the same dishes as before, along with a plate of fried prawn cakes. He assaulted her with questions once again, and Ai Ling answered them politely. After dinner, he asked whether she was interested in walking along the beach—the weather was cool after the rain—but she declined. As they headed back to the hotel, Daniel brushed his hand against Ai Ling's, and when she did not move away or shy from it, he took hold of her hand. As they strolled down the street, Ai Ling wondered how they looked to the other passers-by, who might mistake them for a couple enjoying an evening walk, talking about the quiet, intimate affairs of their lives, and she could not help but imagine the life she could have with this stranger. She wondered whether Daniel wanted children—a boy or a girl, or both. She did not skimp on any detail that would make this imagined life better or richer or more satisfying than the one she had.

Back at the hotel, Daniel asked Ai Ling whether she was up for a drink at the bar. She hesitated, then shook her head. Daniel looked puzzled, thrown off his axis, unable to reconcile what had preceded—a good meal together, the conversation, the hand-holding—with Ai Ling's taciturn behaviour. Not knowing how to extricate herself from the situation, she stretched upwards and kissed him lightly on the cheek. His eyes brightened with a flare of hope, but she was already moving towards the staircase. She heard Daniel calling out to her, but she did not turn around.

In her room, Ai Ling sat on the sofa and gazed out the windows. When her mind had finally settled into its usual flow, she got up and called the reception from the bedside phone, informing them that she would be checking out in the morning and enquiring about the coach schedule back to Bangkok. Done with the call, she started to pack her things.

∞

Early the next morning, Ai Ling woke up feeling nauseated, and threw up. Dousing her face with cold water, Ai Ling tried to hold down the waves of sickness that continued to churn her insides, even when she had nothing left to vomit. The pain came and went like serrating pulses of light. She returned to bed and fell back to sleep. When she woke an hour later, she felt much better, returned to her usual self.

With some time to kill before she had to check out at eleven—she wanted to avoid Daniel by all means—Ai Ling decided to go for a swim in the sea. She put on her one-piece and headed down to the beach. The day held the promise of fair weather, the air skin-sobering cool with a hint of a bite, still retaining the memory of the rain. The beach was empty except for a handful of early risers doing their morning exercise.

Putting her towel down on the sand, Ai Ling surveyed the beach from one end to the other: no other swimmer in sight. She stepped to the water line, then plunged straight in, giving herself entirely to the nerve-numbing shock of the cold water. For a few seconds, her body only registered the biting pain that surrounded it before a blossoming sensation of warmth started to spread out as she moved her arms and legs, pushing her body onwards. She swam for a long time without stopping. When she paused to look back at the shore, everything seemed so distant—the town on the coast, the people, the hills that rose in the south. Apart from her sonorous breaths, the sea was silent. With her feet hovering in a colder, deeper part of the water, Ai Ling could envision the lower regions of the sea, the unknown watery abyss where blind creatures swam, hunted and lived out their existence. Ai Ling suddenly felt infinitesimal, disembodied, her heartbeats insignificant against the mass of countless heartbeats that reverberated in the dark, echoing chamber of the sea. Along with this realisation, she also felt a jolt of surprise, as if she had only now been made known of the significance of her life, an experience so brief in its secret, elusive joy.

The morning sun had spread itself across the surface of the sea, which pulsated with light. Ai Ling stayed in the water, floating on her back, her face open to the sky. Her ears, submerged, picked up the clicking sounds of the sea, a rumbling of its interior, beating with life. The sunlight warmed her face. Ai Ling did not know how long she stayed in this position—her mind had slipped into a state of blissful thoughtlessness—when she heard a sharp sound, rising above the clamour of the sea. She lifted her head and turned towards the shore.

Standing at the edge of the water was the boy who had offered her a drink the day before, gesturing wildly. Ai Ling waved back and looked in the water around her and knew the cause of the boy's excitement. What first looked like a bunch of small, translucent plastic bags discarded into the sea was actually a school of jellyfish, stringy tentacles hanging from the milky dome-like caps of their bodies. They were all around her. The boy's piercing voice carried through the air like a siren.

With slow, measured strokes, Ai Ling made her way carefully between and around the jellyfish, her heart leaping each time she came close to one of the tentacles. Once she was finally clear of them, she pounded her way swiftly through the water, desperate to be back on land. She reached the shore, panting, but the boy was no longer there, only a trail of footsteps in the sand that disappeared further up the beach.

In her ears, Ai Ling could still hear an echo of the boy's voice, fainter and weaker, until it disappeared completely.

22

I change into my old clothes and have a simple breakfast of gruel and salted black beans. Before we set off, the old woman brings me one last bowl of the bitter brew and has me drink it. Carrying the bundle of food she has prepared for me, she leads me out of the compound of the hut, past the furrowed plots of long beans, peas and water spinach, onto the cleared-out path that snakes into the dense forest. I follow her closely. I have no idea where she's taking me, but I do not ask. We walk without stopping until the sun is hovering above the tree line. We finally exit the forest, the hardened-soil path widening out into a gravel-filled road. Coming to a stop at a clearing, the old woman looks at me. With a firm hand gesture, she tells me to stay put. She points to the end of the road, where it disappears down a slope, and stares in the direction for a few seconds. Then, after taking a last glance at me, she turns and re-enters the forest. I watch as she slips between the trees and vanishes out of sight.

No vehicle appears as I stand by the road, waiting. The day is becoming warmer. The dew on the grass has already dried up. The tall Casuarina trees lining the sides of the road stretch into the distance, the leaves rustling with the occasional breeze. The intermittent bursts of sharp trilling from birds hidden amongst the branches provide the only soundtrack to the quiet surroundings. I stretch my legs to work out the kinks. It has to be late morning now. I pick up the bundle by my feet and, glancing in both directions, decide to take the descending route, down the hill.

∞

"I think it's this way," I said, pointing to a branching path that led into a thicket of bushes. We had been walking on the narrow, muddy path for the past twenty minutes and seemed to be heading nowhere. Cody, coming to a stop beside me, glanced at where I was indicating, his face a curtain of sweat.

"You sure?" he asked, taking a bottle of water out from his haversack and passing it to me. He wiped his face on the sleeve of his T-shirt, leaving dark stains. Since I was the one who had suggested the trek on our fourth date, I could not tell him what was worrying me, that we might be lost.

"Yes, it'll lead us to the main route that will bring us back to the starting point," I said.

Cody nodded, took a swig of water and went ahead of me onto the path. Then turning suddenly, he grabbed my hand and pulled me towards him. "You smell good when you sweat." He took a long sniff and kissed my neck.

"Wish I could say the same thing about you," I said.

"Well, guess you have to get used to it then." He hugged me, and I could feel the wetness of his shirt against my body, soaking my shirt, touching my skin.

We walked for another three hours to get out of the Bukit Timah Nature Reserve, having long run out of water and gotten covered with scratches and bites. This incident later became a funny anecdote that Cody would tell our friends over dinners to illustrate the extent he had to go to woo me, that although he had known I had lost the way, he did not have the heart to tell me so.

But would he do it again, he was often asked, and he would say, turning to me, smiling: *maybe, maybe.*

∞

The closely clustered trees tower over me, the thick unruly undergrowth edges out onto the cracked tarmac, the long road curves round a bend before emerging again. My thoughts slip in and out of the crevices of my mind, gaining no real purchase. The sun is now at its zenith, blinding. I take off my shirt and tie it around my waist. My skin feels taut, as if I might burst out of it anytime, like a snake shedding its old skin.

My pace has slowed considerably, and I can feel blisters mushrooming on my torn soles. I glance back occasionally for signs of movement, but there's nothing, only a long grey stretch of road traversing the landscape, winding through the trees. Two dark smudges move through the sky in unison— eagles? One of them lets out a doleful cry, dips low and disappears into the treetops, while the other cuts a straight path ahead. I watch as it flies beyond the hills and vanishes into a bank of low-lying clouds.

∞

For the first three months I was dating Cody, I was also casually seeing another guy on the side. Andy was twenty-eight, and worked as a senior data analyst in a market research firm; we met through a mutual friend. Andy was fine with the arrangement, as he had just got out of a six-year relationship and wasn't looking for anything serious. Because nothing was asked besides mutual pleasure, we enjoyed the sessions we had, with some lasting up to three, four hours. Right from the start, because I knew what I was in for, I did not expect much from him, and was wary of making any unnecessary demands on his time. We met when we were free or bored or horny, and we left the rest of our lives opaque to each other. There was nothing else to hold us together, and we were okay with what we had.

So when Cody asked whether I was seeing anyone else over brunch one morning, I was caught off-guard. I studied his face to see whether his question was asked out of plain interest or suspicion. I could not sense the intention behind his expression.

"Why do you ask?" I said.

"Just curious. You're always checking your mobile phone," he said, biting into his kaya toast, a light dusting of bread crumbs falling onto the tabletop.

"It's a bad habit, I guess. Okay, I promise not to check my phone so much," I said.

"No, no. It's okay with me. I'm just wondering, that's all. So? Are you seeing anyone else?"

I smiled. Cody's look was a mix of anticipation and curiosity.

"Nobody serious. I'm ending it anyway."

"Oh. Who is he?"

"Just a friend. Well, a friend of a friend, actually."

"You like him?"

"He's okay. But he's not you."

"Ah, trying to flatter me?" Cody smiled, looking like he wanted to say more, but in the end he refrained. I deleted Andy's number from my phone and did not answer his calls or messages after that. He persisted for a while, and finally I had to meet him over coffee to explain.

"So that's why you are avoiding me like a plague? You just have to tell me straight. I'll understand," said Andy.

"I just thought perhaps it's better to tell you face to face."

"So this is it? You are serious about this guy?"

"He's decent, and I like him."

"How long have you been seeing him?"

"A few months."

"You should have told me earlier. At least I would have had some time to look around for another fuck buddy." Andy laughed, but there was no mirth in his laughter.

"You will find one soon enough, with your looks."

"I don't know. It's not easy to find someone who is compatible, you know."

"You will, I'm very sure."

After coffee, Andy offered to drive me home. When we reached the block of flats where I lived, Andy pressed me into my seat. "For old time's sake," he said.

"No, better not, people will see."

"Not that it has bothered you before. Come on."

"No," I said, but Andy was already lifting my shirt,

teasing my nipple with his tongue. I dropped my hands to my sides. Andy unzipped my jeans and reached in, stroking my cock against my underwear.

"You'll miss me. You sure you want to give this up?" Andy whispered into my ear, grasping my cock with an assertive firmness. And when he kissed me, dipping his tongue into my mouth, I relented. He bent down and took my cock into his mouth, glancing up at me, silently commanding my attention. When I was about to come, he pushed my cock deeper into his mouth. Unable to hold back, I shot my load, and he swallowed demonstratively.

"You sure you want to give this up?" Andy asked again.

∞

Tattered images cloud my mind as I trudge, my pace slowing to a snail's crawl, the sweltering heat of the afternoon sun dulling my thoughts. Chafing against my worn-out shoes, the blisters on my feet and ankles have swelled to white, soggy patches, leaking blood and pus. Every little movement takes Herculean effort, even keeping my head up to check what's ahead of me. The bundle I'm carrying on my shoulder feels like a bag full of concrete blocks, digging into my flesh.

Feeling faint, I hobble towards the shade of a tall tree with sprawling roots, and collapse in a heap onto the grassy ground. I close my eyes against the shifting light filtering through the tightly-knitted canopy of leaves. Something hard and sharp jabs my shoulder, but I'm too exhausted to move away. My breaths are slow and mechanical, my mouth a burning furnace. I fumble for the bottle of water in the bundle, remove the cap, and pour the contents over my face. The water runs into my mouth and nose; I gag and throw up everything that I've drunk.

Everything starts to slip away from me—I imagine my body slowly disintegrating into the dark soil, sinking into the depths.

∞

Lying in bed in the dark, Cody and I talked about death, the kind of death we envisioned for ourselves.

"Something quick and fast, definitely," Cody said.

"Like what?" I said.

"Like a car crash or a sudden accident, something totally out of the blue."

"So drama, so David Lynch-y."

"Ha, but without the sexual fetishism. Yeah, that way there is no suffering at all, gone, just like that."

"In a blaze of glory?" I said. Cody's laughter echoed in the room. "For me, it's simple. I want to die surrounded by my loved ones."

"That's so cliché, boring. Think of a better one."

"I always have this fantasy that I'll die of an incurable disease. There I am, on my deathbed, and I have just made a terrible confession to my family. There are tears all around, the nervous clasping of hands, and everyone offering kind words, consolation, forgiveness. You know, the whole works. And then I die very slowly, very beautifully."

"What the fuck! What's wrong with you? This is so

fucking Korean drama, so totally unoriginal."

"I know, I know. It's weird. It's just a fantasy."

"I always knew you were such a drama queen!"

"Fuck you." Cody leant in to kiss me on the forehead. I caught the scent of toothpaste on his breath and sought out his lips.

∞

A savage cry pulls me back from the shadow land of dreams into the present. I open my eyes to the bright, piercing sunlight, and look around. Where has the sound come from? Was it a part of my dream? Peering into the dark undergrowth, I can't discern any movement. Perhaps I've conjured it up in my imagination—the sound seemed wild, distorted, unnatural. I push myself upright and lean against the rough trunk of the tree. I survey my surroundings and the quiet road in front of me. Nothing moves.

I pull the bundle into my lap and take out a bun. Its skin has toughened, and already a few ants are crawling on it. I brush the ants aside and sink my teeth into the bun, the fillings spilling out of the corners of my mouth, flecks of vegetable falling on my chest. Within seconds, the bun's gone. I'm tempted to eat another, but hold back, knowing that my supplies are limited. There's no knowing whether I'll be able to find other sources of food when I run out. I reach for the half-empty bottle of water and take a few sips, which barely satisfies my thirst. I have to keep moving. How long before night comes? The sun has hidden behind a strip of gauzy clouds. The insects buzz incessantly in the lethargic afternoon air.

Suddenly, something moves at the edge of my peripheral vision; the skin on my arms prickles. Turning in the direction of the movement, I brace myself—what is it? Across the road, partially hidden behind a tree, a presence—something or someone? How long has it been there, without my knowledge? Its shape remains indistinct, its edges blending into the surrounding darkness. It simply stands there, an outline cut out of the fabric of the forest.

I stare for some time before the image slowly resolves into something that hits me like a punch in the stomach.

It's the boy from the old woman's hut, the one we buried.

I push myself off the ground, my legs unsteady. Leaning against the tree trunk, I blink several times, unable to make sense of what I'm seeing. The boy must be a projection of my fatigued, overheated imagination, I tell myself. Yet, there he is, standing twenty metres away, staring, not moving. Perhaps he is some other boy who lives nearby and has chanced upon me—a stranger in the middle of nowhere; there's absolutely no way he could be the same boy I buried two days ago.

Neither of us makes a move, each staring at the other. My mind is a field of warring thoughts, failing to come up with a plausible explanation. I gather whatever remains of my senses and strength, and take a step forward. The boy immediately takes a step back, moving into the deeper shadow provided by the trees. In the darkness of the foliage, his skin glows with an aura of pale light. With each movement, his figure becomes smaller and smaller, flitting from tree to tree with preternatural ease.

I grab the bundle and move in ungainly steps towards the disappearing boy, not wanting to lose sight of him.

Tripping over rocks and tree roots, I pick up my pace, trying to narrow the distance between us. But no matter how fast I'm going, I'm unable to cover enough ground to reach him. His retreating figure hovers at the margin of my vision, like a fixed point on the horizon, directing me. Ignoring the pain shrieking from every part of my body, I pursue the boy in fits and starts, my lungs on the verge of collapsing, each breath a razor-sharp intake of air. The perspiration stings my eyes and blurs my vision, but still I have the boy in my sights.

Cutting through thick undergrowth and thickets of shrubs and thorny bushes, I finally emerge into a clearing that looks out onto a sloping hill where I see a clutter of huts with wisps of smoke rising from them: a small village. Breathless, and bent with exhaustion, I look for signs of the young boy, but he's nowhere to be found, leaving no tracks or traces of his presence. He has disappeared as simply and swiftly as he first appeared.

∞

"What were you like as a boy?" I asked Cody once.

"I don't know, I can't remember. You ask my sisters next time we go over to their place for dinner."

"Seriously, nothing from your childhood? Like what did you do in school, who were your friends?"

"No, really, I can't remember much of my childhood. Maybe some memories and impressions from here and there, but nothing worth remembering anyway."

"But aren't our impressions what count in how our memories are formed?"

"We embellish our memories all the time, don't we? I mean, we revise them according to how we see and feel about our past at different points of our lives."

"Yes, but they are all we have, right? Anyway, we can't go back in time to relive what we've gone through, so we are stuck with what we can remember. But really you can't remember anything from your childhood?"

"Well, if you are so dying curious to know, I guess you could say I was a weird kid."

"We're all weird in our own ways. When I was like six or seven, I used to catch butterflies and eat them because I thought their wings were so soft and light, like candy floss. Except their bodies were too gooey for my liking, bitter too. But their wings dissolved in my mouth like powdered sugar."

"Damn, Chee Seng. Really?"

"Now you tell me something about your childhood, anything."

"Okay, if you must know, my father always said I was very quiet, sometimes too quiet for my own good. Apparently I could go for days without saying a word. This was after my mother passed away."

"For days?"

"Yes, my father told me I had a so-called 'episode' after she died, though I don't remember anything about it now. He told me it went on for a week, and at the end of it, he was so worried that he even considered admitting me to the hospital, because I wasn't eating or drinking. I just lay in bed the whole time and refused to talk to anyone. And then one night, I simply snapped back to myself and carried on like the past few days had never existed. My father told me all this later on. Like I say, that period of my life is a complete blank. It's not like it's something I'd want to remember."

"You don't remember a single thing from that incident?"

"Nothing. Anyway, it's not important after a while, so why bother?"

∞

By the time the villagers understand where I want to go, I'm exhausted beyond measure, no longer able to stand upright, and I finally collapse. They carry me into a tiny thatched hut and lay me on a dirty straw mat. A cold drink is brought to my lips, and I gag and spit up while trying to swallow. Strange voices fill the air around me as my sight slowly resolves into a series of heavily-creased faces that crowd my vision. The villagers bring out plates of rice and fried vegetables and cajole me to eat, but I decline, my stomach raw. Once again, I seek directions to return to Patong, through a fluttering of hand gestures and an odd word here and there. The men shake their heads and sigh loudly, uttering a stream of words, the gist of which I understand to be: *don't go, stay, wait.* Again, I beseech them for help until they walk away to talk amongst themselves.

A small group of young children in tattered, threadbare rags surrounds me, excited like a litter of puppies, asking question after question, none of which I can decipher. Finally, one of the men comes up to me and takes me down a lane to where a row of houses stands. Women stand at the thresholds, watching us with open curiosity. In front of a small narrow courtyard, the man points to a rusty motorbike with a badly-torn seat, gets on it, and motions for me to hop on. He revs out of the village, a spray of dust trailing behind us. Not wanting to fall off the bike, I grip the man's waist, praying that my strength will hold up for as long as it takes to get us to Patong.

Even before we reach the outer fringe of the town, the road is already jammed with traffic and people moving in both directions, making it almost impassable. Along the way, winding down the hills, I see the full extent of the destruction that has been inflicted on Patong and the beaches that line the coast; from high up, the town looks like a huge debris-clogged swamp, dark brown with large pools of brackish water glistening in the afternoon light, studded with stumps of decimated buildings. The shoreline has cut deeper inland, like the curved edge of a sickle. The sea remains proudly innocuous, placid.

The drive slows to a trickle, sometimes barely moving at all. Occasionally, a shrill vehicle siren sounds out, and a small path suddenly, miraculously, appears, making way for an ambulance or emergency vehicle to pass, and immediately after it has passed, the path would be swallowed up again, the cars and bikes and humans coming together like an organic mass. In a few pick-up trucks, I see piles of blackened bodies, barely covered by flimsy tarpaulins, hands and feet sticking out, stiff as mannequins. The death smell that rises from these bodies is thick and rank and cloying, forcing me to hold down the little that is in my stomach.

The man drops me off at a makeshift medical centre, previously a school with a basketball court and three-storey buildings, a Red Cross sign hanging on the gate. He looks concerned, but after I give him a thumbs-up, he drives off, disappearing around the corner. Standing amidst the sweaty swirl of people, I have no idea where to go, unable to discern the way back to the hotel. From nowhere, someone pushes me roughly aside, issuing a shout, and carries a body into the medical compound—a young girl in the arms of a woman, her head lolling like a broken doll, her ashen face bloated. The woman—mother? sister?—is screaming indiscriminately, her voice cracked and hoarse, until a nurse appears and directs her into one of the tents. The air is abuzz with a taut tension, alive with the flow of movements and cries and smells.

Rooted to the spot, I suddenly feel a sharp jab of longing, to be back in the hut with the old woman, somewhere up in the hills, away from all this misery and death.

23

The coastal town of Patong is in a much worse state than Wei Xiang imagined, from where the boy has led him over the course of the day. Rows of houses and shops that run parallel to the beach have been flattened to rubble; palm trees are slanted at impossible angles or have been ripped out of the earth. Near the beach, the pewter sea water is stagnant and foul-smelling.

From time to time, Wei Xiang catches a glimpse of a bloated body bobbing in the water like discarded flotsam, or caught between staggered piles of debris. The boy does not seem to pay much attention to these distractions, focused only on leading them onwards, still not saying a word. Wei Xiang has somehow concluded that the boy is either deaf or mute, or both, and has given up trying to talk to him. Even without the aid of a common language, he has found it easy, almost effortless, to communicate his intentions to the boy, whether to stop or slow down or make a detour; the boy is able to read him without any trouble or assistance. But when Wei Xiang tries to read the boy's face for signs of distress or fear, he gets nothing—the boy's expression is stone-like, his eyes always looking straight ahead, as if expecting something important to appear any time soon.

Whenever they come to the flooded places, Wei Xiang stoops to lift the boy onto his shoulders, and they wade slowly through the water. The boy's weight feels negligible—a bag of feathers—and Wei Xiang has to hold on to the latter's ankles to keep him steady.

Sometimes they stop to allow small teams of rescuers to pass, hauling bulky bags containing bodies. The rescuers are often so engrossed—frazzled by fatigue perhaps, or numb-shocked by their task, Wei Xiang can't tell—that they rarely look up to take heed of the passers-by who have stopped to stare at them. Wei Xiang holds his breath as they pass, his guts turning at the barest hint of the fetor of death.

They have gone on for hours without rest, and at some point in their seemingly pointless meandering, Wei Xiang has started to question his own actions, this blind ceding of will and reason to a complete stranger—*a boy*—being led to places unknown. What has compelled him to do this—an unexamined motive, or a dark impulse? What is preventing him from staying put, or going in the opposite direction, or more importantly, doing what he ought to have done in the first place—finding Ai Ling?

Wei Xiang stops in mid-stride, and the boy walking beside him stops as well, looking up at him. Wei Xiang flings up his hands in exasperation and shakes his head. The boy watches him for a few moments before reaching out to pull at his hand, tugging him to continue walking.

"No, I can't follow you around all day. I've other things I

need to do," Wei Xiang says. "I need to find my wife, she's missing. I have to find her. Do you understand me?"

The boy gives Wei Xiang a peculiar look, one heavy with sadness, and releases his hand. He drops his shoulders and looks away, as if contemplating his next course of action.

Around them buzz different hives of activity: scores of locals are breaking up the towering stacks of rubble along the streets, frantically searching for missing people; skinny, dark-skinned kids, oblivious to the destruction, are playing in the water, leaping from the shaky peak of a pile of mortar. Wei Xiang feels a deep, fractured sense of disconnection from the scene before him, a man severed from life.

He sits down heavily on the curb and puts his face in his palms. In his bones, he feels the heaviness weighing down on him, the hours and days of mindless exertion and fear, walking the tight rope of desperation and dread. He can't take another step. He rubs his eyes on his sleeve and sinks into himself. Wei Xiang imagines that he looks like one of the survivors he has often come across the past few days—sitting by the roadside or near a collapsed house, a soulless look on their faces, their bodies reduced to hollow shells. He has felt helpless looking at them, and now he is one of them. He shakes off this mental image and looks up, and in his temporarily glazed vision, the world before him suddenly becomes hazy, as if he were looking through thin gauze.

The boy is still standing beside him, hovering at the periphery of his sight, waiting. Wei Xiang stares at the boy's bare feet, caked with mud and streaked with tiny red cuts. They look frail and breakable, like feet of clay hardened in the heat of the sun. Wei Xiang takes off his sandals and places them before the boy, nodding at him. The boy steps into them and starts clomping around clumsily, a faint smile playing at the corners of his mouth. Despite himself, Wei Xiang chuckles and proceeds to tighten the straps of the sandals. The boy moves to take them off but Wei Xiang signals to him to keep them. The boy practises walking around with the sandals, trying not to trip.

Wei Xiang hesitates for a moment as he stands up, uncertain what he should do next or where he ought to go, the gritty grains of sand poking into the soles of his feet. He rubs his feet across the surface of the ground and surveys the surroundings—where is he now? He senses a heavy density in the air, something he has not been conscious of for a while: the briny smell of seawater. The sea must be near.

Narrowing his eyes, Wei Xiang tries to make out the silvery horizon in the distance. Then turning in the opposite direction, he scans the rugged features of Radar Hill—the subtle gradation of green that changes imperceptibly with each shift of sunlight that breaks through the cloud cover—and the deep scars of hiking trails and paths that wind up and round the hill. A thought sneaks into him: Ai Ling planned for a trek through one of the forests in Phuket—was it for today or yesterday? The days are all muddled in his head. In the itinerary, the trek would end up at a lookout with the "best views of Patong and the sea", according to Ai Ling. Wei Xiang feels his chest tighten. A wild thought suggests itself to him: maybe Ai Ling has gone up the hill on her own and lost her way. But she has never been an impulsive person. Still, the thought persists, creeping down a darker path: what's to say that she did not change her mind at the last minute, and run up the hill? Just days before the trip, Ai Ling was behaving rather erratically, acting out of sorts.

Wei Xiang recalls the night before their trip, when she left the house late at night to go to the nearest pharmacy to buy motion-sickness pills; neither of them had ever been ill on their previous trips, let alone from motion sickness. Ai Ling came home empty-handed after an hour. Wei Xiang could not imagine what had possessed Ai Ling to head out alone in the middle of the night to look for something that they would not need, knowing well that the shops in their neighbourhood closed at ten. When she got back, all she offered in explanation was that she was afraid she would get nauseous on the flight. In the end, she bought the medication at a pharmacy in Changi Airport before their flight.

A touch shakes him from his daydream. The boy has nudged him and is pointing at a distant spot towards the sea, signalling for Wei Xiang to follow him. Whatever he's feeling, whatever misgivings or doubts, Wei Xiang can sense the boy's urgency, evident in his animated gestures, beckoning him to take heed. The sun is edging towards the west of the island, tracing the height of the hill; it must be around four o'clock. It would be foolish to turn back now; it's already too late to change to a new course of action.

So, with Wei Xiang's silence as consent, the boy takes off down the street in the sandals. They slip through the ravaged townscape, across fallen, twisted telephone poles, through a flooded backyard filled with bloated bodies of chickens, stiff dark-hued feathers covering every inch of the water surface—Wei Xiang can smell the air getting danker, heavier in density—towards the sea. He feels a charge of adrenaline in his blood, aware that he's running headlong into all kinds of danger, not knowing what will become of him should the waves rise again.

Closer to the sea, he can't differentiate between the brown-and-gunmetal floodwaters and the sea itself, where one ends and the other begins. The water comes up to his knees at times, and then recedes to ankle-height, before another step brings him to a pause on soft, sticky mud. The closer they get to the sea—bare, wasted land around them, quiet and solemn like a cemetery, one or two coconut trees standing in stubborn resistance—the fewer people they see, until there's no one in sight. The wind, pushing in from the Andaman Sea, whips in Wei Xiang's ears, skimming the skin of the water. The boy stops, looks around, and moves to higher ground, away from the tangled roots of the thicket of mangrove they have found themselves in. By this time, Wei Xiang's feet are covered with cuts and scratches, and the sea water is aggravating and numbing these wounds at the same time. Wei Xiang makes a deliberate effort not to look at the cuts, though he's feeling a considerable amount of pain.

Soon they come to a stop and Wei Xiang realises that they are standing at a breakwater, a few metres above sea level, facing out into the expanse of light and water. All around, the unbreakable membrane of silence. He takes in the panoramic view and catches his breath, his lips cracked and bleeding. The boy has barely broken a sweat, his body radiating an otherworldly sheen. Following his gaze, Wei Xiang shields his eyes from the glare of the sun and stares out into the distance, trying to see what the boy is intently looking at.

Along the horizon, towards the northeast, a dark smudge rises out of the water, a hazy ridge of land masses. They must be smaller, outlying islands that pepper the fringe of the main island—hundreds of them, according to Ai Ling, who read up on the geography of Phuket in the guidebook, most of them too small and insignificant for any geographical or historical interest. Ai Ling had wanted to hire a guide and rent a boat to view these islands, to see some of them up close, to know what it's like to step foot on these lands that have rarely seen human existence.

The boy takes a step forward and, without a word, dives into the water. Wei Xiang squats on his haunches, blood rushing to his head, and scans the water for the boy. Nothing, except the rough, continuous lapping of the waves against the cracked stones of the breakwater. He stays motionless, counting the long seconds—sooner or later, the boy will have to come up for air. Still he does not dare to move a muscle; anytime now, the boy will have to emerge.

And then, a few metres from where Wei Xiang is staring, a head pops up out of the water. He gasps and lets out a shout. The boy swims unhurriedly towards him. When he gets to the wall of the breakwater, he grabs onto the gaps between the stones with his fingers and pulls himself out of the water. The wet clothes cling to his scrawny frame with a downward pull, but the boy is unperturbed, his attention focused entirely on the act of scaling the wall—a grip, a tug and a pull, repeat.

When he reaches the top of the breakwater, Wei Xiang stretches out his arm to take hold of the extended hand, and yanks him up with a final pull. Still dripping, the boy steadies himself, his chest heaving. The sandals have disappeared from his feet; they must have fallen off during the dive. Wei Xiang pulls off his T-shirt and puts it over the boy's trembling body. Then on impulse, Wei Xiang hugs the boy. The wetness and rigid coldness of the boy's body goes right through Wei Xiang's shirt and touches his skin, making his heart lurch. He pulls away.

The boy opens up his hand, palm faced upwards. Something glints in the light. Wei Xiang looks at it, and then takes a longer, harder stare. It does not make any sense, this thing the boy's holding in his hand. A silver ring. The boy lifts it higher, as if beseeching Wei Xiang to take a closer look.

Wei Xiang reaches for the ring and looks for the carvings on the inside of the band—the tiny inscription is there: AL + WX. He pinches it in his fingers and glares at the boy, fear mounting. The ground seems to have fallen away from him, and Wei Xiang feels as if he were hovering in mid-air, waiting to hit the ground. The boy returns his stare; something softens in his expression. Tilting his head, he regards Wei Xiang with a puzzled look, and then turns to gaze out into the sea, to where the cluster of islands stands, a mirage of light and land. A few strands of wet hair fall across his eyes.

Wei Xiang collapses to the ground, his mind a gathering storm of dark thoughts. Something catches at the back of his throat. He looks up into the empty sky and feels everything around him coming at him, all at once, with a sharp clarity: the sultry heat, the distant call of a passing seagull, the crash of the waves, the grit of the tiny pebbles embedded in his soles. He thinks about Ai Ling, and the boy, and about the strange, unfathomable ways that life can bring and hold things together—but he can't understand anything, not a single thing.

Wei Xiang closes his fist, holding the ring in the heat of his tightening palm, and brings it up to his face. Ai Ling—her name surfaces like a faraway dream, half-forgotten. He says it again and again, and each repetition of the name brings a certain, fearful finality to it.

Then Wei Xiang feels the light pressure of the boy's body against his side, drawing him back to the present, to the breakwater where he is now. A growing despair is eating its way out of him, and all Wei Xiang can feel is the abysmal sense of coming apart, endlessly.

From somewhere around him, Wei Xiang hears the lilt of a song. It takes him some moments before registering the fact that the boy is singing. He sings for a long time without a break or an end; the song resounds in Wei Xiang's ears, sinking into him, penetrating him. He finally comes apart, in the middle of it.

Even after the heat of the day has drained away, with the sea breeze blowing over them, leaving behind a speckling of salt on their skins, the song goes on uninterrupted, suspending Wei Xiang in a soft, protective spell.

24

CODY

Ai Ling had wanted to get away for the long weekend after their final-year examinations, back in 1991, before she and Cody started looking for full-time jobs. She had saved up for a short trip over the semester, working the evening shift as an assistant in a dental clinic while studying for her finals. She wanted Cody to accompany her—she had just broken up with Ian, and needed to get away for a while—so he agreed. She brought up Bangkok as a destination, since it was within her budget and he could not come up with a better place. They quickly settled on travel dates, and Ai Ling started looking for accommodation and cheap air tickets.

Cody had known her for three years by that point, ever since hitting it off during orientation camp in the first week at university. She was a Social Sciences major, while he was studying English Literature. They got along so well that many of their university friends assumed they were a couple—Ai Ling rarely mentioned Ian even then—and for a while they did not discredit the assumption. Sometimes in lighter moods, Ai Ling and Cody would laugh about it, turning the whole thing into a joke. Ai Ling revealed very little of how she actually felt about him, and they left things platonic, casual and undemanding.

Because they spent so much time together in school, studying at the library during breaks and meeting for lunch, Cody never felt the need to build a friendship with another woman. With Ai Ling around all the time, he had gained a certain social legitimacy that was helpful, even useful, to navigate through university life. He was grateful for the security that came with it. Even at that age, he was still not ready to reveal his other covert self.

They decided to fly out on a Thursday afternoon and come back on Sunday night; the hotel Ai Ling booked was in Silom, in the heart of downtown Bangkok. Because it was her first time taking an overseas trip without her parents, she had to lie and tell them she was going with two female classmates.

"No way was I telling them I'm going with you, they would have killed me," she said.

"Why not?" I asked.

"Well, I'm their good daughter," she replied, "and I don't want them to worry too much about me."

The budget hotel was located on Sala Daeng, a two-lane road that branched off the main thoroughfare of Silom, and when they checked in, Ai Ling asked for a room with two beds; because it was an off-peak season, they were given a room on the fifth floor, facing the road and towering office blocks. Because Cody had been to Bangkok once when he was nineteen, just before entering the army to serve his two and a half years of compulsory National Service, Ai Ling asked him to plan the itinerary; he used the most current Lonely Planet guidebook he could find at the library, which featured the usual tourist spots: Chatuchak weekend market, Wat Arun, Patpong.

Since it was still too early for dinner after checking in, they decided to check out the shops along Silom. Ai Ling was in a good mood, keeping up the chatter as they walked along, peeking into shop windows, restaurants, convenience stores, and catching fragments of music and conversation drifting from staticky radios and dusty televisions. At six-thirty, the street thronged with office workers, street hawkers, beggars and tourists of all stripes, and they stayed close to avoid losing each other. Standing outside one of the massage parlours where the masseuses sat on plastic chairs and talked gregariously, Ai Ling read the massage options available. The masseuses studied Ai Ling with mild curiosity before turning a more direct, practiced look at Cody. Ai Ling asked whether they should give it a try and he shrugged. "Up to you," he said.

"Then let's do it," she said, and approached the counter to book a session for both of them. Without asking, she requested for a male masseur for Cody while she opted for a female masseuse. "No hanky panky," she said, giving him a wink. He smiled and shook his head.

They were both led into a large, dimly-lit back room with several mattresses on the floor; each massage area was separated by thick curtains hanging on rods suspended from the ceiling. Through the curtain, Cody could hear Ai Ling change into the proffered loose shirt and wraparound knee-length shorts. The masseurs arrived shortly, bowing and muttering a soft greeting. Cody kept his eyes closed throughout the massage, unable to relax. When the masseur's hands moved from Cody's feet to his inner thighs, his mind slipped naturally to sex, and thoughts of Terry.

At that point, Cody had known Terry for three months, but nobody else knew of his existence, not even his close friends. They had met at a party at Rascals, a disco located on the ground floor of the Pan Pacific Hotel, exchanged numbers, and Terry had suggested they meet up for drinks shortly after. Despite his initial apprehension, Cody agreed to it. Terry, as it turned out, was more or less the person he was the night they met: frank, affable, candid. Like Cody, he was a student in his second year at a different university, studying electrical engineering. Unlike Cody, he was more outgoing and sporty, a tennis and rock-climbing enthusiast, and even though he was a year younger, he had already had past relationships with much older men. Mostly he talked during the first date and Cody listened. After that, they met up more regularly, sometimes three times a week, usually at cafés or restaurants of Cody's choice. Terry was happy to oblige.

On their third date, Cody suggested a fast-food restaurant in the housing estate where Terry lived with his parents and elder brother. After dinner, Cody asked to visit his place. Since his parents were at home that evening, Terry ushered Cody straight into his bedroom. Barely had he closed the door before they were all over each other. Terry kissed Cody hard and asked whether this was something he wanted, and if he was comfortable with it. The words tripped over one another as Cody uttered them in a thick, hoarse drawl: *Yes, yes, yes.* Terry undressed him and guided him to the bed, and showed him what needed to be done. Against his body, Cody felt dislodged from his own physicality, displaced and removed at a distance even while he was fully in the moment, drinking in every touch and sensation as if it were the first and last pleasure that he would ever experience. He was hungry and voracious and achingly open. When it was over, Cody collapsed onto Terry and began to cry; Terry held Cody and cooed as if mollifying an injured child. From then on, they would end all their dates at Terry's place, having sex at every opportunity. Cody felt constantly ravenous and restless, always fidgeting and frustrated as if making up for what had been hitherto denied to him.

It was the thought of sex with Terry that caused Cody to have an erection while having the massage in Bangkok. In a panic, he jerked upright from the mattress, surprising the masseur, who quickly apologised for his strength. Embarrassing as it was, the erection did not wilt, and when he lay back on the mattress, the cause of his erratic behaviour became apparent to the masseur. The man chuckled to himself and resumed where he had left off. Cody gave him a large tip later when paying. "So generous, he must be really good," Ai Ling said as they were leaving the massage parlour. Cody gave a blank smile and nodded.

∞

The next day, they visited the temples in the morning; to

escape the heat in the afternoon, they headed to Siam Square, navigating the busy alleyways and seeking out hole-in-the-wall restaurants for meals and coffee. At one point, Ai Ling slipped her hand into Cody's and he held it, unquestioningly. They did not talk about what the gesture meant—out of modesty on her part and deliberate obtuseness on his. It meant no more to Cody than an expression of friendship, and he left it at that.

In the evening, they went to Chinatown and ate seafood in a restaurant that was highly recommended in the guidebook: black pepper crab with vermicelli, chilli-fried squid and barbecued tiger prawns. Done with their dinner, they took a taxi back to Silom, alighting at Patpong. The streets were ablaze with noise and neon; the touts, coming out of the woodwork and armed with dog-eared laminated lists of sex shows, were badgering the tourists in loud, beseeching voices, sometimes even tugging them forcibly towards the clubs. Ai Ling and Cody were approached by a young woman in a leopard print mini-dress who waved and rattled off a list of sex acts, pulling Cody's arm playfully. Ai Ling walked faster and dragged him away. "So aggressive," Ai Ling said with a growl. They made their way through the brightly-lit stalls selling 50-baht T-shirts and knockoff designer handbags, purses and watches. At a pirated-VCD stall, they stopped to scan the titles and eventually bought five VCDs for only 200 baht. After drinking some coconut water at a roadside stall, they decided to call it a night.

At the hotel, Ai Ling complained about an upset stomach, and disappeared for long stretches in the toilet. They tried to trace it back to something she had eaten, but Cody had eaten everything that she had. After taking two charcoal pills, she decided to sleep it off while he scanned the television channels with the volume muted. She woke up later feeling better but worn out. They lay on their separate beds and watched *Police Story 2* starring Jackie Chan; during the commercials, Cody would get up to walk around the room or peek out the window, feeling the itch of restlessness. Ai Ling, sensing his agitated state, suggested that perhaps he should go out and do something, rather than stay cooped up in the hotel room with her.

"Just go, don't worry about me. I just need to rest," Ai Ling said.

"I'll go out for a short while and then come back."

"Just go and enjoy yourself. Don't worry, I'm okay. Switch off the lights before you go."

Stepping out of the hotel, Cody took the printout out of his pocket and orientated himself to the streets indicated on the map with his actual location. He had solicited information from acquaintances he got to know at the parties at Rascals: the best go-go shows, the most outrageous theme nights, and the types of men available at different establishments. He had kept the printout in the inner pocket of his backpack, afraid Ai Ling would see it. He did not think he'd be able to visit any of these places since Ai Ling was with him all the time; now her sudden illness left him free to do what he had planned to do secretly without her, and the elation he felt was complicated by a nagging guilt.

At the entrance leading into Boys' Town, Cody paused to look at the colour-saturated clutter of signboards advertising a variety of shows and services, arrows pointing to what was hidden behind the half-closed doors and heavy velvet curtains. A tout approached and brandished a folded, laminated cardboard. "Sir, you want cute boys? You want see fucking shows? I have. Come with me." Cody moved away from him and stepped into Boys' Town.

Keeping a moderate pace, staying in the middle of the lane, not daring to venture too close to any establishment, he caught glimpses of neon-lit flesh. A few of the dancers caught his stares and returned them with virile smiles. He looked away, conscious that his movements had become slow, deliberate and heavy-limbed. The patrons sitting at the tables outside the bars, mostly middle-aged and Caucasian, turned to survey the moving crowd, their hawk-like eyes moving in succession from person to person. A short, strongly-built man wearing a white tank top and a tattoo in Thai script that wrapped around his biceps came up to Cody and shouted into his ear: "We have show now, you want see? Only two-hundred baht, one drink. Muscular men, you like?"

Numbing his nerves, Cody made his way into the club, pushing past the curtain and entering the smoky room. Any sense of order or clarity in his head had dissolved; all he could feel were the pure, dark urges of his physical self. He followed the tattooed man and sat where he indicated. A series of stares came his way, some lingering longer than others, but Cody sat stonily still, unable or perhaps unwilling to acknowledge or reciprocate these looks. Up on the raised podium, oiled-up muscled men in swim trunks labelled with number tags were swinging their hips lazily in a pantomime of seduction. Loud, thumping dance music pounded through the club as repeating patterns of strobe lights wallpapered the lurid interior. Along the perimeter of the podium were three staggered rows of benches, filled with a mixed audience of locals and foreigners. Not daring to let his eyes stay too long on anyone, Cody glanced from one dancer to another, taking everything in but registering nothing.

An announcement came on during a break in the music, and the dancers left the podium single file. The stage lights dimmed for a second, and in the next instant, three men of similar build appeared on the podium, naked, each nursing an erection. Cody held his breath, his insides seizing up, throbbing with an acute, inexplicable ache. One of the men bent over, holding his ass up in the spotlight for a moment, before another man stood behind him and penetrated him slowly, while the third man stuck his dick into the man's mouth.

Over the next twenty minutes, the acts varied only slightly with a change of men and positions, each performing their roles in a parody of lust and exaggerated pleasure. Cody's drink, a Singha beer, came halfway during the show; he took a single sip that left a bitter, corrosive taste in his mouth. When the show ended, he stumbled to his feet and made his way to the exit as if fleeing from a fire or a crime that he had unknowingly committed.

Bursting out of the club, with the night air cooling his heated face, he made ghost tracks back to the hotel, trying to slow the pounding of his heart. The hotel room was dark when he entered; a voice rose from the darkness.

"Cody? Is that you?" Ai Ling said.

"Yes."

"Back so early?"

"Yes, it was too crowded out there."

"I must have fallen asleep immediately after you left." Ai Ling's voice was groggy, sticky with drowsiness.

"How are you feeling?" Cody asked.

"I think I'm okay now. My stomach's not hurting anymore."

"Good. Do you want a drink or something?"

"No, I'm not thirsty."

"Think I'll shower now. Go to sleep, if you're tired."

"I think I've slept enough. What did you do just now?"

"Nothing much. Just walked around and checked out the street stalls."

"Bought anything?"

"No, there was nothing I wanted. Let me shower first, I'm all sweaty."

"Okay."

In the toilet, Cody stripped and threw his clothes into the sink, and then stood under the jet of hot water in the shower. The room quickly filled up with steam. Summoning up images of the men from the sex show, he masturbated and came quickly with a brutal convulsion that left him panting against the wet wall tiles. He caught his blurry reflection in the fogged-up mirror, a dark silhouette moving beneath a cloudy veil of condensation. He washed himself twice over with soap, dried off and put on a clean pair of shorts. He used up a small travel bottle of mouthwash, the insides of his mouth bristling with tiny pins. He dried his mouth with a towel, turned away from the mirror, and stepped back out into the dark bedroom.

"Cody?" Ai Ling called.

"Yes?"

"Can you come over here?"

He padded over to her bed. Moonlight illuminated Ai Ling's face in a warm glow. Cody sat on the edge of her bed, but could not read her expression. Ai Ling reached out and touched his hand, drawing it to her.

"Do you like me?" Ai Ling asked.

"Yes, of course. You're my good friend."

"Only a friend?"

Cody hesitated. "Yes, a very good friend."

"That's all?"

"Yes."

For a long while, they stayed like that. Cody could hear a car passing on the road outside, a rumbling sound that surged and then gradually faded. In the dark, he could sense Ai Ling's thoughts taking several turns across the busy, crowded landscape of her mind. He resisted breaking her train of thought with a sound or movement, even though he wanted desperately to know what she was thinking.

Then, without a word, Ai Ling moved her body aside on the bed, and Cody lay down next to her. She turned her back and pushed herself into him, radiating heat. He put his arms around her shoulders, and she nudged closer to fit into the contours of his body. He inhaled the scent of her hair.

"I'm sorry," he said.

Ai Ling did not say anything, nor did she move away. She drew Cody's arms tightly around her. Cody listened to her falling slowly into sleep, her breaths getting deeper and

longer, and then she disappeared into the world of dreams.
He stayed awake for as long as he could, but soon he too fell
into the void of sleep.

25

"Don't bring so many things. Just travel light. It's only for a few days," I told Cody, two days before the vacation to Phuket, taking out my haversack from the store room, giving it a shake.

"Yes, I'll just bring my underwear because I'm not leaving the hotel at all. I heard the weather is going to be extremely hot," Cody said.

"Okay, sure, whatever suits you, lazy ass. Just don't wear any of my shirts."

Cody was sitting on the sofa in front of the television watching a Channel 8 drama series. The volume was set to low, and from where I was standing, I could barely make out the dialogue.

"When are you going to start packing? We're leaving the day after tomorrow."

"Tomorrow. I'm a fast packer, unlike you, always so slow. I know what to bring. Anyway, it's only for a few days, so I only need three changes of clothes."

"Yes, fast packer, always forgetting things, always asking

me whether I brought extra."

"And you always bring so many things. I'm just trying to help you make full use of all the things you have brought. See, I'm actually helping you in a sense."

"Yeah, and if you forget anything for this trip, you can forget about asking me for it."

"I won't."

It had not been easy living with Cody since we moved in together after getting a place of our own two years ago. I was used to a certain lifestyle with a fixed routine, having lived almost my entire life with my mother and three younger brothers, and it was tough to break away from what had been comfortable for me. In the beginning, it was trying to figure out what worked for both of us, finding the right amount of space—personal and physical—that each of us needed, and coming up with a routine in which we could anchor our lives, together and separately. We quarrelled from time to time, though nothing serious. Because of his work as an editor, the spare room in our flat was converted to a study for him. On one of the walls he had framed some of his freelance features that had appeared in well-known regional travel magazines, pieces on Angkor Wat and Borobudur.

Through trial and error, we had managed to carve out a domesticated living arrangement that was part mutual agreement, part compromise, in which we still had our own freedom, our individual lifestyles. We had, in popular parlance, an "interdependent" relationship, which seemed to be the politically correct way to describe a non-needy, self-sufficient relationship, which in our case, was undeniably true. We had some things in common for sure, and for other things we could not quite come to terms with, we left them as they were or closed our eyes to them, which was the usual way we dealt with things that we could not change. We learnt to live with what we could manage.

"Did you print out the air ticket confirmation?" I asked from the bedroom, after packing my luggage.

"Not yet, can you print it out?" Cody shouted from the sofa, where he was now watching a tennis match on the sports channel.

"I'll use your laptop," I said.

Entering Cody's workspace in the study felt like a minor form of trespassing. It was filled almost entirely with his stuff—books, magazines, CDs—and very little of my own, only a small section of the bookshelf which held my hardcover books, and files full of bills, letters and tax statements. Despite the organised mess in the room, his large work table was relatively clutter-free: only a laptop computer, a note pad, a stationery holder filled with 2B pencils and a drinking glass. The laptop was switched on, and, because Cody had not created a password, I was able to access it. It always felt strange using his computer, which was part of his guarded turf; he never allowed me to read his works until they were published, afraid of jinxing them.

His incoming chat messages were flashing. I clicked on one of them and a message popped into view. Blood drained from my face as I read it; I checked the other messages in the history folder. When I was done, I left the messages as they were, open and exposed. I sat in the swivel chair for some time, unsure how I should react—to confront or to ignore? A deep wariness settled over me, turning my insides cold.

Then, after breaking through the strong grip of my thoughts, I did what I had come in here to do and printed out the ticket confirmation.

That night, after Cody had finished watching the tennis match on TV and I was brushing my teeth, he entered the bathroom and stood behind me, trying to catch my gaze in the mirror. Instead of meeting his eyes, I focused on the foam building up in my mouth, overflowing and dripping into the sink. He wrapped his hands around my waist and rested his chin on my shoulder. I bent to spit out the foam and started to rinse nosily. Cody stood behind me, waiting for me to finish. When I looked up, drawing his eyes to me, he remained silent, unable to utter anything. He must have read my expression: *Don't bother to explain.*

I took one of the pillows and slept on the sofa. At one point, Cody came out and sat near me, his head bent low.

"I'm sorry. It was nothing," he whispered. "Please come to bed."

"No, go away."

"I'm really sorry. It was just a one-time thing, nothing more."

I turned away from him. Cody tried to mutter something, but his words were caught in his throat. He sat beside me through the night, his presence a malignant force. I was wide awake the whole night, keeping up the defence.

The next morning, we followed our own routines determinedly. We had breakfast, read the newspapers, and put away the dishes. One thing we did not do was talk about what had happened, as if nothing was amiss. I did not want to ruin the trip, I rationalised; we would have time to talk about this soon enough, just not now.

∞

There was nothing to stop me from punishing Cody with my silence. On the morning of Christmas Eve, we met Ai Ling and Wei Xiang at the airport to check in together. At the time, I was still not talking to him, distracting myself with the usual drivel with Ai Ling, leaving Cody to Wei Xiang. On the plane, I plugged my earphones into the inflight entertainment system and turned away to look out the window. At one point, Cody leant in to check whether I was asleep and lowered the window shade. When we were waiting for the mini-bus at the airport to take us to the hotel in town, Ai Ling pulled me aside and asked whether everything was okay. I pulled out the excuse of my inability to sleep before an overseas trip, and gave a tired smile. She looked at me, unconvinced, but did not probe further.

In the hotel, after we had got the keys to our adjacent rooms, we arranged to meet half an hour later for a walk to Bangla Road, a few streets away. Alone with Cody in the hotel room, I was unable to face him. It felt like a century had passed since I sat at his work table and read the messages on his laptop; my anger was still there, but somewhat diluted, its edge blunted, and I could not work up the energy to fuel it again. I did not know what I was supposed to feel and act, and so I did nothing.

"Let's not do this," Cody said, coming out of the bathroom, his face wet from a wash.

"I'm not doing anything." I tore into my luggage, tossing clothes on the bed.

"I mean, let's don't fight. I know what I've done and I'm

really sorry, I am."

"Sure, that's easy. Just say sorry and everything is forgiven? It's not that easy."

"Then what do you want me to do?" Cody came up behind me, putting his hand on my shoulder. I flinched and pulled away.

"I don't know. I don't know what you can do." I looked into Cody's face, hoping to find something there to defuse my rising anger. He stepped in front of me and placed his hands at the back of my head, pulling me into the proximity of his body. I fought to break away but he kept his hold on me, his arms tight around my back. I felt suddenly worn out, drained.

"It's not over," I said.

"I know. Let's just do this a step at a time. You can take it out on me later on, if you want. I understand."

Cody pushed aside the luggage on the bed and began to peel off my clothes. Wordlessly, I let him. He nuzzled my neck and kissed my ear. Whatever I felt—anger, resentment—quickly receded into the background, replaced by an inebriating rush of sensations. With little resistance, I yielded, not just to the physical act of sex and its pleasures, but to the familiar, restorative comfort of a lover's touches, a return to safer shores. Perhaps, I sensed, Cody was trying to redeem himself, to assuage his guilt by offering the very thing that I needed—the refuge of his body, its irrepressible hold and heft.

Yet, barely had we finished, after Cody left the bed to shower, that the old feelings came sweeping over me again, like ghosts that had always haunted the dark passageways of my mind. Everything felt forced, useless—my thoughts, our actions, the need to salvage what was lost. In looking for some sort of respite, a truce, I came up blank, hitting a wall. The sounds of showering came to me from the open door of the bathroom, along with the broken snatches of a song that Cody was humming. I stared at my palms, unable to master what I was feeling.

When Cody came out of the bathroom, I got to my feet and started to dress. We were already running late. Ai Ling and Wei Xiang must have been waiting for us in the hotel lobby. Time to move on.

∞

Ai Ling wanted to check out the Banzaan market at Sai Kor Road while Cody and I were keen to head down south to Karon Viewpoint, a short taxi ride away. Ai Ling gave us the address of the hotel, just in case. "Don't get lost," she said.

The taxi driver, sensing that we were new in town, haggled for an exorbitant fare that we managed to cut down by half, and hastily dropped us off a few streets from our destination. With nothing to guide us, we fumbled our way to the location through a maze of small lanes that wound past corrugated tin-roofed houses that hugged close to one another and open plots of knee-high grass where chickens and small dogs wandered, searching for scraps of food. At one of the ramshackle shophouses, we bought two bottles of mineral water and asked the shopkeeper for further directions since there were no signs to indicate where we were. A pack of boys stopped their game of football to watch us pass; one of them lifted an arm to salute us, which Cody returned with a similar gesture. The rich smell of frying food wafted out of windows, along with staccato sounds of canned TV laughter and sudden explosions from action movies. Mosquitoes buzzed around us like a party of persistent, unrequited suitors.

We would have walked past a side entrance leading to the viewpoint if I had not noticed a mangy dog limping out of it, emitting a low, unthreatening growl. A gravel path led upwards into the shaded enclosure of tall trees with signs pointing to different routes. We took the route which would lead us to the promontory that overlooks Kata Noi Bay, and beyond that, the Andaman Sea. Cody went ahead of me and we walked in tandem, breaking the silence when one of us spotted something interesting—a heavy shrub abloom with star-bursts of white-petalled flowers, a patrol line of shiny-shell ants each the size of a fingernail, the sighting of a brightly-feathered bird resting on a branch. From time to time, we would stumble into a clearing, and the sudden touch of sunlight on our sweaty skins felt salubrious. Later, when we slipped back into the comfort of the shade, it felt like we were entering the shallow end of a pool, cool and curative.

When we reached the promontory, the sun was dissolving over the far horizon. The sky was a riot of warm smudgy reds, yellows and oranges. A flock of seagulls clung to the craggy surface of the cliffs, among the rocks jutting out of the coast; from where we stood, we could hear their faint cries. A strong sea wind ruffled the unruly patches of grass that sprouted out of the dry, clayey soil.

We drank from our bottles of water and stared out into the sea. Given the time of the day, nearing evening, we were the only people at the observation point. The silence around us deepened. Cody drew near and stood beside me, his shoulder touching mine.

"I'm glad we did this," he said.

I kept my silence. The trek up the hill was tiring, but it had at least distracted me from my thoughts. Cody's hair was whipping manically in the air, and he tried to placate it with little result. Then he reached for my hand, gripping it. He opened his mouth but before he could say a word, I cut him off.

"No, not now, let's not talk about it now."

In that moment, looking out into the sea, everything seemed impossibly clear, every thought fallen into its rightful place. This glimpse of clarity had a sobering effect on me before it quickly passed, leaving behind a wearying sense of sadness, a new weight in the pit of my gut. But for the moment it lasted, nothing else mattered—my life, Cody's, our relationship.

"This won't last forever, will it? What we have before us now?" I said, nodding my head at the view. The sky had already darkened into heavier shades of its original colours. The winds were getting stronger now, and the air cooler.

This time, it was Cody who remained silent. He released his hand from mine and stepped to the edge of the promontory, looking down at the sea. He picked up a small stone and threw it down. I strained my ears to hear the stone hit something—a rock or the water—but of course, at this height, it was impossible to hear anything. Cody straightened up and turned to me.

"It's beautiful," I said, and then added, "Shall we go? It's getting dark, and it'll take a while to get out of here."

He came up to me and put his arms around me. Closing my eyes, I held the scene in my mind, trying to burn it into memory as if the moment were already a thing of the past, and there was nothing to do but to hold onto its simulacrum. We stayed like this for a short while, the shadows at our feet stretched into dark, slanted lines.

"Let's go," I said, and took a long, hard look at the fading sunset, already tipping into evening. Then I turned and walked towards the gravel path that would take us down the hill, back to Patong, back to the lives we had no choice but to live.

26

WEI XIANG

Awake and lying in bed, Wei Xiang stares at the dusty shafts of light streaming through the curtains, and listens to the filtered sounds of shouting coming from the streets below. He recalls the boy and several scenes from their forages through Phuket over the past few days, how the boy led him through the torn landscape, taken him to the edge of the sea and brought up the ring from the depths. Even as Wei Xiang tries to conjure up the boy's face from memory—a face that can never seem to settle into any set features—he still can't get a full image in his head, only bits and fragments, the deep scar across his left eye. He shoots a glance at the side table where he sees Ai Ling's wedding ring and reaches for it. This is just not possible, yet here it is, the proof right in his hand, irrefutable.

Wei Xiang gets out of bed, refusing to give in to the downward spiral of thoughts that threatens to cripple him into paralysis. Action is better, and to keep in motion—that is the thing he should do. No point thinking about things that lead nowhere. He steadies himself with the thought as he runs through the few places in his head—emergency centres, makeshift hospitals, schools—where he has been the last few days. He was told that there are two new emergency centres, which also serve as drop-off points for dead bodies, located at Phuket Town. After changing into a new set of clothes and gathering up his watch and the well-worn map, Wei Xiang charges out of the room.

As is his habit now, he makes it a point to stop at Chee Seng and Cody's room. He knocks on the door a few times and listens for movement behind the door. No sounds. The day after the flood, Wei Xiang heard a feeble voice when he knocked on the door: Cody. So he's in there; but why is he hiding? And where is Chee Seng? Whatever the case, Wei Xiang is at a loss about what to do with Cody. Isn't he worried about Chee Seng? Shouldn't he be doing something instead of locking himself in the room? Even if he should barge in and force him to come out, Wei Xiang knows it would be pointless if Cody lacks the will or wherewithal to deal with what has happened. And if this is what he has chosen—to hide in the room—there is nothing much Wei Xiang can do. He knocks a couple more times, and when he hears a faint sound from inside, he turns and walks away, ready to begin his day. He stops by the front desk for directions—it will take about an hour to walk to the new, and nearest, emergency centre—and steps out into the noisy street.

The situation in Patong has changed little, even though it has been four days since the tsunami. While the water in many parts of town has subsided, only calf-high at places nearer to the sea, many roads are still blocked by the debris of fallen huts and shops. The decomposing bodies that littered the water-logged streets are slowly disappearing, having been picked up by teams made up of local and foreign volunteers, as well as by residents looking for their lost kin. Yet the stench of death has stayed in the air, like an invisible, malodorous blanket settling over the entire town, and worsens during the long afternoons when the sun bakes everything in sight. Wei Xiang holds his breath when he moves through certain streets, the foul, dank smell of decomposition coming from haphazard piles of rubble. Once, he steps on a severed hand with loose red strips of flesh trailing from its end, and quickly kicks it aside. By refusing to acknowledge what he's seeing, disconnecting the object from its association, he is able to control his stomach from churning; it's something he has to put into practice at every turn, a survival tactic.

With the morning still young, the air is cool, sunlight scattered across the puddles along Bangla Road. Already, people are thronging the main road of the town—lines of rescue workers clearing the collapsed walls of a shophouse, while a demolition crew drills the large sections of the broken structure into smaller, manageable chunks; scattered groups of locals searching under the rubble, still hopeful; ragtag gangs of children running from site to site, curious, craning their necks to see what has been uncovered, shouting lustily. Whenever another body is discovered, Wei Xiang rushes towards it, his heart sick with anticipation and fear. But none of the bodies he has seen so far is Ai Ling.

The new emergency centre, which Wei Xiang took two

detours to locate, is manned by the locals, and try as he might, he can't convey what he wants, but they do not stop him when he goes into the different tents, lifting up the flaps and checking the identity of occupants inside. Once Wei Xiang has exhausted his search among the injured in these tents, he heads for the open compound where there is a long line of bodies enclosed in thick bags of varying size. When he attempts to unwrap one of the bags, a matronly woman with short cropped hair stops him with a raised voice and a stern stare. Wei Xiang tries to explain what he's doing, but the woman shakes her head and points to a notice board where they have taken photographs of the deceased and pinned them up. Scanning the photographs with as much detachment as he can muster, Wei Xiang finds himself holding his breath every time he comes across a grainy photograph of a woman, trying to see beyond the death mask for any familiar features he might recognise. But Ai Ling is not in any of the photographs, a fact that gives Wei Xiang the barest of hope.

Leaving the centre, he checks his map and looks around the street for a prominent landmark from which he can orientate himself, and catches a glance of a man standing in the midst of a crowd, his movements slow, hesitant. Chee Seng. Wei Xiang leaps at the recognition and rushes towards him, shouldering his way through the thick crowd. When he places a hand on Chee Seng's back, the latter whips around, a flash of tense alarm sweeping across his face. Looking at him, Wei Xiang can sense Chee Seng trying to pull something out of his memory, his eyes blank and uncomprehending. He waits for him to break out of his daze, but Chee Seng remains rigidly impassive. Wei Xiang grows exasperated; he pulls him aside, to a less crowded part of the street, where only the facade of a row of shophouses stands; a half-destroyed wall displays a faded monochrome photograph of a young couple in traditional tribal garb, a metal holder nailed under it, filled with the scrawny burnt ends of joss-sticks.

"Chee Seng, are you okay? Where have you been?" Wei Xiang's words trigger no reply. Noticing Chee Seng's cracked lips, Wei Xiang grips his shoulders, speaking firmly into his face, "Wait for me here. Wait here. Don't go anywhere, you hear? I'll be back."

When he returns with the bottle of mineral water, which he has taken from the emergency centre, Chee Seng is still standing in the same spot. He shoves the bottle at him and watches him drink. Apart from a few scars and dark bruises on his face, Chee Seng seems relatively unscathed, at least from what he can see. Where has he been the past few days?

"Where's Ai Ling?" Chee Seng mumbles.

"I don't know. I can't find her."

"What about Cody? Is he with you?"

"He's okay. He's at the hotel."

"Is he injured? Did anything happen to him?"

"He hasn't left the hotel room at all."

"What do you mean?"

"He locked himself in the room on the day of the tsunami, and has not come out at all. But I could still hear him from behind the door this morning. Come, let's go back. You'll see," Wei Xiang says, motioning to Chee Seng to follow him.

It takes almost an hour to reach the hotel; they have to stop a few times so that Chee Seng can catch his breath.

Arriving at the hotel, Wei Xiang sees a porter cleaning the front steps, sweeping up the hardened clumps of soil and debris with a bamboo stick broom, and depositing them into black rubbish bags. The man glances up warily, then recognises Wei Xiang and presses his hands together in a greeting. Wei Xiang smiles and enters the hotel with Chee Seng, walking past a group of Japanese tourists standing around in the lobby, engaged in solemn conversation.

On the fourth storey, they walk along the quiet corridor until they arrive at Cody and Chee Seng's room. Wei Xiang looks at Chee Seng, waiting for him to do something, but he stands rooted to the floor, uncertain. Wei Xiang, sensing his hesitation, says, "He's in there."

Chee Seng returns a perplexed look, but does not make a move. Knowing that there's nothing more he can do, Wei Xiang leaves Chee Seng in front of the room, and walks away.

∞

Standing at the entrance to the hotel once again, Wei Xiang pauses to consider his next step. When he looks around, he sees the boy with the scar standing by a slanted lamppost a street away, in the same clothes he has been wearing for the past few days—a torn white singlet and khaki shorts. For a second, Wei Xiang isn't sure it's the same boy, but as his mind slowly pieces together the features, he runs towards the boy, afraid that he will lose him if he should hesitate a second longer. As he approaches, the boy looks up at him, a thin line of a smile breaking across his lips. Before he can reach him, the boy is already walking away, silently signalling to Wei Xiang to follow.

"Wait, where are we going?"

The boy stops to glance back at Wei Xiang, as if to convey his reply: *Follow me*.

They cut across Phang Muang Sai Kor Road, choked with rescue trucks and medical vans. The local and international news agencies have sent in reporting teams to cover the disaster, descending on the survivors like packs of vultures searching for the best stories, the most memorable soundbites, mikes and audio recorders thrust into the faces of people willing to give interviews. The young boy keeps a steady pace, paying no attention to what is happening around him, weaving through the crowd without stopping. They move south, to Karon, then Kata, through places that reveal new scenes of destruction, the landscape littered with ruins and brokenness. Before long, they are standing at the entrance leading up to Karon Viewpoint. Wei Xiang can faintly recall Cody and Chee Seng mentioning this place in the conversation at their last dinner, something about the views of the sunset. Ai Ling wanted to check out the place the day after their dinner, the day she disappeared. This shard of memory is now as foreign to him as something conjured up by someone from a different time.

The boy does not wait for Wei Xiang to catch up; he slips into the shady canopy of the trees, onto a rock-paved path that ascends in gentle-curving bends. Wei Xiang trails behind him like a shadow. After what seems like a long trek up the hill, they stumble into the blinding light of the afternoon sun, into the clearing of the promontory, the calm, undisturbed sea below them stretching to the vanishing line of the horizon, and in the distance the dark patches of islands. The boy walks to the edge of the cliff and points to somewhere out in the sea. Wei Xiang looks in the direction that he's pointing: a series of small islands scattered at the southeastern side of Phuket. Is this what the boy has wanted him to see? But why?

"What's there? What are you trying to tell me?" Wei Xiang asks. The boy gives no reply.

Wei Xiang looks down at the waves breaking against the sleek walls of the cliff, sending up huge sprays of water, the sound of the impact like a distant rumble of thunder. How many of the dead are still lost at sea? How many will be returned, in the days, weeks or months to follow? Will Ai Ling be one of those returned? Barely has the thought entered his mind that Wei Xiang realises what he has been secretly harbouring in his heart, something he has refused to give utterance to. He shakes his head hard, as if the act of doing so will dispel the thought.

When he turns his face aside, he notices the boy looking intently at him, and in his stare, Wei Xiang sees something akin to sympathy. The boy puts his hand on Wei Xiang's stomach, and again points to the islands. He pats it several times.

"I don't understand what you're trying to tell me," Wei Xiang says, his voice cracking as the words come out of his mouth. "Please help me understand what you're saying. Please."

The boy suddenly looks crestfallen, an expression of helplessness clouding his face. His eyes slowly fill with tears. He opens his mouth but nothing comes out. Unable to articulate what he wants to say, the boy seems stricken. Apart from his furtive gestures, which are barely adequate to convey his intention, they are lost to each other, strangers grasping at shadows.

The boy leans his head on Wei Xiang's stomach, tears wetting the front of his shirt. Wei Xiang holds the boy's head in his hands, stroking his hair. He smells a hint of eucalyptus rising from his shaking body. When the boy breaks from the embrace, he turns to look out at the islands again. And then he gives Wei Xiang a long, thorough look before turning back to walk into the forest, vanishing into the darkness. Wei Xiang watches the boy leave, and in his absence, the promontory feels bare and desolate, a place marked only by silence and emptiness.

After the boy has disappeared, Wei Xiang heads back to Patong. In the recesses of his heart, Wei Xiang knows— without knowing why—that this is the last time he will see the boy, and now it's up to him to make a decision, to act. But to decide what, and to act on what? He can continue to search for Ai Ling and hope that at any moment she will turn up, that things would be all right. But this no longer seems possible to him now, this continual, indeterminate search, in light of what the boy has prompted in his heart.

With no destination in mind, Wei Xiang stands at a junction along Thaweewong Road, with streets branching into several directions. He wants the boy to appear again, to see him standing at the lamppost, signalling to him, showing him what he needs to do. Perhaps, if he waits long enough, the boy will reappear, and, because he wants so much to believe this is true or possible, he is willing to wait for as long as he can. And so he loiters at the junction, the flow of people around him breaking like water over a rock. Then, as afternoon tilts into evening, Wei Xiang is unable to keep up the blind hope any longer. He closes his eyes, forcing himself to snap out of his delusion.

Though he has no clue where he should head next, Wei Xiang turns into one of the alleys and walks to the end of it. He only wants to walk and walk and not turn back, as far and as long as his legs can carry him, before he finally collapses—perhaps to the farthest reach of the island where the land disappears into the sea. In his mouth, he holds onto Ai Ling's name, saying it over and over again, an incantation he hopes will lead him to a specific location, where he can find her at last, until it finally hits him that what he's really doing is trying to take hold of the grief that has only just materialised inside him, a grief that will never let him go. He stops in mid-stride, doubles over, and starts to heave, gasping, as if someone has just punched the air out of him. Then he pulls himself together and staggers on.

Without meaning to, Wei Xiang finds himself back at the edge of the sea. Why is it that everywhere he goes on the island, he returns again and again to the sea, as if it were never out of sight, always present, always here to remind him of what he has lost? Now, looking out across the expanse of water, Wei Xiang can no longer drum up the strength he needs to deal with the doubts that have finally overwhelmed him. He feels utterly sapped, his mind in tatters.

He takes off his shoes and steps into the sea; the waves crawl to meet his feet, cooling his skin. He moves slowly through the water, which embraces him like a tight second skin. It is only when the water comes up to his chest and the ground under him pulls away that he hears someone calling out to him. Wei Xiang cranes his head around, and on the shoreline he sees someone in the subdued afternoon light, a dark figure, waving at him. And Wei Xiang knows that he will not be able to take another step further, that this is as far as he can go.

Even as the voice is calling out to him—louder, more urgent—Wei Xiang remains still, his body swaying in the gentle tug of the waves. For a long time, he stays like this, hoping and waiting for something that is lost to him forever.

27

The room holds the silence well, the walls letting nothing in. As you lie on the floor, time no longer makes any sense. Your thoughts have grown vague, more oblique, worn smooth by repetition. Chee Seng, Ai Ling, Wei Xiang—mere figures that appear like nebulous shadows on the horizon of your perception, disappearing in a flicker of thought. When you do not stir, they stay where they are—dark, ominous creatures strutting across the plains of your mind, wary of one another, yet hungry for contact. Thoughts of them hurt your head, like knife slashes.

Your body's noises: persistent stomach growls, tight pops of the joints in your legs and arms as you turn, breaths inhaled and expelled in long bursts. Your body resists all effort to shut it down, continuing relentlessly, not stopping until every part of you has eventually turned to dust.

A gecko chirps from somewhere in the room—a peal of shots from a toy ray gun. Your heartbeat thumps in your wrist.

∞

The night after the dinner and their big fight, Chee Seng had stormed out of the hotel room. Shortly after, Cody, too, left the room, unable to bear its oppressive silence. He ran after Chee Seng, thinking he could catch up, but by the time he got to the street outside the hotel, Chee Seng was already gone. Droves of people filled the street, stopping to eat at the food carts or play shooting games at the makeshift stalls or surround a street performer guiding his monkey through a series of tricks. Recalling the name of the club that Chee Seng had mentioned earlier, Cody went back into the hotel and asked the receptionist for clear directions. The club was only five streets away, and given that he was still wired from the fight, he decided to walk there.

The evening breeze cooled his skin and brought some relief. He followed a group of locals, dressed in tight T-shirts and jeans, down a side street and found the club, located at the end of a narrow lane; the sign above the entrance was bright and kitschy. He paid a nominal entry fee and entered the club, the tight space of the hall akin to a dark, clammy hole in which strobe lights beamed and sliced and glided over the dancing figures and shaking silhouettes.

It took little effort to find Chee Seng across the huddle of tightly-packed bodies, partially hidden from view. He was talking to a young man, his face pressed close. The man looked at Chee Seng with an overt interest, putting his hand on Chee Seng's chest and shoulder, pulling him into a hug. The moving tableaux of electric lights and shadows across Chee Seng's face gave his expressions a heightened quality, as if he were trying to shape his features according to the moment. On his lover's face, Cody recognised something he had not seen for a long time: a look of unequivocal desire.

To avoid detection, Cody dissolved into a corner of the club, hiding in the dark, his eyes never straying from Chee Seng or the man. They danced for some time before turning to the bar for drinks, with Chee Seng paying for them both. Cody watched, riveted, as if watching a play, two men on a stage with their lines and movements and gestures executed in perfect harmony. He was not sure what he could do at that moment; just the idea of crossing the room and confronting Chee Seng was almost unbearable, a feat that required unimaginable strength that he did not possess. He continued to watch as they danced, and then later left the club, laughing like schoolboys sharing a private joke. Cody followed them, keeping a fair distance. They flitted down several dark lanes, sometimes stopping to kiss, before emerging out onto the beach.

In the darkness, they sneaked under a huge open umbrella and made out on the deck chairs. Cody crept closer— he felt exposed, conspicuous under the milky glow of the moonlight—and he saw everything. They were taking off their clothes, frantic in their urgency, and then one of them stopped suddenly; Cody could not tell which one. Neither moved. After a while, the other man moved away, trudging through the loose sand back towards the road. Cody did not move until he was sure the man was finally gone. From where he was hiding, he could hear the waves hitting the shore, their gentle pulses.

Cody crept over to where Chee Seng was lying on the

deck chair with his eyes closed. He did not move when Cody came closer, perhaps too drunk to notice. Cody blocked the moonlight that shone across Chee Seng's body and waited for him to sense Cody's presence. But there was no sign of movement; he had passed out, dead to the world. Cody stood and waited for his thoughts to straighten themselves out. He shook with fury and sorrow at the state they were in, at how they had allowed things to fall into this mess.

Before he knew it, Cody was weeping, soundlessly and wretchedly, for all that he had lost—there was no way they could stop what was coming. And when he was done crying, he stared at Chee Seng's sleeping form, then turned his back and walked away.

∞

The dreams, when they come, pull you deep into their folds, ensnaring you.

In one of them you're in a room, not unlike your hotel room, and people are passing through it in multitudes, coming and going in such numbers that you have to squeeze your body into a foetal position for fear that you'll be trampled. Yet there is no danger of that, as they never come close enough to even brush against the sides of your body. They walk past and, without looking, throw things at you: a flower, a handful of soil, a tattered book, a plate, a dead snake, a dirty rag, a wad of saliva, a handkerchief embroidered with flying swallows, rice, hair. These things slowly pile up. Yet, even under the cumulative weight of these familiar objects, you do not feel as if you've been weighed down; instead, what you feel in the dream—soft and impenetrable—is a strange sense of security, as if a place of refuge has suddenly been revealed, and it's a place that can take you, broken, into its depths. Each object that covers you carries its own weight of history and significance, one that you somehow know instinctively and exactly; soon, you are completely covered, buried out of sight. The darkness is full and complete and assuring.

In another dream, you find yourself being eaten by a beast twice your size, a cross between a hunchbacked wolf and a steely gargoyle, heavily muscled with matted fur, and wet, yellow pits for eyes. It glances at you, then turns its attention back to the gaping hole in your torso, devouring your insides. There is hardly any blood, and the beast is taking its time, chewing leisurely before swallowing. You can only feel the faintest trace of pain. Somehow, it is the right thing to do, offering yourself up to the beast. You're not afraid. Only when it has eaten its fill do you feel a jolt of desolation, of forlornness, and the sensation is not the pain of self-annihilation or death, but of desertion, of severance. The beast turns its head and glares at you; in its bright enraged eyes, you see how the beast sees you, as a man with nothing to lose. In his stare: pity, contempt, recognition. Then, after shaking its body roughly, the beast rises to its full stature and roars. And without even a final look, it turns and saunters off.

∞

Cody woke early the following morning still in his clothes, the acrid stink of cigarette smoke and alcohol emanating from his body. The sunlight seeping in between the half-drawn curtains was weak and feeble, the sky just starting to lighten. The other half of the bed was empty, though the sheet was roughened up. His mind felt heavy and sodden, unwilling to snap to full wakefulness. Sounds travelled up from the street to reach his ears: an occasional shout, a dog's whiny bark, the revving of a bike.

Was he still where I left him last night? Shouldn't he be back already?

Cody pulled himself out of bed and went over to the balcony, drawing back the curtains and pushing open the glass doors. He blinked and scanned the rusty rooftops of the three- and four-storey houses nearby, most of them bedecked with antennae or satellite dishes. Farther out, the hills rose out of the mist, like a woman casting off her membranous robes for a fresher set of green. The air carried the coolness of the night, and hurt his lungs as he took in a long breath. Leaning against the railing, he glanced down at the street and saw Ai Ling emerge from the hotel, dressed in a white T-shirt and running shorts. For a moment, she stopped and looked around, and Cody wanted to call out to her, but before he could, she was already running down the street, towards the beach. He watched as she turned down a corner and disappeared.

His thoughts went immediately to Chee Seng—they would have to talk about the previous night's dalliance once he returned, and the thought of a potential fight was enough to cast a shadow of weariness over his mind. He sat down on the rattan chair at the balcony and rubbed his face roughly. Then he closed his eyes and leant back in the chair.

Without intending to, he fell into the pit of sleep.

When he woke later, to the sound of something breaking in the near distance, he was thrown momentarily into a state of disorientation. A long series of cries and shouts rang out. As he stumbled to his feet, his vision whitening out for a second or two, he looked out into the streets below.

For a long time, he could not properly register what he was seeing. It felt wrong, as if the images before him had all given up their forms and meanings and purposes, jumbled up into chaos, into spectacular disarray, and nothing could put them back in their rightful places again.

The heavy, mercurial waves, coming in fast and livid, had swept everything up in their wake, and from where he stood he could only feel their full-on urgency. A succession of voices rose and quelled and faded, and then rose again. Hands reached out of the surface of the choppy water, bodies collided with other bodies, smashing into walls and trees and telephone poles. An explosion of birds took to the sky. The tough, unsparing wind carried the wails and cries deeper inland.

Cody did not know how long he stood there watching, but at one point he turned and stumbled back into the room and shut the glass doors. He switched on the television, but it had gone dead, its reflective surface a blank, unresponsive darkness. Then he pulled the curtains shut and lay on the floor and closed his eyes to the world raging outside.

∞

A knock on the door. You're roused from the dark well of sleep. The dim universe of the room materialises before you, light-stripes seeping through the fabric of the curtains. Is it morning or afternoon? You breathe in the dust of the cold floor and imagine it entering your body, settling over tongue and lungs, accumulating in layers of sediment.

The knocks come again. You hold your breath, wishing for them to go away. Your body aches. The room holds the fragile silence even as the knocks penetrate every corner and ricochet against the walls. Three knocks, pause, three knocks.

Go away. Go away, please.

There is a respite, as if the person on the other side of the door has finally given up. You coil up and open your mouth; your tongue feels parched and raw. You utter something; the words vanish under your breath: *Go away.*

The knocks resume. Someone calls out your name: "Cody, it's Chee Seng. Please open the door."

You press your hands to your ears. You shift your body, which feels heavy and ancient and mountainous; your arms and legs move like glaciers, inch by inch, breaking apart in their movements. Three more knocks, fired off like gunshots. You edge yourself up against the wall, your heart jackhammering, your thoughts narrowed to the rigid mechanics of your body. You fold your knees into sharp angles and push yourself up. Every joint in your body flares up in blasts of vengeful mutiny. You hold still and try to straighten your body—nausea seizes you but soon passes— and take a small step. The ground shakes unsteadily, as if about to give way under your weight. You take another step.

The voice again, louder: "It's me, Cody. Open up."

Then you're at the door, leaning against it. The knocks stop. You can feel the person behind the door silently acknowledging your presence, waiting for you to make the next move. You place a hand on the door handle and, with some effort, push it down. The door opens slowly towards you, and, after what seems like a lifetime of missteps and stumbles and doubt, you peer out of the room and hold your breath and never let it go.

28

CHEE SENG

I have come back to Phuket alone every year after the tsunami and stayed at the same hotel, until it closed down several years later. In its place, there is now a large gelato shop and an adjoining playground that draws in hordes of sweaty tourists, mostly parents with children in tow. I have chosen a new hotel along Thaweewong Road, just beside the beach, where I swim every day if the weather permits. Some nights, when the breeze is cool and light, I go for long walks along the beachfront, from one end to the other, looking out at the night sky pierced with sharply blinking stars. On these walks, my mind is crowded with thoughts about the past, though the memories that surface no longer have any hold on me.

They never found Ai Ling, and in the end, after a week of searching and waiting, Cody and I returned to Singapore, leaving Wei Xiang behind to keep up the search.

"She'll turn up," he said. "It's just a matter of time."

He stayed for another week before returning home, heavy with a broken spirit. A small wake was held, where most of the mourners sat quietly in twos and threes, wary of making eye contact with Wei Xiang. Before we departed, I left a note, offering him our condolences. After replying with a thank-you email a few days later, I never heard from Wei Xiang again, though I tried to contact him several times, to meet up for coffee or a meal.

I usually do not have an itinerary when I come to Phuket, preferring to go where I want to go when I feel like it, or stay put in my hotel room reading and sleeping and thinking. My mobile phone is switched off throughout my stay, so there is no way I can be found if I'm lost or missing—a thought I entertain quite frequently. For the first three years after the tsunami, whenever I returned to the island, I would try to find out where the old woman had lived, and whether she was still alive. Though the island is not big—you can complete a car ride along its coast in less than two hours—there are hilly regions in the north and east that are relatively remote, the interiors only known to well-versed locals who have stayed on the island for decades. On the map, there are a multitude of passable vehicular routes, interspersed with small, nondescript villages that all look alike after a while. I would hire a motorbike driver, and using my well-worn map direct him to the places I had marked down. I was lucky, in my third year, to locate the village where I was able to find help after my long walk out of the forest. Through my driver-translator, I was able to get a clearer picture of what had transpired the day I stumbled into the village, though further questions about where I had come from were met with a muted response. Unwilling to give up, I pressed on with the few leads I had, going down every route indicated on the map, looking for signs along the road that would show me a way into the forest, and lead me to the old woman's hut, to the unmarked grave where the young, unknown boy was buried. But all the routes I took ultimately, eventually, led me back to the town, no matter the distance. There was never going to be a way to find what was already lost—this was something that took me much longer to realise, and finally come to terms with.

Yet, every time I come back to Phuket, I can't help but remember the old woman and the dead boy. The long years have passed, but the memories continue to hold strong as if they have already sunk into parts of me that still want to remember. Perhaps, remembering is the hardest part of everything that happened—the constant dredging up of memories that have stayed deep inside me, holding me to the past. They would have crushed me, if I had not learnt to live with them over the years.

My relationship with Cody did not survive after we came back, though we kept at it for another three months before deciding to end it. The separation was easier and more painless than I would have thought. I found a new flat, moved out, and quickly established a quiet life of simple routines. I kept myself busy, and the life I made slowly took on a definite—although not entirely unfulfilling—state, a life I could somehow manage with little disruption. It is strange and oddly easy how one can get used to being single after a period of adjustment.

I was clearing out some old boxes from the storeroom a few months ago and came across Cody's old Motorola phone. The battery was dead so I searched around the flat for the phone charger, and realised later that I had thrown it out—the phone was already many years out of date—along with the other old, unused electronic parts, during my move. I wanted to check what was in the phone, to read the messages, but the urgency passed soon enough, and it seemed rather fatuous after I thought through it.

Yet it does not mean the memories are dead to me. I'll be on the MRT heading to work, or washing the dishes after dinner, and suddenly a random memory sneaks into my thoughts—an image of Cody or the old woman, or sometimes the dead boy. These images flit and linger for a while, but I do not allow them any purchase on my mind; I have learnt to keep a distance from these old memories, to blunt their edges.

It is only during my annual trips to Phuket that I allow myself a deeper introspection, to give myself permission to think about those days back in 2004. I would walk down Bangla Road in Patong and see two men walking towards me, and I would pause and remember a similar scene from that time. Even a glance at a peddler hawking preserved tamarinds and sour plums near a junction was enough to trigger a fragment of memory about the old woman. And there was that time I came across a beggar boy with a shrivelled right foot at the night market in Phuket Town, wearing a tin can strung around his neck, and sitting before a dirty, badly scrawled square of cardboard—there was something about his face, in the tilt of his head, that caused a lurch in my heart; but of course it wasn't him, it couldn't possibly be. For one thing, there was no scar across his left eye. I knew enough to keep my thoughts grounded, to differentiate the real from the imagined. It's not easy though—the pull of the past is a siren's call, beckoning and summoning, and it's inevitable to be tricked from time to time.

On my last trip to Phuket, I visited Phromthep Cape, at the southern tip of the island, having spent the day walking without any particular aim or direction in mind. I had been there a few times over the years, and I always loved the views it offered—the sunset, the outlying islands, the sea. There was still a light crowd at that time of the day, mostly tourists armed with phone cameras, and I made sure to skirt the lighthouse and the shrine, to escape the noise and commotion. I took a narrow footpath down a slope and followed it for a while, as it wound itself up a slight incline, past dry shrubs of calf-height brown grass, and ended at a quiet lookout. From where I was standing, I saw two dark spots—eagles? seagulls?—moving across the sky, one behind the other, punctuating its wide, clear expanse. They never flew close enough to the island for me to identify them. For some time, I watched them glide through the sky before they disappeared, farther out into the sea.

Sitting down, I heard the tall grass swishing around me, and when I listened closely, I could hear the waves—so soft, barely there. Maybe because I was trying hard in such moments not to stir up anything in my head, I heard something: the faint traces of a song. I looked around, straining to catch further wisps of it, but there was nothing but the sound of the waves, and the wind making its way through the grass. I looked out to the sea—already darkening in the dying light—and let my mind quiet itself. Then, turning to my right, looking farther down along the coast, I saw something—a figure, standing at another viewing point along the ridge. I studied the figure for a while—a man, clearly—and waited for him to—to see me? to make a move? to disappear? I could not complete the thought in my head then.

But as I watched the man's solitary figure, his stillness, I could not help but think about Cody and the last time we had stood at such a promontory—was it a lifetime ago?—and looked out at the sea, hearing the waves coming to us as if from another world, breaking into ours. In my mind's eye, I saw both of us standing there, taking in the view, immersed in our own thoughts, alone in our separate worlds.

I could have let my imagination go—to recreate this memory in my head again—but I did not. The memory would not have been real; I would have coloured it with something else, and it would not have done me any good, to confuse what was there with what wasn't. I would have changed Cody in that memory, making him into a man I wished he had been, but of course, he had always been who he was, no matter how I had imagined him in these memories.

I must have been steeped in my thoughts, for when I looked at the man again, I noticed that he had turned in my direction, holding his hand up. For a moment, I thought he was waving at me, and I wanted to return the gesture. But he was merely shielding his eyes from the glare, his gaze trained on something along the distant shoreline, down the coast. I dropped my half-lifted hand to my lap, feeling foolish at my near-mistake.

For whatever reason I could not quite fathom, I continued to watch the man as he cupped his hands around his mouth and shouted into the air. The timbre of his voice caught the lift of the wind, which carried it across the hushed landscape. I imagined those words—I couldn't hear them clearly from where I was sitting—trailing down the slope, off the cliffs, and into the sea, fading and fading until they were no more. The sound, and the echo, gone—the things we lost to the sea.

The man stood for several moments longer, then turned to walk down a path. I waited in the growing dark, watching him leave, holding back something beating wildly inside me that had wanted to chase after him, to tap him on the shoulder, to make him stay. I held back—it was enough to have this longing, it had to be enough.

When he finally disappeared behind the bushes, I stood up and slowly began to make my way down the hilltop, heading towards the lights of the town, from where I had come.

29

Through the thin veil of sleep, Ai Ling heard the faint chirping of birds coming from outside the hotel room. She got quietly out of bed, not wanting to wake Wei Xiang up, who was murmuring in his sleep. She leant over to plant a kiss on his shoulder. Peeking through the half-drawn curtains, she accidentally scared the birds on the window ledge into flight. Standing where she was, she could catch a sliver of the sea. She inhaled deeply; the day was still brimming with newness. She glanced over at the bed, at the sleeping figure of Wei Xiang. She would wake him up later for breakfast, after her run.

Slipping into the toilet, Ai Ling brushed her teeth and doused her face with cold water. She noted that the lines around her eyes had deepened, and the freckles on her cheeks seemed darker after a day under the sun. *What did you expect? You're not getting any younger*, she chided herself. She put on some moisturiser and sunblock, and tied her hair up in a ponytail. Back in the room, she changed into a T-shirt and running shorts. Wei Xiang's dream talk was getting louder now, though Ai Ling could not make out his garbled speech. She made a mental note to check with Wei Xiang about his dream later. Unlike Ai Ling, Wei Xiang could always remember his dreams, able to narrate them with so much detail that it felt like something that had actually happened to him, instead of something culled from the hidden catacombs of his mind. She placed her hand on his arm and kissed his damp forehead, breathing in the muskiness of his sleeping body. She loved this particular smell of Wei Xiang, which had never failed to trigger a physical longing. Her touch promptly calmed Wei Xiang down, his words turning to soft grunts.

Picking up the room key from the bedside table, Ai Ling took another glance at Wei Xiang before leaving. A short run to the beach; she aimed to be back at the hotel before 8.30am, before everyone was up.

They had walked to the beach from the restaurant the night before, after bidding good night to Cody and Chee Seng, who had wanted to return to the hotel to rest before heading out later to check out the bars and dance clubs along Bangla Road. Since it was still early, Wei Xiang suggested a stroll to enjoy the evening breeze. Walking with no destination in mind, they came to a quiet stretch of Patong Beach.

"The moon is hanging really low tonight," Wei Xiang said, nodding towards the sea, where the moon was hovering above the dark sweep of the water. Ai Ling dug her toes into the warm sand, the trapped heat engulfing her feet. Wei Xiang, with his arm around Ai Ling's shoulders, pulled her closer to him.

"Are you okay? You seem distracted," Wei Xiang said. Ai Ling broke away and walked to the edge of the water.

"I'm okay. Just tired, after all the rushing about the whole day," Ai Ling replied. Wei Xiang trailed behind, giving her the space he could sense she wanted. Ai Ling stared up at the moon, feeling the tension slowly easing out of her.

"You want to head back to the hotel now? To rest early?" Wei Xiang asked.

"No, I want to stay here for a while," Ai Ling said.

"Sure, as long as you want."

"Don't you like the sea at night?"

"I do. The sound of the waves is very calming. I could stay here and fall asleep to the sound."

"Do you want to?"

"What?"

"Stay here and sleep on the beach?"

"No, I'm just saying. I don't think that would be safe. Who knows what could happen? We might get robbed."

"Worse, we might get swept up by the waves and cast out into the sea while we sleep."

"Yeah, right. Cast out into the sea."

Ai Ling chuckled and reached for Wei Xiang. They walked farther down the beach, passing other couples lying on the sand or hidden in the shadows, dark moving silhouettes. They nearly tripped over a pair of lovers; the woman let out a cry of annoyance. They apologised and walked away quickly, suppressing their laughter.

"Come on, let's do it here," Wei Xiang said, slipping his arm around Ai Ling's waist, pushing into her for a kiss.

"No, let me go," Ai Ling said, shaking him off.

"Come on, we'll be making love under the moon. So romantic."

"No, it's not! Silly man."

Ai Ling laughed and skipped across the warm sand. Wei Xiang caught up with her and they walked on. The lights and sounds from the bars, cafes and ice-cream shops near the beachfront had faded away, leaving them in near-absolute silence and darkness, except for the waves and the bright moonlight that made the sand glow with a bluish luminescence. Ai Ling looked around her and, for an instant, felt the sharp thrill of solitude, of being separated from everyone else. She relished this sensation much deeper than she expected.

"It's really dark here. Perhaps we should head back," Wei Xiang said.

"No, it's good here. Let's stay for a while more."

They came face to face with a jagged wall of rocks and Ai Ling began to climb it, without checking first with Wei Xiang, who followed. They found a spot among the rocks, overlooking a small inlet that was surrounded by huge boulders and jutting rock formations. Slightly out of breath from the climb, they sat and looked out into the sea. For some time, they were deep in their own thoughts, not speaking. The night heaved around them, holding them still.

∞

The longtail boats anchored a short distance away from the shore were bobbing in the gentle waves. Shading her eyes from the sunlight, Ai Ling peered out to the horizon where the sky dissolved into the sea, into a deeper shade of blue. She fixed her gaze at the dividing line, which seemed so infinite, so far away.

Already there was a small crowd of people on the beach. Young parents with toddlers playing near the water; a few old men casting their fishing rods from the breakwater, handmade cigarettes dangling from their mouths; morning joggers, flushed from the exertion of running on sand. The food hawkers had already set up their stalls along the pavement beside the beach, the smell of frying oil carried into Ai Ling's nose. She felt nausea rise up her throat and suppressed the urge to throw up; her morning sickness was worsening. Removing her shoes, she stepped onto the cool sand of the beach. The receding tide had smoothed out the surface, leaving behind dark trails of seaweed and crushed seashells. Ai Ling picked up the carcass of a tiny crab and examined its exoskeleton. A distant cry of a child broke her concentration; a small Caucasian boy was sitting at the edge of the water, stricken at being overcome by the waves. A young woman ran towards him, extending her arms, laughing.

Ai Ling walked into the surf. Her first contact with the cold water sent a chilling pulse of electricity up her spine. She sank her feet into the wet sand; the waves pulled away for a moment before sweeping over her feet again. She stood stock-still, enjoying the pleasure of the water and the exposure to the cool air. She lifted her head to the sun.

She should have told Wei Xiang about the pregnancy last night when she'd had the chance. Yet her old fears had held her back. She was after all still in the early stages, only six weeks along. She had grown suspicious after a bout of vomiting in the mornings; the doctor later confirmed the fact. She knew she would have to keep the news to herself for the time being, until... until when? She did not know. After the last miscarriage, she had become more fearful of the way life could be taken away indiscriminately. There would certainly be, she knew, another chance to tell Wei Xiang. She had to be patient and wait out her anxiety.

The wavelets chugged at her feet, stronger and more pressing now. The sea birds, which had been resting on the wooden poles impaled along the shoreline, had taken to the sky and were wheeling in the air, their screeching loud and maddening. Ai Ling looked up at them, specks of darkness against the bright sunlight. The wind had picked up as well, tousling Ai Ling's hair and sweeping it across her face.

Yes, it was the right thing to do for now, keeping the pregnancy from Wei Xiang, Ai Ling assured herself one more time before taking another step into the sea, the water coming up to her calves.

∞

The tide drew in and they could hear the splash of the waves against the rocks. Wei Xiang and Ai Ling sat on the sandy ground, leaning against each other. Ai Ling could feel the warmth emanating from his body and wrapped her hands around him, nestling in the heat. Wei Xiang turned to smile at her, his face half in shadow. Ai Ling caught a flash of moonlight in his eyes—alert, watchful.

"You have been so quiet these days," Wei Xiang said.

"Am I?"

"Yes, you are. It's like you're thinking so many things. Care to share some with me?"

"No, I'm not thinking about anything."

Wei Xiang pressed against her, and Ai Ling's body tensed up. "You're really cold," he said. "Why don't we head back to the hotel? You can have a hot shower."

"Sure. But let's sit for a while more. Then we'll head back."

Looking out into the black mass of the sea, Ai Ling pictured her thoughts slipping out of her mind and joining the darkness around them, seeping into the night. If she were to give up her thoughts now, would her mind be lighter, carrying nothing? She had always felt much freer in the dark where she could entertain any thoughts or memories that crossed her mind, without feeling hounded or burdened by them, as if their hold over her were greatly weakened in a different state. She felt almost at peace. At this moment, sitting here with Wei Xiang, a sense of calmness welled up inside Ai Ling, a brief, transient state—she was aware of its fleeting nature—that could be broken at any time. She held firm to the fragile moment.

"Wei Xiang, you know I love you, right?" Ai Ling looked into the night sky, hesitant to face him.

"Of course I know. Why would you say that? Okay, now I'm officially worried. What's going on in that head of yours? Come on, tell me."

Ai Ling laughed softly, the sound fading into the night.

"Nothing's wrong."

"You sure? You very sure?"

"Yes, nothing's wrong."

∞

Standing in the water, Ai Ling stretched her toes and dug her heels into the sand. Craning her face upwards, she closed her eyes, feeling the warm morning sunlight on her skin. The balm of the water and the light felt restorative. She had always loved the sea. When she was eight years old, her parents brought her to East Coast Park for the first time. The noisy rush of the waves as they crashed onto the shore, the broken seashells that lay half-embedded in the wet sand, her headlong dash into the water, the current of fizzy bubbles that moved along the entire length of her body, down her back to her feet. How she had gasped for air, bursting through the surface of the water, yelling for her parents, wanting them to see the great feat she was performing, fighting against the waves and breaking their advance with her might, with the will and strength of her body. Her parents had cheered and clapped, and told her to come back to the shore and not to venture too far. Ai Ling had defied them—she had taken some swimming lessons in school and knew she was a strong swimmer, her swimming coach had told her—and held her head down in the water. Counting the long seconds and fighting the resistance of her body, she finally leapt up and threw her arms into the air, flinging arcs of water from her extended hands. Looking towards the shore, Ai Ling had noticed that her mother was standing so close to the water that the front of her shoes had got wet, a flash of relief breaking across her face. Ai Ling could still remember the calls of her mother then, to come back.

From the chamber of her thoughts, Ai Ling heard an indistinct shout coming from behind her. Glancing back, it took her less than a second to register a young boy standing at the tide line, trying to get her attention, waving his arms and pointing at the horizon. Ai Ling turned to where he was indicating. Far out in the distance, a high wall of water had appeared, quivering like a mirage, dissolving the boundary between the sea and the sky, gaining in height and moving in fast.

Ai Ling tripped over her own feet and fell into the water. She could hear a piercing scream coming from somewhere behind her. She regained her footing and started to run.

∞

When they got back to their hotel room, they sat on the balcony watching the night sky. From the small bag of drinks they had bought at the convenience store next to the hotel, Wei Xiang popped a can of Singha beer and started to drink. The murmur of street sounds rose up to where they were sitting: soft bursts of voices and laughter, the occasional honking of cars, and the deep, almost subterranean beats of music coming from the nearby bars, thumping like a heart under the skin of the night.

When Ai Ling got up to go to bed, Wei Xiang followed. He reached over to turn off the bedside lamp. Shadows stretched long on the ceiling and walls, moving like dark creatures in the slanted blocks of moonlight. When Wei Xiang touched her collarbone with his fingers, Ai Ling felt every part of her rushing to meet the point of contact, her nerves electrified, awakened by a rabid yearning that reached deep into her core, stirring her alive. Wei Xiang traced his fingers down the valley between her breasts and stroked her nipples. Closing her eyes, Ai Ling imagined her body changing into something that was a different version of herself—better, fuller, wilder—and in this new self, she lost all her usual senses. Yet she was not anxious or frightened or fearful; she was beyond all these, floating at the brink of her existence, transformed.

When Wei Xiang entered her, Ai Ling gasped. She held his face close, his breaths landing on her neck, down her shoulders, into her mouth. When she came, she gave in to a dark place that was a void and a death, and in that moment of nothingness, she burnt bright, all aglow.

"I worry about you sometimes. I don't know what you're thinking and it scares me." Wei Xiang had lain down beside her afterwards, and in the dim light, Ai Ling could see his chest rising and falling. She put her hand over his heart, to calm him.

"Don't worry. I'm fine."

"I don't want to lose you."

"You won't. I'm here."

Wei Xiang held Ai Ling's hand in the dark, squeezing it. Ai Ling breathed in deeply and settled into herself. The night drew itself around them, and they fell into slumber.

∞

Ai Ling barely had time to catch her breath as the boy rushed up to her, grabbing her left hand and tugging her in the direction he wanted to go, to higher ground farther up the beach. Close-up, Ai Ling saw the panic in the boy's eyes, full of warning. He muttered something without pausing, the rush of heated words escaping from his mouth, incomprehensible to Ai Ling.

"Where?" Ai Ling said. The boy looked confused, his eyebrows knitted with uncertainty. "I need to get back to my husband."

Ignoring her words, the boy leant backward and tried to yank Ai Ling away. She shook off his hand, taking a few steps back. The wind had whipped up to a deafening speed, howling in her ears. Shrill, frantic birdcalls chorused madly around them. From somewhere, another shout of alarm.

"No, I need to get back to him."

The boy dropped his arms to his sides and stared at Ai Ling. For a brief moment, Ai Ling felt as if they were looking at each other through a distorted glass, across a span of shared history.

The boy turned and sprinted up the beach.

Before Ai Ling could utter another word or form a single thought, the huge wave swept onto shore and lifted her into its embrace, carrying her as far as it could, into the heart of the island, before drawing her back into its depths.

∞

The sun dips slowly into the sea, turning the water vermillion, as darkness creeps its way across the tiny island. The wispy tufts of dry grass shiver in the light breeze, bracing themselves for the night. All is calm. The woman remains perfectly still.

The boy steps out of the water and walks up to the woman on the beach. Water drips from the boy's body onto her back, dotting her shirt with dark splotches. He squats down and puts a hand on the woman's hair, brushing it gently with his fingers, straightening out the kinks, freeing the tangled ends. He wipes the crusted trails of dried blood from the corners of her mouth, and fills the empty eye socket with sand. Then he places his right hand on her bulging stomach and holds it there, fingers splayed.

Closing his eyes, he listens to the world of sounds coming from inside the woman's husk of a body. He listens, and beyond the skin and blood and flesh, he finally hears her. He clenches his hand into a fist on the woman's stomach. He's here—he will always be here.

And the sea, ever present, surrounding them, raging inside them—teeming, roaring, alive with its own dark appetite.

The boy sits on the sand beside the woman, his body touching hers, and looks out across the water. Together, they regard the silence of the island. The sun—now a sliver—slips below the horizon and disappears into the crepuscular folds of the approaching night.

ACKNOWLEDGEMENTS

The life of writing is a long, arduous and solitary one, and impossible without the support and good faith of my family: Pa, Ma, Siew Yen, Harry, Thiam Teck, and Agustiniwati.

For endless inspiration and for keeping my heart in all the right places, the four bright stars of my life: Ryan, Gabriel, Kristine, Gareth.

For their generosity, kindness and constant encouragement, my big-hearted friends: Kok Wei, Jenny, Yew Pin, Angeline, Gavin Ng, Yvonne Lee.

A special callout to the A-team at Epigram Books: Edmund, for his vision and firm belief. My editor, Jason Erik Lundberg, for his invaluable advice, patience and guidance; for shaping and sharpening this book to its current form, you deserve the full credit. And also, to my beloved team of supporters/angels/cheerleaders: Clara, Winston, Lan, Sophia. Always a pleasure working with all of you.

And finally, to my dear readers, for believing and supporting me through the years. This book is for you.

O Thiam Chin is the winner of the inaugural Epigram Books Fiction Prize, the richest literary award in Singapore, with a cash prize of S$20,000 and a publishing contract with Epigram Books. He is also the author of five collections of short fiction: *Free-Falling Man* (2006), *Never Been Better* (2009), *Under The Sun* (2010), *The Rest Of Your Life and Everything That Comes With It* (2011) and *Love, Or Something Like Love* (2013, shortlisted for the 2014 Singapore Literature Prize for English Fiction).

His short stories have appeared in *Mānoa*, *World Literature Today*, *The International Literary Quarterly*, *Asia Literary Review*, *Quarterly Literary Review Singapore*, *Cha: An Asian Literary Journal*, *Kyoto Journal*, *The Jakarta Post*, *The New Straits Times*, *Asiatic* and *Esquire (Singapore)*. His short fiction was also selected for the first two volumes of *The Epigram Books Collection of Best New Singaporean Short Stories* anthology series.

O was an honorary fellow of the Iowa International Writing Program in 2010, a recipient of the NAC Young Artist Award in 2012, and has been thrice longlisted for the Frank O'Connor International Short Story Award. He has appeared frequently at writers' festivals in Australia, Indonesia and Singapore.

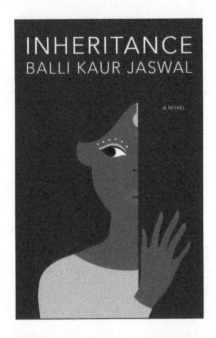

INHERITANCE BY BALLI KAUR JASWAL

- Winner of the 2014 Best Young Australian Novelist Award -

In 1971, a teenage girl briefly disappears from her house in the middle of the night, only to return a different person, causing fissures that threaten to fracture her Punjabi Sikh family. As Singapore's political and social landscapes evolve, the family must cope with shifting attitudes towards castes, youth culture, sex and gender roles, identity and belonging. _Inheritance_ examines each family member's struggles to either preserve or buck tradition in the face of a changing nation.

ISBN: 978-191-2098-00-2
PUBLICATION DATE: May 2017

KAPPA QUARTET BY DARYL QILIN YAM

Kevin is a young man without a soul, holidaying in Tokyo; Mr Five, the enigmatic kappa, is the man he happens to meet. Little does Kevin know that kappas—the river demons of Japanese folklore—desire nothing more than the souls of other humans. Set between Singapore and Japan, Kappa Quartet is split into eight discrete sections, tracing the rippling effects of this chance encounter across a host of other characters, connected and bound to one another in ways both strange and serendipitous.

ISBN: 978-191-2098-72-9
PUBLICATION DATE: May 2017

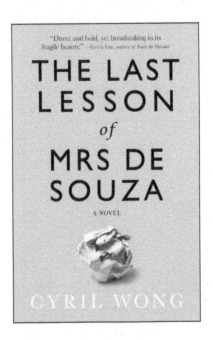

THE LAST LESSON OF MRS DE SOUZA BY CYRIL WONG

One last time and on her birthday, Rose de Souza is returning to school to give a final lesson to her classroom of secondary school boys before retiring from her long teaching career. What ensues is an unexpected confession in which she recounts the tragic and traumatic story of Amir, a student from her past who overturned the way she saw herself as a teacher, and changed her life forever.

ISBN: 978-191-2098-70-5
PUBLICATION DATE: July 2017

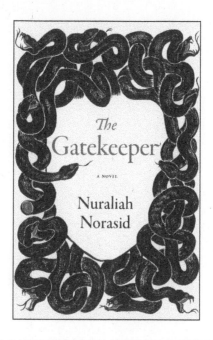

THE GATEKEEPER BY NURALIAH NORASID

- Winner of the 2016 Epigram Books Fiction Prize -

The Gatekeeper tells the story of a ten-year-old Gorgon girl named Ria, who petrifies an entire village of innocents with her gaze. Together with her sister, she flees the jungle of Manticura to the underground city of Nelroote, where society's marginalised members live. Years later, the subterranean habitat is threatened when Ria, now the gatekeeper, befriends a man from the outside.

ISBN: 978-191-2098-68-2
PUBLICATION DATE: September 2017

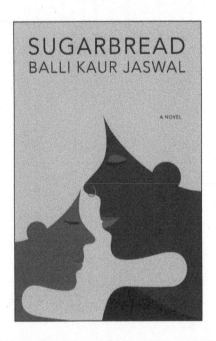

SUGARBREAD BY BALLI KAUR JASWAL

- Finalist for the 2015 Epigram Books Fiction Prize -

Pin must not become like her mother, but nobody will tell her why. She seeks clues in Ma's cooking and when she's not fighting other battles — being a bursary girl at an elite school and facing racial taunts from the bus uncle. Then her meddlesome grandmother moves in, installing a portrait of a watchful Sikh guru and a new set of house rules. Old secrets begin to surface, but can Pin handle the truth?

ISBN: 978-191-2098-66-8
PUBLICATION DATE: September 2017

STATE OF EMERGENCY BY JEREMY TIANG

- Finalist for the 2016 Epigram Books Fiction Prize -

A woman finds herself questioned for a conspiracy she did not take part in. A son flees to London to escape from a father, wracked by betrayal. A journalist seeks to uncover the truth of the place she once called home. A young wife leaves her husband and children behind to fight for freedom in the jungles of Malaya. *State of Emergency* traces the leftist movements of Singapore and Malaysia from the 1940s to the present day, centring on a family trying to navigate the choppy political currents of the region.

ISBN: 978-191-2098-65-1
PUBLICATION DATE: November 2017

LET'S GIVE IT UP FOR GIMME LAO! BY SEBASTIAN SIM

- Finalist for the 2015 Epigram Books Fiction Prize -

Born on the night of the nation's independence, Gimme Lao is cheated of the honour of being Singapore's firstborn son by a vindictive nurse. This forms the first of three things Gimme never knows about himself, the second being the circumstances surrounding his parents' marriage, and the third being the profound (but often unintentional) impact he has on other people's lives. Tracing social, economic and political issues over the past 50 years, this humorous novel uses Gimme as a hapless centre to expose all of Singapore's ambitions, dirty linen and secret moments of tender humanity.

ISBN: 978-191-2098-67-5
PUBLICATION DATE: November 2017